# SPY
# WITHOUT
# A CAUSE

By the same author:

*All Through the Night*
and
*Keeping the Lid On*

# Spy Without a Cause

## Neil Thomas

THOROGOOD

Published by Thorogood
10-12 Rivington Street
London EC2A 3DU

Telephone: 020 7749 4748
Email: info@thorogoodpublishing.co.uk
Web: www.thorogoodpublishing.co.uk

A CIP catalogue record for this book is available
from the British Library.

ISBN: paperback: 9781854189127
ISBN eBook: 9781854189134

Printed and bound in Great Britain by
Marston Book Services Ltd

# Who's who

| | |
|---|---|
| Marie-Louise Audran | French Vice-Consul, Hong Kong (HK) |
| Miguel Bentoz | Journalist, Singapore |
| Chuck Besky | FAO field worker, Philippines |
| Nigel Bland | CEO of Spreadworths, UK publishers |
| Rodney Bolt | Tax advisor, Singapore |
| Bill Brumby, Tong Lim | Book Distribution co-owners |
| Jimmy Chan | Entrepreneur, HK |
| Betty Chan | Jimmy's estranged wife |
| Elizabeth Chan | Jimmy's daughter |
| Clive Castle, Katy Covington | Advertising and video execs, HK |
| Nick Dale | Accountant, Manila |
| Davina Farmer | PR, HK |
| Laurence Farmer | Travel exec, HK |
| Ferdinand 'Ferdy' Graeme | CEO of Langleys, UK publishers |
| Gavin Gordon | Tax lawyer, Sydney and HK |
| Richard 'Dickie' Hart | Advisor to the Governor, HK |
| Stanley Ho | Gold dealer, Bangkok and Antwerp |

| | |
|---|---|
| Khoo Ah Au | Chinese Communist Party – senior trade official |
| Craig 'Tufty' McMasters | Conference MD, HK |
| Kenneth Minter | Events consultant, HK |
| Michael 'Mike' Moreno IV | US diplomat |
| Eric Old | British Council, Singapore |
| Jeffrey Parker | International sales director |
| Simon Perkins | Taxman, HK |
| Richard 'Rich' Rowlands | British publisher |
| Ramiro and Ramon | Café owner and son, Manila |
| Martin Rochester | Journalist, HK |
| Tan Siow Mong | Accountant, Manila |
| Ting Tack Chee/ 'Lane Crawford' | Bagman for Jimmy Chan, HK |
| Billy Ting | Ting Tack Chee's brother |
| Will Tomkins | Military Intelligence, HK |

*The setting is the early 1980s*

PART ONE
# HONG KONG

*Again, the devil took him to a very high mountain and*
*showed him all the kingdoms of the world and their glory.*

MATTHEW 4:8

# 1

I'D HAD QUITE A DAY OF IT. Jet-lagged after the flight from London, I'd been met in one of the Rolls-Royce cars of The Mandarin hotel and whisked through the Airport Tunnel from Kai Tak International and then through the Cross-Harbour Tunnel from Kowloon to Hong Kong Island. I saw quite a few Rolls-Royces even on that shortish journey. Wealth in this place was clearly to be flaunted, especially on four wheels. I'd heard that the ultimate for the richer Chinese women was to be in a luxury car wearing an expensive fur coat, especially in the humid heat of the place, to show off that they had money, no conscience and a swanky car with air-conditioning.

The speed, the frantic driving on all sides, the heat, the noise and the people, yes, the sheer number of people – everywhere, including in the tiny foreign exchange kiosks at the airport, which seemed to have dozens and dozens of staff squeezed into the smallest of spaces – all combined to pressure-cook the atmosphere of the place.

Even the wobbly and frightening descent of the plane, with the close-quarter view of overcrowded apartments in the surrounding high-rise tenement buildings, had played its part in giving me more than a little bit of a headache.

I felt no better, and a whole lot worse, after a glass or two of Dom Pérignon in the Captain's Bar of the hotel. My host – a printer that my bosses at Langleys wanted me to vet for them, as I thought – was Jimmy Chan, who clearly wanted to impress on me, right from my arrival in his city, that this was a typical day for him, that his expenses could stand it, that he had exquisite taste and was generous to a fault. It was a pity he failed on all counts. I'd not taken to him at all. Nor him to me, for that matter – he'd coughed out a curious and unpleasant sneering laugh when I told him it was my first trip to Hong Kong.

Still, we managed to exchange some pleasantries – him, going through the motions of doing so, putting on the same performance, I imagined, as he trotted out for every visitor he met; me, trying to let him see what a bright spark he had on his hands this time.

He looked like he was really thinking, another British twit out to lord it over the 'colonials'. I was matching him, thinking him a gifted actor paying lip service to the uncomfortable role of benevolent host to another arrogant Westerner.

We'd just arranged, very politely, to meet the following day for lunch when, fortunately, a member of the hotel reception team came to tell me my room was ready. She didn't look particularly surprised to be greeted with an, 'I expect a really good harbour view room for Mr Rowlands,' which was rudely offered to her by my host.

I was happy to get away from the bar, to be away from Mr Chan and to get checked in.

My room, when I got to it on the seventeenth floor, gave me an incredible view, a real picture window onto *The World of Suzie Wong* – up until that point, my only other visual reference to the scene before me.

It's the kind of view – across the water to Kowloon – you can look at forever. Chuffed to have got a decent room – and only momentarily wondering if I would have got it anyway or if Mr Chan really did have that kind of leverage here – I couldn't resist singing a few bars of the song 'How about you?' … 'I like Hong Kong in June, Harbour View?'

A couple of drinks that evening, a light room-service supper whilst unpacking, a late breakfast the next morning, all delivered by the knock, knock 'room boy!'

and a leisurely read of the local paper and my selection of guide books, saw me ready, feeling the benefit of a good night's sleep, to go and meet with Jimmy and take in that promised lunch.

But first, I thought I'd better do some shopping. I was already too late to be the lucky first customer in any shop, reducing my haggle room, but I managed to buy a neat, brown-leather document folder with an identical one thrown in free. I realised straight away that I'd clearly failed in my first negotiation test and I'd probably paid for three!

In the second shop I went into, they welcomed me with open arms – maybe they hadn't had any paying customers before me – and I fared better, managing to get hold of two Minox EC cameras, with films, for the price of only one and a half. Of course, it helped that I didn't know what on earth I was buying, as I was acting on precise instructions from a friend I was going to be seeing in the Philippines. Fortunately, they mistook my total ignorance for hard-headedness when they tried, and failed, to interest me in other more expensive cameras and, by the end, they were itching to see the back of me.

I'd been told, very specifically, 'Get the black Minox EC. It's the smallest. Get two – one for yourself. I'll show you how to use it. It's known as the poor man's spy camera. You'll find it useful to film any papers and documents you can't remove from places. With all your publishing activity, I'm sure it'll save you heaps of time and having one will be a life-saver, literally, for me.'

I didn't know what he was on about, but was pleased with myself for getting hold of them and intrigued by their dinky size and what they might mean to him and the uses he had in mind. As soon as I held one, I could see the potential. A bit of secrecy if I came across something I wanted to copy but didn't like to ask! Yes, I got that.

It was only after I'd bought the cameras, my main purpose of going into the shop in the first place having seen them displayed in the window, that I realised there were other goods on offer, ranging from ivory carvings, cork-carved scenes in black-and-glass frames and a whole bizarre range of Chinese medicine products to cure every ailment under the sun. What really caught my eye was a cheap-looking Sony Walkman copy and a range of bootleg cassettes. Perfect, I thought, to give some escape from the din of the streets and make travelling more relaxing. I then bought one of the players and a David Bowie bootleg tape of the *Let's Dance* album with 'China Girl' as one of the tracks. Little did I know how significant that might become.

I'd barely got back to the hotel and left my shopping bags with reception, when it was time to meet Jimmy.

\*      \*      \*

He picked me up on foot from the hotel and, walking into the thronging streets, led me along a few crowded alleys, before diving off ahead of me through a shabby doorway. We went up some stairs, in a fairly nondescript building, and into what I assumed was going to be some dingy first-floor office, but turned out to be a dim sum restaurant of considerable size. There, we were ushered rather ceremoniously to a corner table, such as any self-respecting leader of a tong would expect, with suitable fawning from the staff seemingly being all part of the service.

Certainly that's what you would think Jimmy was, on first meeting him, an out-and-out crook. He had a nasty face, broken with yellowing teeth and a mop of black hair that you would swear was a wig, but wouldn't dare joke about! How can we possibly be doing business with him, I kept thinking. If he's got any good points, I can't think what they are, other than his obvious aggression and having the look of someone you'd never want to cross.

He spat Cantonese out of the side of his mouth in guttural bursts at the waiter, who turned on his heels and shot back into the kitchen. That's how you order off menu here, is it?

He then turned to me and was most polite, despite the staccato way he had of speaking English with a strange New York accent, but he couldn't disguise how false his bonhomie, in reality, was.

'When you start using me print all your books?'

No preamble then. Straight down to business.

'And what you drink? Brandy and 7-up? Whisky is my drink. Same for you?'

I thought about the advice I'd been given before I'd left the UK. Drink J&B, no ice; brush your teeth in it and you won't go far wrong, wherever you are. But others had said that the water in Hong Kong was fine to drink – it's part of the Empire after all! Surely I'd look a plonker if I didn't join in with the whisky and I'd get marked down as a soft touch. I couldn't think of anything worse than a whisky with a Chinese lunch, but clearly this was a test. I thought again about the lines in the *The Maltese Falcon*: 'I distrust a man who says "when". If he's got to be careful not to drink too much, it's because he's not to be trusted when he does.'

So, lunch or not, here goes.

'Alright.'

Jimmy raised a hand, flapped it a bit and then, when he had the waiter's attention, indulged in a little more snapping of his fingers before turning to snap at me.

'I'm waiting. When first order coming?'

I knew he was talking to me as well as the waiter who'd just turned tail and headed for the kitchen.

'It's not as easy as that. We've been using a company in Singapore for the past few years for my division's printing. I can't just yank all our work from them, even though you've done a lot of work for the rest of the group.'

'Why not? They no good. Let me speak to them. They Chinese like me?'

'Yes, they are, but not Chinese like you, not really. They're very polite and take everything very slowly and they like building trust and all that, just as we do.'

'Polite Chinese are not to be trusted. They play you for a fool. I've no time for that. We already have trust. Your bosses know already. You want save money? Yes, no. Simple as that.'

'Yes, we do.'

'Exactly.'

'And that's why I'm here, to research what's on offer. I'll have to see at least three other printers here in Hong Kong and get quotes and details of the service level arrangements from all of them, you included, and report back to my Board to keep them happy.'

'Cover your back. Insulting. We are best. Better than the best of the rest.'

'And, of course, I'll need to take up references, a couple of trade ones and one from your bankers, oh, and to see some of your recent company accounts, all to check on your bona fides and corporate stability.'

'What? You can get all the quotes and references and paperwork you like. What you do then? Shuffle them? Is that what you are? Someone who collects documents and can't make a decision on what is best for you. What are you? Some kind of paper tiger? Nobody sees my accounts, not even shareholders. They all trust me. If you want to see what we do, you come sit in our factory for a week and count in and out all our print jobs. See for yourself what we making. Check the quality. Talk to workers. That's enough for other big publishers from the UK. That's all we do for you.'

Jimmy looked at me with a good hard stare and I could tell what he was thinking. Why have they sent me this shit-shovelling low-grade editor?

I didn't mind. It suited me that he obviously thought that way – you can always flatter some prat's ego by a bit of self-deprecation. I told him, 'Of course, I'll have to check it all with the powers-that-be back at the office.' Sometimes, when you're played for a fool, it's better to accept the typecasting.

This calmed him down, I thought, because he switched to asking me whether I knew people in Hong Kong. Naturally I told him I didn't really. Suddenly, he offered to write any letters of introduction I needed, make any appointments for me and to give me the lowdown on anyone I wanted to meet. I bet you would, Jimmy.

I turned down his offer of a translator to accompany me on any meetings I was having. I'm not that stupid, Jimmy.

'I don't think that'll be necessary, but thanks for the offer and I'll take you up on it if I get into language difficulties.' This is Hong Kong, Jimmy! And it would be mighty odd to find a businessman who didn't speak English.

This annoyed him, clearly, and his livid expression was the very opposite of the difficult-to-read Chinese face that I'd been warned about encountering in negotiations. Quiet and inscrutable? No. Make that noisy and very 'scrutable'.

Fortunately at that point the food started arriving ... and arriving ... and the whisky bottle was barked for and delivered to our table and poured ... and poured.

He'd lectured me all the while on why he was the best businessman in Hong Kong and how we'd landed on our feet when we'd met him.

Just as well that the guide books had warned me that slurping and making noises is considered correct etiquette by the Chinese, for Jimmy was extremely polite by these standards. And, as with any other customer, I assumed, he quickly swigged every drink that arrived and expected me to do the same and, like a fool, I did – draining every glass to match him.

'*Yum sing*,' he would mumble every time he drained his glass and was clearly expecting me to do the same. I finally twigged it must be Chinese for 'down the hatch'.

Each *yum sing* he said made it increasingly obvious that he was more and more irritated by me.

That's what made my headache a whole lot worse, but I held my own, and my ground. At the end of the meal, a furious Jimmy went off in one direction and I jumped in a red and white taxi conveniently parked outside the restaurant and asked for Victoria Peak. I wanted to tick off one sight, if only to break my habit of never actually seeing much of where I was. I thought it might ease my throbbing head.

\*         \*         \*

Some hope! The taxi driver drove like a lunatic and seemed to hit every pothole as if trying to finish off both me and his already useless suspension.

'Hey! Slow down! What's the rush?'

All I got for that intervention was a glare of pure hatred from the cabbie, whose eyes, scarred face and curled mouth were visible in the driver's mirror. He looked like the knifeman in Jimmy's tong. Perhaps he was.

Macho driving, mean looks and a rush to get anywhere was something I would have to get used to, but as we sped along the winding residential roads, I took in the desirable properties of those who had literally reached the top of society in this frantic city.

There was no doubt, from their facial expressions, especially the eyes, that not only this taxi-driver, but also Jimmy – and, from what I'd read, probably every single Chinese inhabitant of the colony – had only utter contempt for us *gweilos*. What they failed to realise is that this made even the most ghastly of the Westerners that they despised, seem to me, in comparison with them, like the sole surviving inhabitants of the last bastion of human decency.

And I knew, both from one friend who now worked in the Hong Kong Inland Revenue Department and from another, who worked as a diplomat in the Governor's office, that Jimmy was a tricky customer. I'd found that out when I'd phoned them in advance of my trip. How difficult was that going to make my job of assessing whether or not to give him an even bigger chunk of our printing work?

I realised that I would have to do business with him. More meetings and yet more lunches. What could possibly go 'wong'?

\*       \*       \*

I suppose the view from The Peak, down over Victoria Harbour – with its innumerable ships of all sizes – and across to the New Territories, *is* pretty amazing, if you've a head for heights and like looking down on the glorification of greed. I'm right up there on both counts.

Seeing it for the first time, I kept thinking what an annoying growth – a carbuncle of commerce – Hong Kong must be to the People's Republic of China; something extremely itchy at the very least, maybe a boil to be lanced at best, or even a malignant tumour to be surgically removed at worst. If you're a self-respecting communist, having Hong Kong on your doorstep must be like having the neighbour from hell move in to the semi-detached next door. I could imagine the Beijing mandarins peeking out in despair and revulsion from behind their bamboo curtain.

I'd come up to take in the promised panorama and I wasn't disappointed. It was easy to marvel at how the British had got away with it for such a long time, since 1841 – apart, of course, from the short and vile interlude when the Japs had taken over in the Second World War. That occupation had set the colonial rulers' bar so low it made the British, in comparison, seem like the benevolent winners of an Empire Games medal for political and social rectitude.

Already, I, for one, knew I wouldn't be in the least bit sad to see it all come to an end in 1997, when the famous 99-year lease of parts of the mainland was going to terminate, which would render the in-perpetuity ownership of Hong Kong Island itself completely unviable.

This underlined for me how ridiculous it was that the whole place existed at all. OK, sure, it had enjoyed and fully exploited its status as an entrepôt between East and West, but in the main, its success was down to it being a free port and enjoying artificial tax advantages. In a way, you could do the same for Grimsby and sit back and see the skyscrapers proliferate.

No surprise then, that Hong Kong had become a melting pot of greed and ruthlessness, with its unsavoury residents all glooped together in a kind of wanton wonton soup, the main ingredients being sundry unscrupulous individuals from the four corners of the earth and the dregs of society from the far ends of the world. Little wonder that the British ex-pats were called the FILTH, failed-in-London-trying-Hong Kong. That just about got it right.

As I gazed down again at the view over the 'fragrant harbour', the irony of the English meaning of the words 'Hong Kong' wasn't lost on me.

\*       \*       \*

Back in the hotel, I was still fixated with the view out of the window. The evening rush hour was well underway, with ant-like hordes of people pushing and shoving on and off the Star Ferries criss-crossing backwards and forwards across the waters of Victoria Harbour, between

Central Pier down below me and Tsim Sha Tsui on the other side.

The phone rang just as the tea I'd ordered only seconds before was being delivered, and it was all I could do to both hand over a tip and answer the call.

It was the London office on the line, and I didn't even have a chance to say hello, never mind any other pleasantries.

'What the hell have you said to Jimmy Chan?'

'What do you mean, "what have I said"?'

'It's eleven-thirty at night here and I've just had a very angry CEO ring me from The Garrick. Jimmy is saying he can't deal with you. You're too junior and he wants to see the CEO himself. That's out of the question. This is your first day. I repeat. What the hell did you say to him?'

'I made it plain that we'd be getting other quotes. I can't see why that should faze him.'

'He's ranting about being asked for his accounts. Did you ask to see them?'

'I was trying to show him we might be doing some due diligence.'

'Are you mad? This is Jimmy Chan we're dealing with.'

'And it's a multi-million pound contract we're talking about. I think we're in the driving seat. It's what we'll be asking the others.'

'What others? We've been working with Jimmy for yonks. The CEO and him go back years and years. We haven't had him in a competitive tender ever. No wonder he's doing a number.'

'Why is he so upset? Don't you think we should be suspicious of that? If he's got nothing to hide and hasn't been ripping us off all this time, what's his worry?'

'The CEO has reassured him that we have to go through the ritual of looking at other suppliers, but he hasn't got anything to worry about. He told him you would run through the processes, but it would come out right in the end.'

'I don't actually agree with that at all. Jimmy ran through his terms of trade, which seem pretty unorthodox to me, with things like all purchase orders to go through his private company, JC Pty, and some future payments to be in bearer bonds – something about having to oil the wheels with printers in China. Very fishy. And he even insists that all of our travel and shipping arrangements are to be made through Elizabeth Chan Ltd in Gerrard Street. It all sounds rum to me.'

'Jimmy likes to play the Big Man, that's all. Take what he says with a pinch of monosodium glutamate. He's trying to show off. Don't rock the boat, that's all I'm saying. And, if you like, you can *act* like we're not an easy touch.'

'But, at the same time, show him we are!'

'Cock this up and it'll be your last trip to Hong Kong. Have you got that? I need a brandy after all this. I suggest you have a night on the town, enjoy yourself and relax. You're not there to change the world. Don't be too keen.'

# 2

I'D BEEN ORDERED TO HAVE a night out on the town – on expenses was how I'd taken it. After a call and a freshen up, I'd arranged to meet Simon Perkins on the Kowloon side of the Star Ferry. He was a friend and former UK Inspector of Taxes, now working in the Hong Kong tax office.

Once outside the hotel, the pungent smells of the city hit me a bit like opening an oven door and getting a greasy faceful of something hot and steamy. Early evening crowds quickly swept me along through the ticket office and then onto the crowded boat. The noises of the engine and the hubbub on board gave a bubbling soundtrack to match the lights of the buildings and their reflections in the water. What a place. What a pace.

Simon was just as I remembered him. He always stood out in a crowd with his unusual blond hair and that made him easy to spot in the middle of a sea of dark-haired Chinese. He was dressed simply in a polo shirt and chinos, as always, for an outing. No wallet clearly visible – a card and some Hong Kong dollars, no doubt, in his back pocket. With a wry smile on his lips and an extravagant wink, he held his hand out to greet me. His sharp blue eyes were looking everywhere, like someone bored at a cocktail party desperately looking for someone more interesting than you to talk to.

'Just checking you're not being followed!' he offered by way of hello.

'And?'

'If you've been with Jimmy Chan, I'd expect it.'

'Really?'

'Yes and I can see a Chinese guy carrying a Lane Crawford carrier bag, and hanging back studying the timetable. Locals never study the timetable. We'll let him follow us and see what happens. Anyway, nice to see you. How's the jet lag?'

'Fine now. This place certainly gets the adrenalin flowing. That should keep me going. Where are we off to?'

'Ah. I thought I'd take you to the famous Bottoms Up club, you know, the place that featured in *The Man with the Golden Gun*.'

'Really?'

'Yes, it really *does* exist,' he said, ignoring my ironic prudery. 'Come on! This way.'

As we marched off, it seemed like we were going on one of our old pub crawls. After asking me what I thought of Hong Kong so far, Simon was off, telling me about the history of the club and it being a haven for the tortured souls of American GIs on R&R trips up from Vietnam, in the days before the war finally ended.

'Isn't it the place that *Private Eye's* Ned Twinkie said you could order "one on the rocks and one off the wrist"?'

'I shouldn't doubt it. But please don't ask for either.'

As we walked, Simon talked, much as long-time residents everywhere do to first-time visitors, annoyingly assuming total ignorance in the listener. Actually, I didn't mind and was happily looking in whatever direction he pointed and trying to take it all in.

We turned left off Salisbury Road just before The Peninsula Hotel and into Hankow Road. Further up that sign-infested, neon-lit street, we found the street entrance of the basement club. Seedy or what?

'Don't worry, we'll order a beer each – one drink apiece – and pay for them. That way, we can't get stung for more. You can have a look at the place and then we'll head off,' Simon turned and assured me as we went down the stairs.

The place was heaving. Men and topless bars – a ghastly cocktail mix all over the world. Of course, I'd read the guide book description of 'four circular bars, exotic topless girls and lots of friendly people'. I could only take issue with the last of these, until I spotted, and wasn't at all surprised at doing so, the unusually smiley face of Jimmy Chan waving at me. He was surrounded by three Western businessmen and he was beckoning me over.

It seemed fitting he was there. After all, apart from showing me a few sights on our walk to the club, Simon had been telling me what he made of Jimmy. I now knew him to be a person of interest to the taxman in Hong Kong and elsewhere – someone whose financial affairs were adulterated and whose books were works of fiction. According to Simon, Jimmy took creative accounting to Booker prize-winning levels and even members of the Revenue reluctantly had to admire his chutzpah.

In one set of year-end figures, submitted when he was running a small grocery business, Jimmy's entry in the books of 'Kia-Ora' in Purchases nearly went unchallenged, despite it being a huge sum in Hong Kong dollars to spend on orange juice – even for a grocer – until one bright tax officer said he'd checked where Jimmy lived and found Kia-Ora was the name of his new house. He'd bought his home through the business! They'd taxed him on it as a result.

It seemed that every set of accounts from Jimmy's companies was examined with a fine-tooth comb by the Hong Kong Revenue, and large tax settlements, often with penalties and interest resulted. Simon had never actually met him and inevitably, when I approached Jimmy and his party, who Simon was and how I knew him were the first words that greeted me.

He seemed happy to know he was an old friend and in his rush to introduce his guests, forgot to ask what Simon did in Hong Kong, something he'd recall and regret later, no doubt.

The three stooges with Jimmy turned out to be directors of Spreadworths, a large legal publishing competitor of ours, based in London, who started telling me how they would save a fortune by moving all their printing to the Far East and how Jimmy was the man to do it for them. It looked like their decision was based more on the greater fun they could have on business trips to Hong Kong than to William Clowes, printers, in Beccles, Suffolk. I can't remember any of their names except for one tall, silver-haired, rather patrician-aired hooray in red trousers and a blazer, who introduced himself with words he'd doubtless been drilled to say by his careers master at Charterhouse, or some such, 'Hello. I'm Nigel Bland.' Right on both counts!

Fortunately, they quickly got bored of me, just as soon as the girls got bored with not having their rapt attention and, telling Jimmy I'd be in touch, I went back to join Simon, who was busy buying, or rather negotiating, a price for, our drinks.

'You'd better not tell him what I do.'

'I'm not that daft. Worse, I'm picking up your ultra-suspicious mind, because the guy who has just joined Jimmy and his gang is the same one you said might be following us at the Star Ferry, isn't he?'

'The very same! Well spotted.'

'Maybe he was just on his way here anyway and we've jumped to the wrong conclusion.'

'You'll learn there are no simple coincidences with Jimmy. Now he knows who you're with, we're off the hook for the moment, but you'll be grilled about who I am at some point. We'd better have a decent cover story.'

'I've said we were old friends. He might let it go at that.'

'You might think so. I don't. He could have someone tail me and if he sees me going in and out of Windsor House, he might guess I'm with the Hong Kong Revenue. If he asks my name, give it out as Parkins, that way you're not lying, just mispronouncing. And don't be specific about what I do. Say it's nothing remotely helpful to what you do, something boring like insurance, you think, for the civil service departments.'

'I think you'd better tell me a bit more about Jimmy Chan.'

'I'll only tell you what is a matter of public record.'

'I wouldn't expect anything more.'

'Listen carefully and hear between the lines. Jimmy is a very successful businessman with fingers in lots of pies. We've lost count of the number of 'cousins' who front up his many businesses. He personifies the Chinese concept of *guanxi*, which is the idea that you only do business with people you know. That doesn't work for him when some poor executive like you turns up representing a company headed up by an old friend. You're an unknown quantity and he doesn't like it one bit.'

'What kind of businesses does he own?'

'The list is endless, but things like an ivory emporium, a Chinese medicine specialist plus various other shops and, oh, he likes to have wholesaling as well as retailing in any business he follows. He's cosy with the top auction houses out here and sells all manner of artefacts that he claims are family heirlooms, but that's a whole other story. What'll be more familiar to you is his printing operation, but he has direct mail houses and even a small publishing business too. Those are the ones he owns, for sure, but we also know he operates some gambling clubs through supposed relatives, strictly under the radar of the authorities, and he travels a hell of a lot overseas where he has even more cousins.'

'Has he ever fallen foul of the law?'

'Not yet, but we're working on it. I've friends in the police who are as interested in him as we are and they think he has real ownership of nightclubs but, again, nothing on paper. It's all hearsay, nothing provable. A recent spate of damage to competitor establishments is interesting, shall we say, and the police are pursuing certain lines of enquiry, but nothing concrete as yet.'

'I'd heard he'd had some business dealings with my company in Nigeria that went a bit wrong – did you know about that?'

'Yes, it was reported here in the *South China Morning Post* – a joint venture with your lot in a printing and warehouse facility in Lagos that went up in smoke with a big insurance pay-out. According to the newspaper report, the local police investigated and surprise, surprise could find no sign of arson, only a faulty office fan!'

'We've all been suspicious about that for some time and the production director responsible for Nigeria left for pastures new soon after, but we were told very firmly not to draw our own conclusions.'

'That's our Jimmy. Talk about pin the tail on the donkey!'

'I need more background – can you dig a bit more with the police and see what you can find out?'

'Sure, but don't hold your breath – he's as slippery as a plate of garlic eel. Which reminds me, I bet he takes you to eat down at Aberdeen Harbour during your visit, especially as you're the new boy in town! I had thought of taking you, but I think I'll leave it to him. You'll see why!'

We stayed for a couple more drinks, largely making rude comments to each other about the other people and why they were there, forgetting we were in there too, before heading back on the Star Ferry, with Lane Crawford bag man once again in tow.

*     *     *

I'd managed to get myself invited onto The Peninsula-owned and crewed junk for the Saturday – a friend of a friend was the PR for the iconic hotel across the water on Kowloon side. At ten o'clock in the morning I presented myself in the splendour of the white and gold-columned lobby, with its potted palms and white uniformed bellhops, to be greeted by a mixed bag of assorted expats and blow-ins. I fitted in only too well. The odd assortment of shorts on the flabby men and the slick dresses of the elegant women told its own story of the overseas outpost.

We picked up the junk a shortish stroll away and I struck up a conversation with a guy with thinning clumps of bright red hair. We introduced ourselves and he told me he was in the conference business and ran his company from his own yacht in the harbour.

'Non-resident you see and non-domiciled, I don't even have to pay the local taxes. Pretty damn good arrangement. I'll run a year's worth of events here, set up an office to carry on without me and then I'll be heading down to Sydney to test out the Aussie appetite for business meetings. What about you, what game are you in?'

Not wanting to give too much away, as I knew about him and suspected he would know about me, I said I was in publishing. That usually shuts people up as they think of fuddy-duddy, dry-as-dust intellectuals pumping out tomes of boring fiction, or even more tedious non-fiction, but it didn't work on this chap, who pressed me with more questions.

'Like what sort of topics do you cover?'

'Tax and legal publishing, actually, and a bit of government contract stuff.'

'Fascinating,' was not the response I was used to getting. 'Maybe we could work together, share some mailing lists, that sort of thing, as we do a lot of legal seminars and I'm interested in the tax avoidance area too.'

'Yes, maybe we could. Give me your card and I'll give you a call.'

He hadn't asked me who I worked for. He obviously knew already.

We arrived at the junk, just in time to avoid any detailed arrangements for meeting again, and I sidled up to the glamorous PR who was hosting the day, Davina Farmer. Not for nothing was her nickname 'Legs'.

'Thanks for inviting me, Davina. I've just met Craig McMasters – is everyone here like him or is it going to be a relaxing, fun day?'

'Fun with me, darling,' she laughed, 'but this is Hong Kong. Everything's business. Making contacts, signing contracts. That's why you're here, be honest. The hotel has only let me have the junk on the proviso it's not a junket!'

She giggled – almost at the surprise of having made a joke – and turned to take a drink from the on-board butler and to talk to a lively couple I later learned were flight staff with Cathay Pacific.

'Abandoned you already, has she?' asked a friendly looking man in shorts, t-shirt and deck shoes who'd just tapped me on the elbow.

'Don't worry, she'll get back round to you and maybe even me. I'm Laurence, Davina's other half, well, actually her husband. She can afford to ignore me. She'll keep you onside in her PR way, you'll see.'

'How long have you two been out here?'

'A year, almost to the day, and I hate it. She wanted to come for this fantastic PR job, which turns out to be no more than being a lobby girl as I call it, although she calls it guest relations. I tagged along and managed to get some drudge work for a travel company based here. Most of the time, I'm flying all over the place. Just as well. That's why I don't get Hong Kong fever.'

'I was talking to Craig McMasters – do you know him? I've only been here a couple of days and everyone is new to me,' I lied.

'The chap in the pink shorts with the clashing ginger hair?'

'Yes, that's him.'

'He's a real operator for sure. Making quite a name for himself out here. Runs all his conferences in The Peninsula. That's why he's almost guest of honour today. The hotel's hospitality guys want him wined and dined in order to keep his work, but between you and me, he doesn't seem to pay his speakers much, if at all, and he certainly doesn't pay the banqueting department's invoices with any sense of due dates.'

'Thanks for that tip. He was trying to sound me out about doing some mailings.'

'What shared costs? Piggy-backing? That sort of thing?'

'I guess so.'

'Avoid him would be my advice. He'll nick your ideas and pinch your customers, but don't quote me. Look, I'd better mingle, but join us for dinner tonight. I know Davina wants to have a proper chat, you know, and catch up on our mutual friends back in the UK. We can give you the low-down on a few folk we know out here and can introduce you to some of our real friends.'

I avoided Craig McMasters after that, but couldn't prevent him seeking me out later that afternoon and giving me his card. I thanked him and smilingly waved him off the boat, thinking that in doing so I was as much of a two-faced tosser as he was.

I'd spent the trip over to Lantau Island and back, in between swims off the junk in Discovery Bay and drinking beer, talking on the front deck with a couple of married advertising execs, Katy Covington and Clive Castle, who made commercials and training films together. She was ultra glam in what must be the latest swimwear and transparent wrap whilst he was good-looking in an understated way, but was constantly blinking which I put down to an allergy or an eye infection. They were a relaxed pair and I managed to forget all about work and hustling and was glad to hear about their life in Hong Kong. For FILTH, they seemed to be doing exceptionally well. Or maybe they were just good at the tricks of product advertising.

As an extra, they pointed out various sights as we passed and seemed happy to do so, colouring their commentary with local knowledge. A tall building with hundreds of round windows on each floor next to The Mandarin, they informed me was 'Jardine House, or the House of a Thousand Arseholes, as it's known to us locals'.

They shared my jaundiced view of bankers and had nicknames for everything and everyone, no doubt perfected by sitting around all day dreaming up ad campaigns. No wonder it's said that all jokes not made up at The Stock Exchange originate in advertising agencies. Would I ever again be able to think of the Hong Kong and Shanghai Bank other than in their words, as staffed by 'Honkers' and 'Shankers'.

I was pleased to learn they were going to be joining us for dinner that evening which, thanks to Davina's contacts, was going to be at the Foreign Correspondents' Club.

Unfortunately, the dinner group was going to include a rather grand older chap who was drunk even before lunch and went round introducing himself as a great friend of the Hong Kong Tourist Association, saying to anyone who would listen that he spent his time going to 'conferences about conferences'. In between falling asleep on the deck cushions, I'd seen that he and Craig had struck up some kind of friendship. I thought that, if all else failed that evening, I could ask what he'd found out about our globe-yachting events organiser.

\*     \*     \*

It was easy to find the Foreign Correspondents' Club from my hotel. After a wash and brush up, I'd enjoyed a short walk through the thronging Saturday evening streets to Lower Albert Road and quickly spotted the distinctive building, with its horizontal candy-striped façade and round upper windows, bearing the legend 'FCC' in large lettering above the portico entrance.

Last to arrive, unfortunately, as I thought, but fortunately as it turned out, I had to take the one remaining seat at the large round table, between the sleepy guy from the boat and someone I didn't know. He quickly introduced himself to me as Martin Rochester, a journalist whose work I knew, but he was evidently deep in conversation with Davina, who sat on his other side, for he'd turned back to monopolise her as soon as I sat down.

The place was so loud, cacophonous in fact, that I knew conversation with all ten people round the table was going to be impossible. I'd be lucky to hear what the person next to me was saying and, anyway, I only knew Davina and Laurence and Katy and Clive from the boat. The others, being self-assured, assorted Hong Kong wealthy young things, were interested in nobody else but themselves, and barely gave me a glance as I joined their evening.

I set to, as the wine was poured for me, to find out what else I could about Craig McMasters, who thankfully wasn't there. My brand-new friend seated on my left seemed jolly enough and, introducing ourselves, I learnt he was Kenneth Minter who looked like a poor man's Michael Winner. He turned out to be a mine of information about everyone round the table and skewered them all with pithy barbs about their appearance or status.

Katy and Clive were dismissed with, 'He knows that a relationship with her is the price he has to pay for sex with a blonde bombshell like her and she knows that sex with him is the price she must pay to have a relationship with a guy like him with prospects until a better bet comes along.'

Davina he singled out for, 'Love her dearly, and she's gorgeous, but she's too dim to know how dim she is, bless her, and she doesn't even realise that there are people round the table who are only here because she's a source of freebies. They're not real friends like me! I mean look at the brunette opposite. She sweats her assets, don't you think? I mean, her dress is so revealing, you can practically see everything. What a funny place to keep a hairbrush.'

Laurence fared no better. 'He's a no-hoper, really, who married way above his station and is just clinging on for the ride, which must be good, don't you think?'

What he would be later saying about me, I could only wonder. However, he clearly loved talking and was more than happy to do so. Accurately sensing my main interest, he quickly settled on telling me all he knew about Craig, or Tufty McMasters as he called him. Seemingly he'd known of him in London. In no time at all, I knew a lot more than I had done about Tufty, especially his reputation in the conference business of being a 'shrewd businessman, but for that read shifty shyster', as my surprisingly entertaining dinner companion put it.

'He certainly practises what he preaches and half the stuff he puts on is about tax avoidance, offshore investment and looking after the wealth of high net-worth individuals. He must have sailed to every tax haven there is, ticking them all off in some kind of Munro-bagging for money-grubbers.'

'How does he get away with it?'

'He's always sailing off into the sunset before anybody can catch up with him, that's how, and he's repeatedly said one day he'll sell up and settle down, somewhere like Bermuda.'

'I thought you and he seemed to be getting on like a house on fire this afternoon.'

'Oh, did you now? That's what I wanted him to think too, because a friend of mine has asked me to find out what else he does on that boat of his. Handy way of transferring cash around the place, to say nothing of any other smuggling, if you ask me.'

'Should you be telling me this?'

'Davina's already told me you're a friend of hers. That's good enough for me. And you obviously know about this sort of thing. You're not exactly as green as Kermit's bum are you? Tufty was asking about you, incidentally. Didn't like it that you did some legal and tax publishing and ran the odd conference. Very sensitive about competition is our Tufty and he'd been told to watch out for you by some guy called Jimmy Chan, I think he said. With the pair of them interested in you, be careful, especially with whom you meet and where you go, oh, and what you leave lying around in your room. They're not above paying the hotel staff for a bit of snooping. After all, Tufty pays a dollar, US, per name, to get hold of delegate lists from rival events. Take a tip from me, if you're writing down names of contacts, don't use the real names, fudge it a bit and doctor the telephone numbers. Note addresses separately without names. For example Laurence and Davina Farmer you'd enter, not literally of course, that would be gross, as David and Lavinia Grazer. You get the idea. Write telephone numbers with the last digit being one less than the actual number.'

'Really? That is interesting. Thanks Kenneth, I appreciate that. But tell me, what do you really do? I mean really, really do. All that stuff about "meetings about meetings" and "conferences about conferences", what does that cover?'

'If I told you, you wouldn't believe me. No, seriously, there's nothing sinister about what I do. I run an international conference association. I'm in with all the big venues and the tourist boards and they all want me to see their tedious facilities and sample their simply ghastly catering offerings. That's why I'm travelling all the time. I'm off to Singapore and KL next week.'

'How on earth did you get into that line of business?'

'Fell into it really. Used to work for a flaky organisation that sold video recorders that were going to be the next big thing, except the format was wrong. It doesn't pay to be a pioneer. You're better off being in the guard's van than the vanguard when it comes to technological change. We did do a lot of promotional events which I found myself organising in the US and Japan and throughout the Asia-Pacific region. We used to get accused of being a front for the CIA, just because we had a couple of ex-CIA guys and a former SOE old bird on our Board.'

'That does sound a bit obvious. Are you sure it wasn't a front?'

'If it was, it fooled me. No, there's nothing cloak and dagger about me. The firm went bust in the end and I happened to find myself applying for the job I've now got. I can speak a few languages and can pick up a few words in the ones I can't. I'm the walking, talking personification of what Peter Ustinov's father is supposed to have said, you know, "a man who speaks many languages has nothing of interest to say in any of them". In other words, I can bullshit my way through and that's what's needed to schmooze in this game.'

Somehow, I wasn't convinced by Kenneth Minter's clean-as-a-whistle claims. He'd told me he'd been to a minor public school, which turned out to be Winchester. He'd have been well drilled in fitting in and surviving. There was more to him than met the eye, for, with his background, you could bet he would have mastered the art of not drawing unwelcome attention to himself and keeping his real self hidden. I'd no sooner had those thoughts, when Kenneth turned to talk to Laurence sitting on his left, which prompted Martin Rochester to glance at me and, in true journalist style, ask me directly: 'And what brings you to Hong Kong, Rich? I've just been asking Davina and she doesn't have a clue what exactly you're doing here.'

Apart from Jimmy, whose name kept cropping up and who I was fed up talking about, I had nothing to hide. I told him what I was up to, thinking that he might be a useful source of information for me – more useful than I was going to be to him.

'I've got to sign off on a couple of printing contracts for my firm of publishers, Langleys.'

'Yes, they're big aren't they, especially in this part of the world?'

'But *my* area, really, is business publishing and I run some tax planning and government contract seminars amongst other things. I'm here to sign up a few more authors if I can, and I'm trying to get some other international journals started, maybe some regional ones on tax and a big one in defence contracting.'

'Ah, you'll cross swords with Craig McMasters – careful or Davina's loyalties will be compromised.'

'I doubt that. He won't worry about small fry like me.'

'Don't be too sure. He doesn't like any other fish at all swimming around in his feeding grounds. And to continue the analogy, you should see him as the shark and not feed him or antagonise him or he'll bite your arm off.'

'I'll bear that in mind. But actually, I'm far more interested in what you're working on than talking about the boring things I'm following up. I used to enjoy reading you in *The Times* and *The Sunday Times*, but not so much recently. Who are you writing for these days?'

'Anyone who'll pay me enough to get by in this overcrowded mecca for mindless misfits. Sorry, that's my usual pat answer. Actually I've carved out a bit of a niche for myself with the *Far Eastern Economic Review and the South China Morning Post* as well as syndicated pieces for the rather naff *International Herald Tribune*.'

'Isn't that staffed by CIA guys all over the world?'

'That's common knowledge. No marks for insight there, but I'll write for whoever will pay me.'

'Sorry, I get that. It's just that I'm seeing subterfuge and intrigue wherever I look and it's easy to fall into the conspiracy theory trap.'

'I'm just a jobbing journalist, earning a crust and trying to write some books on the back of my magazine and newspaper efforts.'

'What are you working on at the moment?'

'I'm writing a piece about the legacy of the Opium Wars. It's part of a series supporting my history as revenge theory. The Chinese want some payback from

Britain – that's why they'll happily take back Hong Kong in 1997.'

'Why do you think they are still exercised by what the Brits did all those years ago with the opium trade?'

'Simple answer – by the early twentieth century a quarter of male adults in China were users of narcotics from the disarmingly pretty opium poppy. That's millions of men – enough to weaken the nation. A proud country that saw itself as the centre of the world, and not as 'Eastern' or made up of a bunch of 'Orientals' as we saw things, and who battled to defeat the opium smugglers and dealers only to lose to the West, mainly Britain. The Chinese only got the legacy drug problem more under control by the time of the Second World War. Forcing the weakened Manchu government to legalise opium, which, incidentally, is what we British did, had led to the impoverishment of the Chinese economy and ultimately to the peasant movements and the rise of communism. I'd want revenge for that, wouldn't you?'

'Put like that, yes, I can see why they might feel so inclined.'

'It's personal too. Did you know that the founding fathers of Jardine Matheson were the leading opium sellers in the early nineteenth century, with one of them describing the Chinese as "a people characterised by a marvellous degree of imbecility" who occupied "a vast portion of the most desirable parts of the earth"? I'd want revenge for that too.'

'The Chinese are having the last laugh though, aren't they? They must be laughing that the drug trade is now an out-of-control Western problem. Part of your thesis, I suppose, is that the drug cartels from Latin America and the gangs throughout Europe and the US are no worse than the East India Company?'

'Quite so. And, since Nixon, China now is beginning to flood the West with plastic tat much as we did to them with drugs. But enough about me.' He'd obviously had enough of my helpful 'input'. He continued with another question. 'Where are you off to after Hong Kong. Back to the UK?'

'Not immediately, no. I'm going to the Philippines and maybe Singapore.'

'No? Really? I can put you in touch with a few good people who might be useful to combat the shit and derision you'll meet in Manila and the sterile soul-free zone of Singapore. In return, if you come across any interesting stories on your travels that I could craft into some award-winning piece of reportage, I'd be in your debt. Might even stand you lunch.'

He gave me his card and as I looked at it, I thought I'd mention something that was very much on my mind.

'Actually, there is one story you might like to follow up, centred on the Philippines and the whole thing about corruption in overseas aid.'

'Tell me more.'

'Have you read about the FAO guy who was probably murdered in Manila, although the authorities say he committed suicide whilst drunk?'

'Chuck something or other, wasn't it?'

'That's right! Chuck Besky. American guy working for the UN's Food and Agriculture Organisation and doing some feasibility stuff on third-world agricultural projects for the World Bank. I met him in Cambridge some years back and we've kept in touch. He was a cynical kind of guy and was always banging on about corruption, both in those that gave out the money and those that received it. It seems likely he'd trodden on a few toes, maybe even enough to get himself bumped off.'

'Go on, sounds interesting.'

'I suspect he was onto something in the Philippines and not just the obvious with the huge funds going into the agricultural sector. He was taking a look at the movement of rare and banned goods in relation to the traditional Chinese medicine trade.'

'What's your interest?'

'I want to try and find out more when I'm there and maybe stir up a bit of interest in things being further investigated.'

'If you find out anything detailed, I'd like to do a piece on him. Can you dig out anything he wrote, maybe in articles or even reports?'

'I'll do my best, but his wife, sorry, widow, is probably the one to approach for background as she understands his research and shares his passion to make the world a better place. You should contact her. She still works on a consultancy basis for the FAO, but spends most of her time, not out in the field as Chuck did, but desk-bound in the amazing building in Rome.'

'Isn't that the one built by the Fascists with the double staircase designed so that different groups of visiting dignitaries from Italian Africa could move up and down the stairs without passing each other?'

'Exactly – like the double helix version in the Vatican. You know the one, the Bramante Staircase I think it's called. But I only know about the FAO one because Chuck showed it to me when I visited him there. How do you know about it?'

'Oh, I once did a piece about fat-cat salaries in the UN and organisations like the FAO and I was in Rome myself. It went down well! I'm now blacklisted there and at the World Bank. But give me any info on that and anything similar and I'd be happy to follow it up. It would give me a chance to have another go at them and get banned for life, with any luck.'

I barely had time to thank him, when Clive was up on his hind legs and tapping his glass with a spoon to subdue the noisy table. Clearly some kind of announcement was in the offing.

'Sit down, Clive. You're rocking the boat,' shouted Davina, but Clive stayed, swayed a little and, obviously 'tired and emotional', started his little speech.

'You all know that Katy and I have been together quite a while now. She can't shake me off, no matter how hard she tries.'

'He followed me to Hong Kong when I thought I'd done a Garbo on him and got away,' she piped up.

'Yes, that's right, I did follow you out here, because when you left London, you gave me an ultimatum. You said you wanted nothing more to do with me unless I lost some weight and stopped wearing glasses.'

Despite cries of, 'Short-sighted of you' from Kenneth and 'Shame' and 'Aw' from others, Clive carried on.

'Six months later, I came out here after you, the new svelte, contact lens wearing me, and we've been together ever since. But what d'you know? She has just this minute refused to marry me. Again. For the third time.'

Davina got up and walked round the table, arms outstretched to give Clive a hug, and an awkward silence fell. I was puzzled at this turn of events, given how well he and Katy had seemed to get on with each other when they chatted to me on the junk that afternoon. Holding

Clive's arm, Davina leant down and, cleavage to cleavage, spoke to Katy and then said to the table, 'Katy wants you to forget this. It wasn't the occasion for a proposal and she's really embarrassed by what's happened.' So much had been drunk during the meal that the table immediately forgot about the embarrassing incident as they all resumed their noisy conversations.

Clive slipped quietly away at this point and nobody tried to stop him.

'She's found some richer bloke, I've heard, an established film producer, only she hasn't quite got round to telling Clive,' Kenneth whispered in my ear. 'Poor sod. That's what it's like out here. Happens all the time. He'll no doubt get some Chinese girl to lick his wounds, but even she'll keep trading up blokes, like some kind of property dealer of male flesh, until she manages to get a passport out of here.'

'I thought they were made for each other,' I replied.

'She'll twig that when it's all too late. He's better off out of it.'

'Nothing is quite what it seems out here, is it?'

'Too right it ain't. And take another warning, watch out for your new journalist friend, Martin Rochester – he'll rip you off at the drop of a hat. His only loyalty is to his byline.'

The evening wound down quickly after that and, although most of the others accepted Kenneth's invitation

to a post-prandial drink at his flat, I'd been warned
by Martin – how nice people were about each other
in Hong Kong! – that they were noisy, messy, drunken
affairs, involving opera played at full volume and incredibly strong champagne cocktails. I made my excuses and
left as I knew I had to be awake bright and early on the
Sunday to head over to Stanley Market.

# 3

I WAS UP AND FEELING relatively refreshed that following Sunday morning and nearly choked on my fresh tropical fruit at breakfast in my room as I read, in the *Sunday Morning Post*, the name of the latest appointment as French Vice-Consul General in Hong Kong. The accompanying picture alongside confirmed it was certainly the woman I knew. Petite and dark-haired, with the sultry look of a French film star, there on the page in front of me was Marie-Louise Audran, someone else I'd met in Cambridge. She'd been there doing a summer school in linguistics at Maldwyn College. She'd had a fling with a pal of mine who loved Noam Chomsky as much as she did and they both went around dressed head to toe in white all the time. They'd split up and then she'd been involved with Dickie Hart, another friend who was now working as a diplomat in Hong Kong. Any connection still between them? So, this is what's happened to her. I'd have to get in touch, that's for sure, but for now I was already late to meet Simon in the lobby for our day searching out bargains at the market.

When I got downstairs, I was surprised to see him talking to a tall, upright, military type – with ultra-short brown hair – who turned out to be just that.

Simon turned as I approached and introduced us.

'Rich, this is my chum Will Tomkins, attached to the Hong Kong police. Don't let that put you off, though, as he's British military through and through and, ironically, it's no secret that he's on the intelligence side, not the sort of dull things you'll be getting up to like drunkenness and minor customs infringements.'

Will was friendly and open, immediately putting me at my ease and, as with most army guys, he stood squarely facing us both as if he was about to give a briefing about today's mission.

'Exactly so! Simon's got it right as usual, but on that last point, might I suggest you mail back to the UK any receipts you get for purchases you make. Don't keep them with you to be found on you when you return. And always unwrap stuff like new clothes and stuff them in your suitcase and say you've had them ages if asked.'

'Blimey, you'll make a smuggler of Rich yet, Will. Right, let's get this show on the road, shall we? It's going to be the three of us for part of today, which I thought might be fun. You'll learn a lot about Hong Kong, Rich, that's certain. Even if you don't buy anything in the market, you'll pick up some bargain information on the way.'

It was a relief to be driven well in a comfortable car, a blue Bristol 411 that Will had had specially shipped over from England, it turned out. He handled the wild traffic and the tortuous route we took with considerable ease. I had to comment on it and got more information than I bargained for.

'Actually the army trained me as a driver and put me through all sorts of specialist sessions including a defensive driving course which I did out in the Middle East.'

'What on earth is defensive driving?' I might have guessed that the reply would be delivered as if he was addressing an army class.

'I'll detail a few aspects for you if you like. For a start, you position your main passenger in the back, of course, and directly behind the driver. That way if we get shot from the front, the driver will cop it first. You're OK because you're in the back and either Simon or me will take the hit for you.

'Secondly, never leave your vehicle. Not like in all the daft cop shows you see on TV where, at the first sign of trouble, they jump out of their cars and use the open door as a shield to fire through the opened windows. No. You stay in the car and drive on or reverse at speed and get the hell out of there. They got it right in one of the early sequences of the film *The Day of the Jackal*, for that street attempt at assassinating De Gaulle. Despite the rammings and the gunfire, the car carrying the President swept on. The car is your best weapon of defence, and offence, for as long as it is driveable.'

'I feel reassured, but panicked at the same time. Let's hope we won't need to deploy your skills in Hong Kong.'

'I already have on a few occasions like once when we were chasing some border infiltration by a gang that were, allegedly, doing some business with the guy that Simon says is your best friend, Mr Jimmy Chan.'

'Did you get them?'

'No. They must have done the same course and got a distinction to my merit. We just couldn't catch them. Jimmy's got a few madcap drivers who must have done the additional, offensive driving diploma, the way they drive. You'll find them in taxis mostly.'

'Really. I had a mad one straight after I'd met Jimmy for lunch.'

'Yep, that'll be one of them for sure. Jimmy has his own taxi and uses it as a trick to avoid the usual difficulty in tailing someone. He'll just have them picked up in his own vehicle asset and driven to wherever they want to go. That way he knows where the target is going and he gets to take the taxi fare as a bonus. My advice: change taxis on every journey and make sure the first one isn't following.'

'Is Hong Kong as bad as all that?'

'It is if you're in the wrong business or involved with the wrong sort of people, which you are with Jimmy. And Hong Kong has loads of covert action going on. It's a melting pot, with Russians, Chinese, French and UK intelligence up to all sorts, not forgetting the Yanks charging around the place being anything but inconspicuous. Hong Kong is a bit of a hub for intelligence gathering in the Far East and South East Asia, just like Vienna was for Central and Eastern Europe in the late 1940s. Its unique legal and immigration systems have made it the most ideal centre to collect and exchange sensitive and secret information. Travellers from too many countries can come and go without a visa. And if you're resident in Hong Kong, you can do what you please, it seems to me.'

'But my Head Office people think Jimmy's a legit, hard-working company director who does a good job for us and cuts a good deal for them.'

'Do they really? I mean, *really?*' Will was disconcertingly sceptical.

Is he right? Of course Head Office must know a whole lot more about Jimmy than they've told me. What does that mean – they trust Jimmy more than they trust me? Or, they know too much about Jimmy, more than they feel safe to entrust to me? And what does that say about how much trust I should put in them? To say nothing of my loyalty to them. Once trust is impeached, then loyalty is misplaced and if you are betrayed, then your trust and loyalty must be written off.

Simon cut in at this point.

'This is why I thought it might be useful for you to meet Will for a chat and I know you'll keep what he says to yourself.'

Will carried on with his impromptu briefing.

'Jimmy will want to know more about you to make sure that you are as much of a sap as all your colleagues seem to be.'

'Charming. But I'm on the level. I really am. I'm just a simple publisher trying to get stuff published that sells and makes money, who's looking out for good authors and always trying to cut our costs without compromising quality.'

'Yes, that's a textbook business school approach, but you're trying to do it in Jimmy's world and that makes it different. You're not dealing with a printer in the home counties whose only dodge might be to print a few copies less than you've paid for, or who uses a lower grade paper than you've ordered, hoping you won't notice. This is all about giving a respectable front to a lot of very dodgy activity. Believe me, you don't want to know what you could get involved in. Keep it to the publishing and play it straight with Jimmy and you'll be OK.'

Little did I know I was into something much deeper than I could have imagined.

'I've already told him I'll be looking at other suppliers.'

'Dear oh dear. He won't like that.'

'He's already demonstrated that.'

'He won't let it happen. Just wait and see.'

I was rather glad that, at that point, we arrived at Stanley Market and Will dropped us off.

'This is where I leave you guys to your shopping. See you around one o'clock, in the same place. Then we can head for lunch.' With that, he was off.

I couldn't really concentrate on all the knock-off bargains that were on offer, but managed to buy a few top-label shirts. This was especially pleasing as Simon said, although a lot were copies, some were genuine, having been siphoned off from the actual production line of the labels concerned. In other words, the factory had deliberately over-produced, supplying the customer company's order as per the purchase order and then flogging off the extras they'd made in the market to boost their local cash. Perversely, I would have preferred them all to be proper fakes, I think, but for that, Simon said, I'd have to go to Bangkok.

In between walking around the stalls and handling the merchandise, I tried unsuccessfully to engage Simon further about Will's activities in Hong Kong, but he kept giving me the brush off and, finally, in an exasperated tone, told me 'not here, not now' which shut me up.

The whole place got busier and busier with bargain hunters, but compared with the north coast of Hong Kong Island, it had a more restful atmosphere, almost like a holiday resort, with the nearby beaches crowded and the South China Sea looking very tempting. No wonder lots of expats chose to live over this side, in the high-rise apartment blocks that were, to me, spoiling what must have been a pleasant fishing village at one time.

After a late lunch on the terrace of the Repulse Bay Hotel with Will, who'd driven us there, he left Simon and I to make our own way back because he lived round the corner on the Stanley side of the island. We headed back to the hotel, changing taxis, naturally, on the way. I was dropped off first and, en route, we'd arranged a time for me to go to Simon's offices the following day.

I was facing up to a week that now looked like it was going to be hard work and a bit different from what I'd expected. Still, provided I didn't do anything daft, nothing would really happen in Hong Kong, would it? I could get on and do what I needed to do and then head off to Manila, as planned, without getting into any difficulties.

\*     \*     \*

After breakfast that Monday morning, I sat at the desk in my room staring out at the sensational harbour, but an overcast sky and a choppy sea made the day look decidedly stormy. The weather warnings had promised lashings of rain. Not in a rush to go anywhere, I sat and made a few calls.

The first was to Marie-Louise at the French Consulate who surprised me by picking up the phone herself. Just how big was that office? She seemed pleased at first to hear from me and to know I was in Hong Kong, but gradually it became quite apparent that she was not sufficiently interested in seeing me to be able to fix to meet up this week, but 'maybe when you're next passing through'. Why the brush off?

'Sure,' I replied. 'Look forward to that and good luck in your new job.'

I didn't say I would be coming back in a week or less. That would have been pushing it. I'd just see what reception I got when I surprised her and got back in touch sooner than she'd expected.

I then tried to confirm the meetings for that day and the next with the other suppliers that had been set up in advance when I was in London. Strangely, none of the people I spoke to could make any time to see me, or felt they could take on the type of work we did, or could work with us without a conflict of interests with our competitors. It was difficult not to think that they'd all been got at. I wondered who by?

My week was disintegrating fast and a call from – guess who, that's right, Jimmy Chan – found me on the back foot.

'Hello, Jimmy. To what do I owe the pleasure?'

'I hope you had a nice weekend on the junk and at Stanley?'

No longer shocked that he knew my movements, I was blasé in my reply.

'Nice, thanks. Met some interesting people and bought a few nice shirts, Ralph Lauren, that type of thing,' I said, knowing that's what he wore and letting him know I now knew where he probably bought his. 'How can I help?'

'You can help by coming with me tonight to Aberdeen Harbour.' Simon was right. 'I take you to the Jumbo Restaurant. Very famous. Very big. They know me. We get star treatment. I'll have a car pick you up at seven at The Mandarin.'

'That's not necessary, Mr Chan. I'm not sure what I'm doing tonight yet.'

'I am very sure, Mr Richard Rowlands, what you are doing tonight. You are coming with me for dinner. You will not be doing anything better with your time and of that, I am very, very sure indeed.'

Sensing defeat and not wishing to antagonise him any more than strictly necessary, I could only reply, 'If you insist. Thank you! It's most generous of you.'

'I do insist and it is nothing for me to entertain such an important visitor to Hong Kong. Your taipan back at home knows I am seeing you.' That was to make sure I toed the line. 'See you tonight. Goodbye.'

How did he get away with this kind of nonsense? It beggared belief that he could still think it wasn't obvious how he behaved. That wasn't *his* problem though, was it? All he cared about was getting what he wanted and as long as he did, why should he care what people like me thought?

It all made sense now, of course. The cancelled meetings with other suppliers and the floating restaurant dinner arranged for Jimmy to do a bit of gloating. That would be putting me in my place.

It was raining cats and dogs as I left the hotel. My heavyweight golf brolly from the hotel was struggling with the downpour as I caught a taxi – deliberately not the first one to see me – which had swerved towards the kerb, in a Jimmy's driver's style. I ran past that one to the one behind it. I asked for Windsor House, the tax office building that housed Simon Perkins and his Inland Revenue colleagues. The taxi did a dangerous U-turn, leaving what must have been one of Jimmy's taxis stationary at the kerbside, with a bunch of tourists attempting to get into it. We then made a left and headed off along the Gloucester Road. It was only a relatively short distance from the hotel, but the weather made it seem like an achievement to get there.

Simon was not at all surprised to hear all my appointments had been cancelled.

'Look, isn't it easier to just go along with Jimmy? That's what your bosses want. Why make life difficult for yourself?'

'I don't like being pushed around by a supplier and I like being bossed about by fools even less. I'll see what I feel. I still have the option to pull all the printing from Hong Kong and put it into Singapore. Jimmy's reach doesn't get that far, does it?'

'You'd be surprised. He's got relatives everywhere and he moves around Singapore, the Philippines, Indonesia, Malaysia and Thailand – all the ASEAN countries in other words – with ease, his way greased by deals and bribes and all kinds of trading relationships. You could be getting into further trouble. If you're not careful, you'll get bogged down by trying to "play" Jimmy and you won't do all the other things you want to do.'

'You're right, as usual. I keep forgetting I'm here to try and sign up tax specialist authors for various publications, including a new big encyclopaedia on tax havens and tax planning.'

'You mean on tax avoidance and tax evasion. Why not say it?'

'That's calling a spade a bloody shovel.'

'OK! But that reminds me. I do know that "no man in the country is under the smallest obligation, moral or other, so to arrange his legal relations to his business or property as to enable the Inland Revenue to put the largest possible shovel in his stores", as Lord Clyde said in the tax case that all us final exam Inspectors of Taxes had to learn off by heart.'

'Look, despite that, I know you really take a dim view of the obsession the wealthy have with tax mitigation, strongly believing that if everybody paid their taxes, we'd each pay lower tax rates and solve all the problems of society and all that jazz.'

'That's about it. What's wrong with that?'

'It takes no account of greed and selfish greed at that, nor of all the professional advisors who love the fact that tax systems are so complicated that they can charge whatever fees they like. And that's where I come in. Supplying tips, tricks and techniques to help companies and individuals lower the tax take from their hard-earned incomes.'

'Then, why should I help you make the job of the Revenues around the world and mine in particular even more difficult than it already is?'

'Look, all I'm asking for are the names of those who you think have the sharpest tax brains in Hong Kong and maybe in these ASEAN countries. But not out-and-out crooks. Just those who could keep readers up to date with current legislation and practice and maybe point out a few pitfalls for the unwary.'

'You make it sound like you're doing a sterling service supporting the underdog when what you're doing is spoon-feeding jackals. What am I going to get in return?'

'I haven't got much to bargain with, I admit. What have you got in mind? I know you can't – and wouldn't anyway – accept a fee, and a free subscription could even count as a bribe. That limits me to doing nothing, but knowing you, you'll have thought of something.'

'Actually, I have. Clearly you know we're looking at Mr James Chan and we think he is doing various things through the Philippines. Can you get your accountant mate down there to find out anything about who Jimmy deals with – we need names and addresses, particularly company or partnership names, sets of accounts, anything. We've tried approaching the Revenue services in Manila, but they more or less told us, in a spirit of international cooperation, to get lost.'

'OK, I'll do that, but only because I'm interested too, and I promise that if I come across any other tax scams on my travels that even I think are too immoral to write about and promote, I'll let you know, especially if there's a Hong Kong angle. I take it you're not interested in what happens in Vanuatu or the Cayman Islands?'

'Not unless it involves money from Hong Kong. But, all right then, I'll write out a list of tax experts I respect and leave it at the hotel. It's a short list. I'm not posting it to you. Don't keep it lying around. It didn't come from me. I'll even disguise my writing.'

'Thanks, Mr Bond. Try and leave it tonight or first thing in the morning, because I'm thinking that if I can change my hotel bookings, I'll rearrange my flight out of here for tomorrow. Since my meetings have disappeared, I might as well get down to Manila. Then I'll go on to Singapore and come back here to try and pick things up again after today's set-back with my appointments.'

'When you come back, you might like to meet up with your old university pal, Richard Hart, or Dickie Hart as you, very wittily, call him. He hates that, incidentally, and has tried to shed it now that he's something big in the political office of the Governor's. Between you and me, I think he's probably Our Man in Hong Kong, or at least his deputy.'

'What makes you say that?'

'Oh. Come off it. You're not that naïve. Think about it. Modern Languages at Cambridge, picked for the Foreign Office. Straight back to Cambridge on the Russian course, then a couple of years later at SOAS on the Mandarin course, then off to Beijing, now in Hong Kong. Stacks up doesn't it?'

'Yes, that does sound pretty conclusive, but I haven't seen him for a few years. I didn't know you were in touch with him.'

'It's kinda difficult to avoid meeting up with people in Hong Kong. Will knows him too and we all meet up to exchange notes on people. We'll have a session on Jimmy again soon. Dickie is much more interested in all the stuff he does here and in his ins and outs of China, naturally enough, than in what he gets up to elsewhere.'

'Did I tell you I was having dinner with Jimmy tonight? I couldn't get out of it.'

'That's good. Where's he taking you?'

'The Aberdeen Jumbo, as you predicted.'

'The full works then, carved carrots, seafood by the shell-full. You'll be lucky to be able to talk with all the noise.'

'That's a good thing as far as I'm concerned. I just want to get it over with and I'm going to have to think about what to say to him.'

'I can help there. We're interested in why people connected with him have so many companies registered in Hong Kong where the accounts submitted to Companies House look too good to be true. Those companies are unknown to us and have no tax history. We know those companies then get a good credit rating based on those accounts and they use that rating to purchase goods from regular companies who send out the goods on credit, because the credit checks they do don't throw up anything to worry about. Stay with me ...

' ... Then after the goods are supplied, the supplying companies try and get payment, but their big new customer has disappeared and when they go and look at the registered office, the bird has flown, as it were.'

'How can I find out about that, for Christ's sake?'

'Tell him you're thinking of setting up on your own, but are afraid everyone will ask for money up front. Ask him if he has any advice.'

'Are you mad? If I tell him that, he'll tell my bosses.'

'Exactly. So tell him you're telling him in confidence and you trust him. He'll then think he's got leverage on you as well as you being an extra client, because he thinks your current firm is in the bag.'

'I could come the innocent. It's what he thinks already, after all.'

There was a whole load more of this, now the rain had stopped and the pavements were steaming, over a hastily taken street-food lunch that I found unappetising, mainly because I was looking beyond the stall to where the quick knife-work in a restaurant window showed a chef to be skinning snakes. He'd hold them aloft before throwing them, rope like, over a horizontal metal pole suspended from the ceiling. Lots of dead snakes hanging like tights drying on a clothesline.

Promising to keep Simon informed of anything interesting, I went off back to the hotel. There I ordered some jasmine tea, tried to stop picturing skinless snakes slithering around the room and took a seat, instinctively with my feet up off the floor, in my room with a view.

Actually, Simon was right about setting up on my own. I had been toying with the idea. I jotted down some thoughts and numbers for a business plan to publish a few new journals backed up with some specialist business reports, stressing the Far East, and I even added breaking into China as a milestone in the strategy. Concluding that it just might actually work, I sketched out a way that, with a few useful staff appointments, a small team could get things underway, and could publish some profitable titles quite quickly.

It was totally absorbing, so much so that it was suddenly six o'clock. I changed quickly and thought I'd better head down to the Captain's Bar and have a drink to prepare me for my night with Mr Chan.

In the bar, there ahead of me, perched on three bar stools, were the group of Australian tax lawyers that I kept bumping into at the tax planning conferences I'd attended in my search for authors and customers.

They hadn't seen me, but I knew there was no avoidance or evasion possible where these guys were concerned. They'd taken me under their wing in Brussels and insisted I went with them to some swanky Michelin-star restaurant out in the country where we drank Romanée-Conti and Chateau d'Yquem.

I'd told them I couldn't go as my expense account at my pay grade just wouldn't stand a large entertaining claim, but they wouldn't have any of it. I *must* go with them and their little trust fund based in the British Virgin Islands would foot the bill.

Some of their stories came flooding back to me, including their practical joking even on people they liked. 'And we gave him a big breakfast', seemed to be a favourite punch line and when I'd asked naively what it was, I'd found out it involved changing the signed room service breakfast order left hanging outside a room by the victim, who would wake to several trolleys of multiple orders of orange juices, porridges, toasts, full Englishes and coffees, all delivered a couple of hours earlier than expected. What a laugh! They thought.

But they were a lively bunch and, despite the heavy drinking, were always up early the following morning to go for a jog. Very Australian.

Still, tonight, I could have a quick drink or two and then Jimmy would be my excuse for leaving them to it.

One thing was certain. I would not be leaving a room service breakfast card outside my room tonight, or any other night.

They clocked me just as I raised my arm to wave at them.

'Well, well, well. Rich Rowlands.'

'Of all the bars ... '

'... our Pommie friend has to walk into ... '

'... How's tricks. Are you rich yet?'

'He's always been Rich to us!'

'What brings you three musketeers to Hong Kong?' I managed to say.

'Nice to see you too.'

'What are you drinking?'

'Are you staying here?'

'What's your room number?'

'And let you charge all your drinks to me?'

'As if ... '

'Come on, we're on the Dom Pérignon.'

'We're paying, natch.'

'At least our trust fund is and we've got to blow it all this week before we wind it up. The girls have found out about it and aren't best pleased.'

'All good things come to an end.'

'Rich has gone all religious. Give him a drink quick before he tries to convert us.'

That all went on until I had to leave them to it. I think they valued me as an audience, putting it charitably, but once they knew it was a business meeting I had to go to, they backed off and let me go quite quietly in the end. We agreed to be in touch and I asked them to do some writing for me. They were, despite all the macho bravado, incredibly knowledgeable about tax planning and handled some very high net worth international businessmen and celebrities. Serious about work and even more serious about fun – one of them, Gavin, a barrister, originally from Scotland, even played 'Free Bird' by Lynyrd Skynyrd at full blast whilst he was working on a brief – you could almost forgive them for the financially dubious world they operated in. But like most tax avoidance, the money saved by their schemes was frittered away as much by them as by their clients.

'Who are you meeting?' one of them asked.

'Jimmy Chan,' I replied. 'Do you know him?'

They exchanged meaningful looks.

'What?' I pressed them.

'Professional confidence,' they all seemed to mouth or speak at the same time.

*     *     *

The Jumbo experience was unpleasant, I won't lie. A vast, green, floating pagoda-style Chinese food ship, lying at berth in Aberdeen Harbour, the JUMBO, as its huge neon sign on the top deck announced, was packed on all levels with large tables of noisy diners, and it made me feel very small and insignificant. What on earth did I matter to the life of Hong Kong?

Jimmy was playing the BIG I AM all evening by barking at the waiters, insisting we were shown all the fish before it was cooked and taking me down to the lower-deck kitchen and storage areas. That's where the restaurant kept huge glass tanks, each full to the brim with hundreds of fish, in barely enough space to breathe, all stacked up, one on top of the other with only their mouths moving. It was like looking at the aquarium version of a sardine tin, with barely alive fish. It was a sickening sight and I realised for the first time that fish, by and large, are really ugly blighters. I swore then and there I'd never go scuba diving and what's more, maybe I'd give snorkelling a swerve and likewise any sea-world attraction.

It seemed easier to let Jimmy do the ordering and it was the same routine as at our lunch. He snarled the orders and the staff ran around, falling over themselves to keep him happy.

It's painful to remember the conversation as Jimmy enjoyed sensing my humiliation, particularly when I had to admit that I was actually seeing none of his competitors in Hong Kong for the business we were seeking to place. I tried unsuccessfully to suggest I might try and place some of the work in Singapore, but he pointedly said I must look up a cousin of his who knew most of the printers in Singapore and Malaysia. The threat was implicit.

Stymied, I tried to pick his brains about setting up on my own and as predicted he was surprisingly helpful and said he would be happy to help. He told me exactly how to get a good credit rating – Simon's outlined scam was bang on – and was proud of his skills at outwitting other businessmen, banks and the Revenue. He told me how to move funds around without breaching Exchange Controls. (This wasn't sophisticated or complicated as it largely involved gofers carrying suitcases full of cash and handing out bribes to customs officials where these weren't 'cousins'.)

He told me how much he could help me getting to see top officials in China to get in on the act of publishing for, or with, the Chinese, as he, strangely it seemed, called them. He didn't appear to care whether that was for my current firm or for me when I set up on my own.

The sting in the tail came when he offered to finance my start-up and base the company in Hong Kong, where he said it would be better for him to be a main share-holder to start with, and to be a director. I bet it would, Jimmy, but no thanks.

'That's exceptionally generous of you, Mr Chan.'

'Jimmy. You call me Jimmy.'

'You've given me a lot to think about and if I decide to start my own business, you'll be the first person I'll call.' Like hell you will.

I felt stuffed with seafood and it was fairly late. I said I thought I'd better be going as I had an early start. What he said then disturbed me and chilled me to the core, which, considering I was still sweating from the really hot chilli crab I'd eaten, was some feat.

'You go to Manila tomorrow.' I hadn't told him.

'Yes, that's right. I was going later in the week, but I've brought it forward.'

'Will you be taking the Minox cameras you bought?' He must have a cousin in the shop. It seemed pointless to even ask how he knew.

'Yes, my friend in Manila told me to get hold of them for him.' Why did I tell him that. I ordered myself to keep what you tell him to a minimum and don't let the brandy talk.

'Is he a spy?'

'No. Good Lord, no. Last time I looked he was a boring accountant.'

'What's his name? I could use a good accounting man in the Philippines.' That was a question too far.

'I don't know the name of his firm. I'll get hold of his contact details and let you know.' He'd know I was being cute here.

'How do you contact him?'

'I use his personal number, but I don't feel at liberty to give that out, any more than I'd give out your personal number.'

'You don't have my personal number.'

'Exactly. My point, exactly.' What could he have said to that?

Jimmy Chan was now smiling, this time inscrutably. A cliché, yes, but scary! I didn't know if I'd just put my friend in harm's way.

## PART TWO

# MANILA

*There's one for you, nineteen for me ...*

GEORGE HARRISON

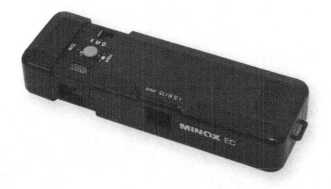

# 4

THE MANILA HOTEL WAS, it turned out, a bit of a sheltered harbour in a sea of sordid contrasts. Outside, the rough and the smooth, the rich and the poor, the elite and the exploited were evident enough, what with the gated compounds and the shanty towns, but in the hotel, apart from the blue-uniformed armed guards in the lobby and stationed on every floor by the lift, it was a five-star flambé-and-American-Express kind of place.

The hotel had been home to General MacArthur when he was military advisor to the Philippines before the Second World War. Of course the place had had to be rebuilt, after it was burnt down by the Japanese, but it still boasted the 'MacArthur Suite' as if it was the original and not the carefully reconstructed reproduction it actually was. The ante lobby was elegant with extravagant chandeliers, marble floors, potted palms and lots of white-liveried staff rushing around. Owned by the government – for that read, 'the Marcos family' – you could see how it had been styled with their influence. Imelda was supposed to use the restaurants of the hotel regularly herself and even sing with the band.

I'd arrived at the Manila International Airport, collected my luggage and trolleyed it outside to be surrounded by people, third-world style, hassling for money and offering services. Getting, finally, into a taxi was a relief and the drive to the hotel was mercifully short, along what I was told was the Boulevard of Broken Dreams. A poetic driver.

The humidity and the smell of the local mahogany that lined the elegant bedrooms was OK by me and I'd arrived in time, after a quick unpack, to go down to the Manila Restaurant to have dinner and catch the cabaret.

Performing, as I walked in and up to the maitre d', was The Family Birth Control Band, obviously, for that's what it said on the easel-mounted sign by her lectern-style desk. They could have fooled me – the girl singers were lusty and thrusty – leaving me in no doubt that they would be only too willing to take the band's name in vain.

'Will sir be dining with us this evening?'

'Yes, certainly.'

'Are you alone, sir, or expecting company?'

'A table for one please and not too close to the stage, thanks.'

'Very well, sir. Table fourteen,' she said as an aside to the waitress standing by to show me the way.

The food was very American. You could have 'feel-ay' of any animal or fish offered every which way. You could have food from everywhere, to go with the music from all over the world. In the time it took to order and serve my Chicken Binakol, the most authentic-sounding Filipino dish, I heard the band play authentic-sounding country, soul, Latin and rock n' roll. Weird.

The service was slick for me and for every other table, you could tell. The highlight though, apart from the incredible covers of hits performed by the singers in the band, was the cigar-lighting ritual which you could witness taking place from time to time at certain tables: first choosing one from a trolley like the French do their cheeses, then the slicing off of the capped-end with a silver guillotine, the dipping of the sucking end in brandy, the lighting with the flame of a candle and the amazingly rapid wrist movements to draw the air through the cigar and light it, before it was handed ceremoniously over. Ah, did Churchill ever have it so good? How could I not have one? And I don't even smoke. Or I didn't then. I hadn't needed to.

It had been a slightly unrelaxing day, what with being convinced I was being followed both to, and inside, the airport in Hong Kong and then hoping to find a calm, luxury hotel in Manila, but disconcertingly encountering armed guards outside my room. The band was, I suppose, merely strangely appropriate; desperately talented singers who could sing any song in any style, but totally devoid of any soul, all in the cause of promoting their name to encourage population control. It was just a pity that their target market couldn't afford to be dining in such surroundings.

The evening was going to get a whole lot stranger.

*       *       *

Nick Dale had arranged to meet me at the hotel. I'd telephoned his office when I'd arrived and received my orders.

'I'll pick you up after dinner. Just wear casual clothes, shirt, trousers, loafers, that sort of thing and take some pesos – not many and no credit cards.'

'You're frightening me now, Nick,' I'd said, trying not to sound too alarmed. 'Is it safe?'

'Well, yes ... and ... no. The hotel is fine. Armed guards and all that, but it's best to take no chances. We'll look like tourists or some bums off the rigs out for a night on the town. That makes us targets. And a lot of people carry guns.'

He'd arrived as arranged at nine and in he walked to the hotel, with the confidence of a prosperous local. He'd aged a lot, and his shoulders, always hunched, seemingly through years of dedicated deskwork, were even more rounded than I remembered. His dark hair was thinning, but his lop-sided grin was there, just as before. Apart from his Western features, the way he was dressed gave him the look of a Filipino accountant, ready for a night out, which was, after all, what he was.

We sauntered out of the main lobby across the turning area and through the guarded main gate. We skirted round the edge of the square of Rizal Park joining the paseo, with Nick, humorous as ever, saying that the large stone monument we could see was there because it was the site of the execution of José Rizal, the great national hero. So what could the locals possibly have in store for us?

He pointed across to the US Embassy opposite the hotel and, at the far end of the park, the buildings of the Ministry of Finance and the Ministry of Tourism, the 'twin preoccupations of our dictator and his missus'.

He was then straight into satirical mode, riffing on his favourite subject, the personal failings of Ferdinand and Imelda Marcos.

'I've started referring to them as "The Cashews".'

'Why? Because they're both nuts?'

'No. Because one's all about cash and the other's all about ...

'Shoes!' He'd let me shout out the punch line.

'Yes.'

'Very satirical. Say that in public, though, and you'll get yourself arrested. Insulting the First Lady like that. You should be ashamed of yourself.'

'That's why we're going to walk around this square a couple of times until I get a few things off my chest. I'm serious about how bad this guy leading the Philippines is. He's probably stashed away millions of dollars for every pair of shoes she has.'

'How do you know that for sure?'

'Look, his official salary hasn't budged from $13,500 a year and we know he's got property and assets everywhere. That salary wouldn't cover a morning's outgoings. You should see what I've uncovered. The guy is a kleptocrat of mega proportions. He's been skimming off the top of Japanese reparations from the war and thieving international aid money. He's stolen gold from the Central Bank, taken loans from international banks and dollars from US military aid that he'll never pay back. He's even taken great dollops of cash from the levy he charged the poor old coconut farmers that he'd told them was to improve their industry – the very same industry in which he's already gifted most of the trade to his own companies. And, as if that wasn't enough, he even took kickbacks on the government contracts that were awarded under the levy.'

'I repeat. How do you know this stuff?'

'The curious thing is it turns out that your international tax planning journal is required reading by the finance guy who handles everything for the Marcoses. He saw my name listed as Philippines Bureaux rep and called me in to pick my brains about tax havens – Switzerland and the Cayman Islands in particular, but Hong Kong and Macau featured strongly. He had me sign a Filipino Official Secrets Act form.'

'You're kidding? He actually made you sign something?'

'Not actually, no, but he looked me in the eye and said that if I told anyone about anything he discussed with me, he would have me killed. So, a bit stronger than signing a piece of paper, don't you think?'

'God. This gets worse and worse. But what's the link with Hong Kong?'

'Apart from Marcos claiming to be descended from a sixteenth-century Chinese pirate called Lim-A-Hong, there's a whole Chinese/Filipino thing and they're looking to Hong Kong to shelter some cash and maybe set up a raft of companies to shift aid, loans, gold and hot money through. I'm well in there now, but I was careful to tell them I was only giving advice as I had my own accountancy and tax business to attend to and I couldn't compromise my independent professional advisor status.'

'Where did you have the meeting?'

'Wait, it gets even better. I was invited to the Malacañang Palace.'

'Did you meet the Marcoses?'

'No, sadly. He was having one of his kidney treatments and she was in the US on a shopping spree when I first went there, but I got given a walk-through of the hideously kitsch rooms of the palace. It felt like I was on the set of a third-rate film. You should see it. Priceless works of art like Goya's portrait of the Marquesa de Santa Cruz. They've even got a throne room, with a hideous mural of Imelda painted behind, where they can sit on their carved armchairs, in front of Odeon-style curtains in gold, to set them off. It looks like they got it all, apart from the old masters, cheap from the Woolworths' Versailles range. The whole thing is a fraudsters' paradise.'

'How have you pieced together the scale of all this fraud from one meeting?'

'It's not just one meeting. And I still haven't bumped into the Marcoses. I was given access to all the files and just told to familiarise myself with them. I've seen handwritten summaries by the King of Kelptomaniacs himself and, supposedly, he has the most phenomenal memory and knows where everything is. He's like a squirrel who keeps squiggled notes of where he's hidden his nuts. I spent most of last week at the palace. That's why it's fresh in my mind. I'm not allowed to take any papers in or any papers out. Each night I've been writing up some coded stuff just to remember what I've seen. I found, when I was allowed to wander around, a large filing cabinet with a small safe in it. Ludicrously, they'd pasted the combination lock's number on the inside of the drawer. In that safe were records of umpteen Swiss and Canadian bank accounts, share certificates and letters signed by Marcos. And that's why I need the Minox.'

'What are you going to do with this info?'

'Give it to you, of course, and God knows what you can do with it. Publish it anonymously somewhere. Get it into the right hands. That might be Aquino in exile in the US. Anything. I don't want it. It's all hotting up here too much. I've got to be careful. Marcos himself has only survived because, thanks to him being paranoid and ruthless, we've had martial law up until recently to damp down revolt and the threat of a communist take-over. That's why the Chinese government is keeping an eye on what happens here and is getting active and that makes it more interesting still.'

'My Hong Kong party might be a player in something fishy down here, I suspect. He was itching to find out why I was coming here and who I was seeing. You know, the one whose firm I told you on the phone I was likely to use as a printer.'

'You're right about that. He is. I found a couple of strange references to him only today in some of the papers I was given to look at. One piece of paper, in the Marcos scribble, names Jimmy Chan as his agent for dealing with precious art and *objets* with a top auction house in Hong Kong and New York. Another was permission for Jimmy to export marine turtles for the purposes of medical research. That's code for letting him take an already endangered species to sell for use in traditional Chinese medicine. And it turns out your Jimmy Chan – the one you say Simon wants me to find some dirt on – is a director and owner, supposedly, of one of Marcos's coconut companies. I've seen the deed that transferred ownership of sixty per cent of the business with a blank space for the name, but Marcos himself holds the deed. He's the real owner. Your Jimmy is just a sleeping partner or a front.'

'But no proof then that Marcos owns it, or whether Jimmy owns any of it?'

'Exactly. No real evidence. Everything is about secrecy. That's why they want all the ins and outs of what the rules are in various jurisdictions. They love the "anything goes, no regulation" style of Hong Kong, where corporations doing business in China can set up Hong Kong companies with secret shareholdings. The worse I describe it, the better they like it. Boy, they loved me quoting a US crime-fighter that Hong Kong is where most of the corruption in China is accomplished.'

'Christ, Nick, you're right in deep with all this. You'd better be careful ...'

'I will. I'm only doing my job and that's mostly helping rich fuckers to hide their wealth from prying eyes, and I have to close my own eyes to the moral questions of who they've screwed over to acquire that wealth in the first place. The elite here send enough money overseas to repay the national debt several times over and they go offshore without any conscience at all.'

He paused and glanced around him rather shiftily.

'Don't look now, but we're being followed,' he continued. 'There's a guy fifty yards behind us in a yellow Baro shirt. They all wear them. It's national dress, the Filipino Barong to give it its proper name. In other words, he's a Marcos goon. And it's not just wearing the same shirt – they will insist on keeping their army boots on and that's the identity clincher ... I've been followed everywhere by a whole series of them after my accounting visits to the Malacañang Palace.'

'They'll have clocked me?'

'Oh, not just that, but your room in the hotel will be searched whilst we're out.'

'What are they looking for?'

'What will they find?'

'A list of my official appointments.'

'They'll thank you for that. As will the people listed. They'll all get a visit and a grilling. Probably before you get to see them. Don't be surprised if they're less than friendly when you meet them, reluctant to say much and keener on finding out exactly what you're up to. What else did you leave lying around?'

'A few of our publications – you know – books, newsletters, a copy of the dummy for the *Asia Pacific Tax Review*, with one of your articles in it actually. Oh, and one of our tax book catalogues.'

'That's good, but the goons can only spot names on a list, they'd only be able to read a Tagalog ca-ta-logue!'

'Very amusing and very calm. Aren't you worried?'

'Of course I am. They're killers, for sure. Marcos himself, when he was only eighteen, shot a political rival and has been mixed up with violence and threats ever since. Once a gangster, always a gangster, only now he has thugs in uniform to back up his threats and carry out his orders. But I'm careful. That's why we're walking round this ruddy square and it's why we're then going to go out for an old friends' bar crawl.'

'All they'll get from going through my papers is that I plan to see a Revenue official or two and some accountants here in Manila, to try and get them to give us some updates on tax matters in the Philippines and maybe even buy some of our books and periodicals. They'll also find a list of our country correspondents, including the tax departments of regional countries.'

'Who's on your list?

'For a start, you are.'

'Listed as what?'

'I put you down as a very old friend and contact from school, listed all your accounting credentials and put you in as a local expert based in Manila with experience of tax planning in the region and internationally.'

'Nothing more incriminating than that?'

'No.'

'Are you sure?'

'Yes, positive. And any other names of casual contacts I've put down in a kind of code because of something someone said to me in Hong Kong. And I made no mention of Chuck.'

'I suppose that's something.'

'And where did you leave the Minox cameras?'

'I'm glad you've reminded me. Jimmy knows I have them.'

'How the hell does he know that? Did you show him?'

'Of course not! He must own the shop I got them from or else he has a contact in there. He thought they were for me.'

'But, don't tell me, you said they were for your friend in the Philippines.'

'Look, I didn't know what you were up to, did I?'

'What else did you tell him?'

'Just that you were an accountant and an old school friend.'

'Christ, Rich.'

'Jimmy thinks I'm a nobody and even if he knew who you were and what you did, I don't think he'd think I was clever enough to be a threat.'

'Well, where are they then? Please tell me they're not still in the room?'

'No, no, I did what you told me. They're in a cardboard box of brochures I've left with reception.'

'Good. Anyway, we can get back to all this tomorrow. Let's go and get that promised drink.'

\*　　　\*　　　\*

We'd skirted round the park, onto Taft Avenue and past the Ministry of Foreign Affairs and Nick described the area we went into, with its grid of busy streets, as Malate. We dived into a 'rough as fuck' bar and had a San Miguel each. It was a pick-up bar and full of unsavoury beer-swilling older guys with shirt-busting paunches, negotiating with the pretty 'hostitutes' for all the extras on offer.

'I wanted you to see this. The Philippines at its worst. The girls here are totally exploited. Most are from worn out, economically depressed places in Visayas or Mindanao. They'll be taken to bed-rent places nearby and then come back for more customers. These are girls from the barrio, which, to the Filipinos, means the rural villages. They're all dirt poor, badly educated and attracted to the bright lights of the city. Shocking. If you're seated in a booth here, don't whatever you do ask for a "beer and a special" unless you want a drink, and a BJ under the table.

'We won't stay here, of course, unless you want to have a practical course in foreign affairs and pick up a dose of God knows what,' Nick shouted at me as we headed for the door and strolled outside in the humid night air.

'I'll take you to a more relaxed bar on Remedio Circle – it's less of a joint than the others around here, a bit more bohemian, and it doubles as an art gallery. The other bars in that part of town are more café society than sleaze, especially those on Adriatico and Bocobo streets. I know the manager of the Penguin, the one we're going to, and I gave his son some accountancy training to help him do the books for his dad, so I'm accepted. The dad's a good guy to know and have on your side. In fact, we'll hire the son to drive us around in the next day or two. I can show you some of the sights and it'll give us time to talk.'

Nick was right and it was quiet enough to chat when, eventually, we managed to stop the owner, Ramiro, and his son, Ramon, talking at us, especially Ramon about our day tour. They were lively characters and looked like a Filipino father-and-son, Elvis-impersonating act that you'd see in a local cabaret club.

Maybe I shouldn't have asked Nick about the disappearance of Chuck Besky. It served as a cue for another rant on the Marcos regime. I had to try and keep him calm and quiet.

'Don't worry about that,' he assured me, 'people in here feel the same.'

Getting back to Chuck, I asked him if he knew any more and told him I'd got Martin Rochester interested in following it up as a story. If Nick was willing to talk to him, he could feed in some of the Marcos background, off the record.

'OK, I can tell him what I know, but that's not a lot, and he can't as much as say he's got a source on the ground, or it could land me in trouble.'

'But did you have any direct contact with Chuck?'

'No, thankfully I didn't, although we spoke on the phone. He was always careful about that. I'd ring him from here and we'd even arranged to meet here before he went missing. He failed to show, but I thought nothing of it as he'd warned me it might happen and, if it did, I should try the same time on subsequent nights.'

'How did you find out what had happened to him?'

'I still don't know.'

'I mean, how did you find out he was dead?'

'All I know is what was in the papers; he'd been found dead in some scuzzy by-the-hour hotel in Ermita and that he died from alcohol poisoning. But that isn't the real story.'

'What was he doing in Manila? I thought he was up-country. The last address I had was the Banaue Hotel, where he was doing a study of the area's incredible rice terraces and their man-made waterfalls.'

'Yes, he told me he was working on a study of the Ifugao culture of that region and he'd come across some macabre stories about their headhunting ancestors. Nowadays, they dress up in tribal gear and perform their ritual dances in the hotel after dinner, would you believe? Needless to say the Banaue Hotel is government owned. Maybe an informer overheard or saw something and reported back.'

'Why do you think that happened?'

'He'd been compiling a report on Marcos-driven corrupt activities, mainly in the agricultural sector, I suppose. God knows how he found out what he did on the outside. Most of what happens is well hidden from public view and I've been amazed at what I've seen on the inside. Chuck was supposed to be looking at irrigation projects and funding and he told me he didn't like what he'd found. He was rambling on about gold shipment, drug smuggling and rare species poaching. Now I know a bit more myself about things like the marine turtles, I can see he was onto something, but at the time, I must admit, I thought he sounded like he was suffering from a dose of jungle fever. He told me that an interim report was in draft in longhand and he wanted to give it to me to get it typed up. That's why, I presume, he wanted to see me, only he didn't make it.'

'We're going to have to try and find out more. What do you suggest?'

'Anybody asking questions of the press or the government departments about him is going to get the third degree immediately. Let's try the US Embassy. After all, Chuck's a US citizen, they must care what's happened to him. There's one guy I know, and think I can trust, who we could use and I'll tell him our position. We can't afford to be seen to be interested, but we are.'

'Nick. What am I getting involved in? What are you doing poking around in all this shit? I'm beginning to think I'm completely naïve. I came on this trip hoping to sign up a few contributors, discuss new publishing ideas and tidy up a few printing contracts for Langleys. What's happening to me? All I see is corruption and crooked deals. Are the Chinese really the shittiest people to do business with in the world? And now the Filipinos? I think I just want to get finished on the few things I set out to achieve and get back home. The UK never looked so good.'

'Glad you got that off your chest? That's better. It's a stage you're going through. I know I did. I was posted out here and came because I thought it would be more exciting than walking over London Bridge every day. I was right there and I don't regret it. I came out here all

British about it, thinking I could do a good job in a developing country and learn a lot in the process.'

'Did you start by trusting everybody as I've mistakenly done?'

'Of course I did. That's a basic human instinct and it helps to come from a country where you don't have to fight for every last bowl of rice or worry about who you tread on to get it. There's a different mindset here. Trust no one until they've proved themselves and even then be suspicious. Keep your own counsel. You have to learn that.'

'And don't get caught up in things that don't concern us?'

'That's easier said than done. I mean, take the Philippines; how can you see the gangster government of Marcos and not feel sympathy for the rest of the Filipino people who I like a lot?'

'But this is dangerous. Chuck is dead!'

'We don't know that for sure.'

'This is a new twist. Why do you say that?'

'There's no body been produced for a start and people disappear all the time.'

'But the newspaper report? And why would they fake it?'

'I'm not saying they have, but just as you're realising, you can't take anything at face value. We'd better discuss it with the US Embassy guy when we see him. They'll want to know about Chuck, even if it's for the sake of the family and repatriating the body.'

'All this is exhausting. I think I'd better get back to the hotel, have a good night's sleep, get my head ready for tomorrow's appointments and generally psych myself up to think that they're all up to no good.'

'OK, I'll walk you back. I can't see you tomorrow evening, unfortunately, but the day after we have our little tour. Are you going to be able to manage without me?'

'I think so. I'll try to pretend I'm having normal business meetings with regular people and no hidden agendas. It might be easier to do that without you reminding me to watch my back all the time.'

'But you will, won't you? You have to. Your life could depend on it. And mine!'

'Yes, yes. I'll stay alert and suspicious at all times and give nothing away. That's easy in my case, because I know absolutely nothing.'

\*       \*       \*

Back at the hotel, the imposing lobby was reassuring, but the guard in the corridor outside my room spooked me and I tossed and turned all night and woke up with a sore neck and a pounding head. My mouth felt like the proverbial camel's jockstrap and I'd no enthusiasm for the day's meetings. I hoped they wouldn't be too dull.

# 5

I NEEDN'T HAVE WORRIED.

My appointments were all timed carefully and, with the taxi booked to me for the whole morning, getting to and from them all was easy.

In case you think that sounds as dull as I'd feared, let me explain what happened.

My first session was over at the tax offices in Quezon City, with a senior Bureau of Internal Revenue guy who at first welcomed me in a friendly way. His desk was piled high with files that he moved to a side table, which was also covered in files. He plonked them on top. I'd been walked to his office through a general office of shy officials all hiding behind similarly high mounds of files. Do that many people pay tax here, I thought to myself?

Tax offices everywhere tend to look the same, as if it's a worldwide brand. The quantity of manila – no pun intended – envelopes, files and cheap brown furniture give them a uniform and bureaucratic, franchisee appearance.

The staff could be the same too: dedicated everyman and everywoman with those that rise to the top being that bit smarter, but not quite free-thinking enough to leave. I had a prime example in front of me. A likeable, no doubt hard-working, middle-aged man, with greying hair and sad eyes, anxious to keep his nose clean and his family fed.

Just as we were starting the meeting, he said that he'd asked a senior official to join him in welcoming me to the Bureau of Internal Revenue. He gestured toward the office door, as if summoning someone in. I turned and, through the window in the door, saw a figure outside who yanked open the door and marched in.

Now I've seen a lot of different people in a lot of different tax offices in a great many different countries, but I've never seen a tax official like this one.

The suit was cheap, and in the Philippines that means nasty. It was blue. It didn't fit. And you could see that he was carrying some kind of gun in a shoulder holster and I don't even know what a gun in a shoulder holster should look like. But it was that obvious. He had an uncanny resemblance to Marcos himself. Family perhaps? Or a body double maybe? Like Marcos, he was slight of build, but menacing, with a vain, cocky, junior gangster air about him. He took a seat and took over the meeting.

'Why are you in the Philippines?'

I had to explain about our international tax publications which were designed to keep professional advisors and their clients informed of the different tax regimes of countries where they had, or were thinking of having, business interests. My job, I told him, was to recruit good local correspondents who could provide me with accurate, up-to-date details of the tax code in their country.

He couldn't care less about that. He wanted to know who else I was seeing and how I knew Nick Dale. Clearly he already knew I'd met Nick. The goon had reported that accurately.

I explained calmly that he was an old school friend who was a contributor and wrote articles for us about local accountancy rules and regulations and that I could show him some of Nick's work if he was interested. He wasn't. Presumably he already knew about that too.

He asked me if Nick had ever discussed his work in Manila with me and I hoped for Nick's sake that I convinced him that client confidentiality was never compromised, because Nick refused to talk about any of his clients, even to tell me who they were. He looked sceptical, which is a fancy way of saying he looked at me with utter contempt.

Calmly, I moved on and told him that I had some other people to see after this meeting who were with accountancy firms based here, that I was leaving in a day or so, that this was my first visit to Manila and that I hoped I might return, if business went well. The poor Bureau guy said he was interested in writing, but was quickly silenced with his guest saying that there was no way that they would help with a commercial enterprise trying to make money out of official government information and that full-time staff were not allowed to take external jobs. Despite me saying we would not be paying for any information, he just shook his head and told me he was sorry I'd had a wasted journey.

Slightly pissed off by now, I then merely and politely asked what his job was at the Bureau. Mistake.

He got up angrily, walked around the desk and hit me across the face with the back of his hand. He walked out without another word. So, that was his job!

You always think that if anything like that happens to you, you'd fight back, but let me tell you what your reaction is. The surprise is total, but a survival button clicks on and tells you that if you were to slap him back it will escalate and you'd end up hanging by your thumbs in some squalid prison on a remote island. A double take would have to do as my retaliation.

A strained half-smile on the face of the real tax official and a shrug practised during all the years of being a yes-man yearning to be free, was all I got by way of an apology.

'Who is that guy?'

'A colleague.'

I saw his eye flick to the corner of the room and noticed the camera. That would explain the tight-lipped response to an outrageous incident.

'No input from your department in our publications?'

'No.'

'Your international colleagues from your fellow ASEAN tax authorities are signed up, or will be shortly. Would that change your mind? You might lose face.' That would work with the Chinese, but would it work with a Filipino?

'Put it in writing to me when they are all signed up.' That was his apology and my tactic hadn't worked.

'What shall I say in the next publication? That the Philippines has a friendly tax regime where the government officials are proud of their open-door policy which welcomes business from overseas?'

He replied without the slightest hint of irony, 'That would be a nice comment and will be looked upon favourably in any further request.'

Just to keep his credentials with those watching well and truly polished, he asked me to notify him personally of any copies of any of our publications sold in the Philippines to enable him to assess any taxation due.

'Of course,' I replied, playing the game for the camera, but not knowing what he was talking about.

I fared no better with my remaining appointments for the rest of the morning. They were with professional outposts of the large international accountancy firms – each located near each other in Makati, the financial district of Manila. All were careful to point out that they could supply information on the tax legislation, but would not be able to contribute articles outlining any ways in which their firms approached the legislation for tax planning purposes. The search of my room had been used against me, but they'd told me, in so many words, that they broke the rules on a regular basis to avoid tax.

I headed back to the hotel with my tail between my legs and my cheek stinging from my brief encounter with a Marcos enforcer.

Over a club sandwich and a beer in the Ilang Ilang café at the hotel, I licked my wounds and tried to take stock of where I was at.

Progress on business matters; not good.

Knowledge of the Philippines; poor.

Introduction to corrupt regimes; painful.

My concept of doing business; challenged.

\*     \*     \*

I went back up to my room and thought I'd have a lie-down. I was pretending to myself I was tired and needed a power nap, although I knew I was just fed up and sleep seemed a better option than banging my head against a brick wall.

No rest was going to be possible for me. The room had been searched again and not as subtly. They wanted me to know it had been searched. I rang the concierge who came up immediately and answered my questions very succinctly.

No, housekeeping would not do this.

No, the guard in the corridor had seen nothing.

Yes, they would report the matter to the police, but was anything actually missing?

No.

Then there seemed little point in bothering the very busy police service did there?

No.

Would a bottle of champagne by way of an apology for any inconvenience be acceptable?

Yes.

Would he please tell the guard to keep a better watch?

Yes, of course, sir.

\*        \*        \*

With the urge for an afternoon nap now no longer clouding my brain, I tidied up my room and was on the point of calling Nick when the phone rang, and the concierge told me a Mr Dale was waiting for me down in reception and asked should he be sent up.

A few minutes later, I was walking around Rizal Park, again, with Nick and I going through the events of the morning with me warning him they'd likely be watching what he was up to.

'You now see what I mean, Rich,' he said. 'You either stay uninvolved, keep your nose clean and get on with things, turning a blind eye to everything, or you start, bit by bit, and ignoring the likely consequences, to get engaged.'

'Oh, don't start all that all over again. Anyway, why did you come and see me? I thought you were busy today and this evening, and now you're making me walk around this wretched square again. I assume it's all hush-hush.'

'Right. Here goes. Steady yourself. Chuck is still alive!'

'What?'

'I got a call from the Penguin at breakfast time this morning, telling me to drop in if I was passing. That's code for urgent. I legged it there, smartish, and my man Ramiro had an envelope for me which had been pushed through his door during the night.'

'Come on, what did it say?'

'Simply this – "Still alive. In hiding. Meet me at Hidden Valley Springs tomorrow lunchtime." It was signed, "Chuck".'

'Do you think it's from him? You've taught me this much, not to believe anything here in Manila. How do you know it's genuine? Is it a set-up? Trust no one. Your words.'

'It's genuine all right. He and I spoke in the past about Hidden Valley as a possible meeting place.'

'Where the hell is it?'

'In Alaminos, over in Laguna, on the southern slope of Mount Makiling.'

'That means nothing to me. How far is it?'

'This is the good part. We can fit it in as part of our tour tomorrow. It's a lovely spot – hot, cold and soda springs in the crater of an extinct volcano with pools and a waterfall. Tourists love it and the family that own it are friends of Ramiro at the Penguin and can be trusted.'

'It's good to know you've arranged a nice little day's sightseeing then, with the added attraction of meeting up with a dead man walking. I can't wait.'

'He's your contact. It's only thanks to you that I was in touch with him in the first place.'

'You're right of course. How can we not meet him? What's your plan?'

'I've arranged for Michael Moreno from the US Embassy to come with us. I had to meet him quickly because I couldn't risk saying anything much over the phone. I've just seen him. We'll need him to help with all this.'

'Is that what Chuck wants?'

'I guess so, but I can't exactly ask him, can I.'

'But won't we be followed?'

'Probably, if they saw us leave from the hotel, and that's why you'll tell the concierge, today, that we're going on a sightseeing tour tomorrow and calling in at the Pagsanjan Rapids Hotel. The owner is a government informer according to Moreno. The concierge'll just report where we're headed and they'll use someone at the Rapids Hotel to keep an eye on us, with any luck not bothering to send a car to tail us. When we don't show at Pagsanjan, that might start a few alarm bells ringing, I suppose, but by then we'll be back here.'

'Nothing like adding a certain piquancy to our peep at the island.'

'I'd better get back to my day. I'm going to the Malacañang this afternoon. I'll come back with you now to your hotel and pick up the cameras. That's why I've brought this local carrier bag to arrive and leave with. It's less suspicious than carrying cameras and more relaxed than coming to see you with a briefcase. They don't search me anymore on my way in or out, especially not if I'm carrying shopping bags. I'll keep both cameras for the time being – they might come in handy tomorrow.'

'What time does our Chuck "You Only Live Twice" daytrip start?'

'Meet me at Penguin tomorrow at ten. We can leave together and pick Moreno up en route. He's told me where, not far from Remedio Circle. He'll be lurking unseen outside the entrance to Manila Zoo and will only approach us when he knows we aren't being followed.'

The rest of the afternoon, I laid low in the hotel and sat in the lobby drinking endless cups of tea. That way, they, whoever *they* were, would know where I was and could see I wasn't meeting or speaking to anyone. I worked on the contents of the next few issues of our tax planning newsletter. For a moment or two, corporate tax avoidance seemed like a civilized intellectual pursuit, until I realised that it was actually all part and parcel of the subterfuge that greed engenders, and was actually crossing the same moral line that money launderers, embezzlers, smugglers, Mafiosi and corrupt political leaders did without any worries at all. Pretend all I might, I was still part of the racket.

*       *       *

I went over to the Penguin for breakfast that next day and was ready for Nick when he strode in, looking as excited as I was apprehensive.

Ramiro and he chatted at our table until his son, Ramon, came in looking a little flustered. Problems with the car, it seemed, but now all fixed and ready to go.

We then went through a complicated payment procedure. I was asked for my American Express card.

'Do you take American Express then?'

'Most certainly.'

Nick pointed out that the day's hire charge was the same amount as an average Filipino would earn in six months.

Then, taking my card, Ramon put it on the counter and placed a piece of paper on top of it. Holding both down, he gently rubbed a pencil over the paper so that the embossed card details were visible, reversed out, like a modern-day brass rubbing. I got to sign the finished artwork.

'Will that go through?' I asked.

'Of course! We submit them to the local Amex office and they pay up, less their commission. More important, if anyone asks about today, we have a record,' he said, waving the piece of paper, 'otherwise, I'd get you to pay cash as I normally would. I'll write on this piece of paper the words, "Vehicle and driver hire for day tour for two persons".'

'I can see why you do the bookkeeping. Did you teach him this, Nick?'

'No. He taught me!'

\*     \*     \*

Nick sat in the front with Ramon. The car, an old Mercedes, was not very comfortable. It looked the part, but nothing much seemed to work as intended, particularly the air-conditioning, which seemed to be pumping hot air into the cab.

'Isn't there air-conditioning?' I asked.

'Of course,' Ramon replied, 'all the windows can be opened.'

It was a short ride to the zoo and even we could tell we weren't being followed. In no time at all, 'Call me Mike' Moreno was alongside me in the back and we were heading off on the South Luzon Expressway, with Ramon cheerfully pointing out, without a hint of animosity, some luxury, gated-and-guarded compounds, lived in by the rich and successful Filipinos.

'Let's get our story straight,' Nick turned to speak to us all. 'We didn't go to the Pagsanjan because Ramon here persuaded us to go to Hidden Valley, telling us the lunch is better and because we suspect he gets a better tip from the owners.'

'Whatever you say, Mr Nick,' agreed Ramon.

'Does the driver know the purpose of our trip?' asked Moreno, slightly taken aback.

'Of course! And he knows how dangerous the information is, so, for his own wellbeing, he has no knowledge of it whatsoever do you, Ramon?' suggested Nick.

'Like you say, I was hired to give you a decent tour of the countryside and that is what I'm doing. You can talk and I will hear nothing.'

The mugginess of Manila suggested it, but the flora confirmed it – we were driving through a tropical country. Beautiful but blighted, it was dotted with poor, subsistence-level, slum-like dwellings that brought you down to earth after the new developments in Manila and the luxury real estate that existed in pockets in the capital and on its outskirts.

Mike Moreno was clean-cut, preppy and all-American, with light brown hair cut short, horn-rimmed glasses, wearing a dark blue suit, white button-collar shirt and a bright blue tie. In that heat! Whilst *we* were in casuals! He looked, in other words, like a Mormon and just when I'd decided I didn't want to hear what he had to say, as if he'd just turned up on my doorstep, he started his analysis of our predicament and I found myself hanging on his every word like a new convert. Chuck had paid for the sins of the world and we would only be able to save him and the Philippines by our atonement. Therefore, we must keep the faith. That's what it sounded like to me as I gazed out of the window.

What he had said was that we must get our hands on Chuck's bible of information or photograph it if he wouldn't hand it over. The original, if we could get it, or the film, he would get it to Hong Kong in the diplomatic bag for it to be assessed. Getting Chuck out of the Philippines would be more problematical and would require a miracle. He had us worried at this point, maybe even praying to the Mormon founder, Joseph Smith. But after a pause, he said that basically, that meant that he, Mike, would take him to the USA's Clark Air Base on Luzon Island and fly him out to Hong Kong at the earliest opportunity, typhoons permitting. That easy!

'We can lose him at the base. Fifteen thousand live there. It's got its own shops, schools and every kind of facility. He'll be OK. Provided he plays ball.'

'You don't know Chuck, do you?' I asked. 'If you did, you'd know he's his own man. He's not a team player. He might have other ideas.'

'I can help him if he trusts me. He can go to hell if he doesn't. But he'd be a fool not to give us the report, for he runs the risk that it'll be lost for ever – and all his digging around will have gone to waste – if he doesn't. As far as him wanting to live or not, the regime has made it clear they consider him dead already. Now, he can live to tell the tale by trusting me, or he'll be killed for sure. Why die a martyr's death, unnecessarily, like some crazed latter-day saint?' I was beginning to think that maybe he really was a Mormon.

That, then, was the plan and we drove on pretty much in silence except when, after ten minutes or so, Mike asked me what I was actually doing in the Philippines.

Prompted by my telling him about the conferences we ran, it turned out he was an expert in US defence contracting and had worked as a lawyer for a big swanky firm in Washington DC – Keiser, Mott, Moreno & DuPlessis. His father had started it and was still the senior partner. Mike had moved on to work for government on secondment, doing some defence contracting consultancy work. He was full of himself, telling me that he thought his name (which he proudly stated in full was 'Colonel Michael J Moreno the Fourth'), his experience and his contacts would make him a box office draw for any delegates. He'd be very happy to speak for us at our conferences and could offer us Spanish, Italian, French and German as languages in which he would happily conduct a two-day seminar. Crikey!

I caught Nick's eye and knew we could each read each other's thoughts. His echoed mine.

This guy is as CIA as you can get. I'm glad we picked him from the Embassy's pool of available talent. Shit, I bet he's got a gun too.

I turned around nonchalantly to look out of the rear window. He followed my glance.

'Yes, we're now being tailed,' he said, sensing my next question. 'Some of my guys, just in case.'

'That's reassuring, but is it necessary?'

'We'll find that out. Don't worry, they'll be discreet. They'll mingle with the tourists, but they'll be keeping our backs.'

He grilled me in a gentle way. Softening me up for what? Where did I travel? What were my plans for visits to places in the region? Did I know people in those places? Like who? He was interested because he knew people in those places too. They might know each other or be the same people. I doubted that, but he kept pressing me, shaking his head every time I mentioned any tax experts until I said 'Jimmy Chan' which warranted a raised eyebrow nod and 'Dickie Hart' which got both a smile and a nod.

'Do you know Jimmy?' It was my turn to probe.

'Yes, but it may not be the same one. You can never tell. All the names are common.' He knew Jimmy, for sure.

'What does your Jimmy do? Mine's a printer with fingers in lots of different pies.'

'Mine is a friend of Mr Marcos.' (He annoyingly pronounced him 'Mar-cose'.) 'We think he moves gold in and out for Marcos. We don't know yet how he does it. We know he flies in from time to time for a weekend of cock-fighting at the Marikina Cockpit in Metro Manila and the La Loma Cockpit in Quezon City. A lot of money changes hands and he uses it as a meeting place to get handed brown envelopes of cash that he passes off as either large bets or mega winnings. He does the same at the Manila Casino. Then he spends a lot at The Playboy Club of Manila on Roxas Boulevard. He's a very clever operator. He's not a printer. Maybe not the same guy?' He knows he is, but he doesn't want to tell me. Who cares? It's his job not mine. I'm finding it difficult enough to do my own, without worrying about anyone else's.

'Hang on a minute,' Nick turned to join in the conversation. 'Mike, does your Jimmy own a printing works here in Manila?'

'Not sure that's public knowledge or even correct,' replied Moreno trying not to look like he'd been caught out. 'What are you referring to? I've got to be careful here with burdening you with too much sensitive information,' he waffled.

'My Jimmy didn't mention a print works here to me. He knew I was coming to the Philippines and since we were talking printing contracts, he would surely have mentioned it, if he had a factory here.' I tried to sound in the loop.

Mike looked at me and then at Nick who was still craning around trying to look for an answer. Nick continued, happy to have shocked both of us.

'There was a reference to Chan Printing Inc. – you know, inc as in ink – which I thought a jokey name on some boxes of books at the Malacañang Palace, giving a local address near the University of Santo Thomas. May be worth checking out, if you ask me.'

'Sure,' said a non-committal Mike. 'I still don't think it's the same guy.'

He knows it's the same guy – we all do – and Colonel Michael J Moreno the Fourth, now more CIA than Mormon, had been caught out not knowing something pretty vital. Given that Jimmy didn't tell me he printed in the Philippines, that meant it could hardly be legit. The car fell silent again as we all contemplated what Jimmy could do with a factory here in Manila. The look of realisation that he could be using it as a cover to smuggle whatever he liked in crates of heavy books seemed to dawn on all of us at the same time, to judge by the two slack jaws I could see and the one I could feel, but we kept it to ourselves. We weren't going to be sharing secrets. Anyway the priority wasn't Jimmy, it was Chuck.

'Sorry to be a bit dense here,' I ventured timidly, 'but how does it play out for the regime if they haven't actually got Chuck? How do they explain away the press announcement of his death? Chuck's an American citizen. Can't you ask them to explain themselves?'

Back to being the Mormon on the doorstep outlining the role of Brigham Young, Mike explained it for me in simple terms that I could accept and believe.

'They'll say they made a mistake. The body wasn't
Chuck. They'll report that they'd found papers that they
now know to be false on the body of a dead Western man
in a dive in downtown Manila. They'll say that maybe
the deceased had stolen papers from Chuck and been
killed in a botched robbery. Maybe, they'll impute Chuck
murdered him. They'll say Chuck has disappeared and
meanwhile they'll be hunting him down like a dog to
make sure he has, if you take my point. That's why we
gotta get to him before they do.'

I knew I hadn't shared my thoughts with Mike, but
equally he hadn't divulged much to me. Having seen him
as our knight in shining armour, I was starting to have a
few doubts. What if the Yanks just didn't like what Chuck
had been up to and wanted to snatch him and give him
up to Marcos. They'd cosied up to the regime for years
and the Nixon administration had consented to his introduction of martial law, after which, the regime could do
whatever the hell it liked. Lyndon Johnson and Reagan
were fans. How could the Americans now let anything
undermine what they were playing at here with Marcos?
Did that mean they might not like what Nick was doing
either, if they knew? Had he told them? I should shut him
up somehow and stop him saying anything further about
what he was up to. Surely I was too suspicious? Then I
kept thinking what a mess the Americans had made with
their meddling in the Middle East, Africa, Afghanistan

and South East Asia. Add to that list the Philippines, likely damaged for all time by their support of Marcos in the plundering of its wealth. For all their hatred of the old colonial powers, the Americans were the most inter-fering of them all. I'd like to be talking to Nick right now instead of stuck in the back of what seemed to me to be a Mercedes sauna-class paddy wagon, with a Mormon prison guard who had his own agenda.

After some more staring out of the window, Mike, sure enough, asked Nick directly.

'Say, Nick. Exactly what have you been finding out at the Malacañang?'

Nick, fortunately, had not heard above the noise of some passing lorries and jeepneys engaged in a horn duel, allowing me to jump in: 'Nick was telling me he's managed to sell some of my publications that he writes for to the Marcos accountants who work out of the palace. That's right, isn't it, Nick?'

'Yes, that's right.' Nick had got the message. 'They called me in after seeing my name in a copy that they got as a free insert in an international accountancy magazine. That's when I saw the boxes of books with Jimmy's name on. We had a little general chat about UK tax and exchange controls and they've subscribed to a few journals and loose-leaf tax encyclopaedias.'

'Christ, that sounds dull,' said the Mormon.

I must be wrong, mustn't I? The Americans are the world's good guys, they tell us, stepping forward unselfishly to act as the unpaid police force on the world stage. They see themselves as second-to-none in the goodness stakes with an independent and democratic history and a strong moral code of what is right and wrong. I mean, weren't the good guys in Westerns all Americans like Mike? Then I remembered – all the bad guys in Westerns were Americans too. Like Mike?

'Driver.' Mike suddenly shouted. 'Pull in up ahead. You can park off the road. You don't mind, do you? I need to have a word with my crew following.'

'Sure,' said Nick to Ramon, who duly glided to a halt in a kind of unofficial lay-by up ahead.

Mike jumped out and walked back to the black jeep that pulled up about twenty yards behind us and he leant in at the driver's window to address his troops.

Nick and I got out whilst Ramon lit a cigarette and sat in the car. I voiced some of my fears to Nick who told me not to be ridiculous – yes he'd long suspected Mike was CIA, as, indeed, were most of the US Embassy staff, but everybody told him that he was one of the good guys and was as angry about the Marcos regime as anybody he'd ever met in the Philippines. He thought, however, that Mike was now bound to lean on him to get information, even if he'd believed his lie about his activity on the inside of the Malacañang Palace.

'But what do we do if Chuck throws a wobbly and won't go with Mike?'

'It's too late for that to worry us. That's going to happen with us or without us. Chuck will be better off in Hong Kong. You've got to make him see that. Can you use any contacts you have to get him looked after, assuming we can get Mike to part with a fellow countryman and "resource" as they'll no doubt see him as after today?'

'I can speak to Simon and see if he can get his mate Will Tomkins who is in Military Intelligence or something, attached to the Hong Kong police, to help with Chuck. Maybe he can give him some protection if and when he gets there, but Mike will have to be willing to cooperate. Maybe we should find out exactly what Mike is up to.'

Just then Ramon came over to where we were standing and pointed towards Mike walking back to our car.

'We'd better go,' he said to us whilst stubbing out his cigarette carefully on the ground until he was sure it was out, 'don't want to start a fire.'

'Ramon,' I asked, pointing at what looked like a collapsed wooden shack growing out of the ground amongst the palms and papayas. 'What tree is that?'

'A banyan tree. Many Filipinos think they are home to spirits, mostly bad. Not good if you believe in bad luck.'

That helped my positive outlook a lot.

We returned to the car at the same time as Mike did and were soon underway.

'What's the plan for Chuck?' I asked Mike.

'I want him off the island and quick. We can get him to Hong Kong. I've spoken about him recently with a British diplomat there. You mentioned his name a while back. Seems you Brits all went to the same school, didn't you? You know him – Richard Hart – with the very curly black hair, a great guy.'

'Yes, I know him,' I said, 'but not from school. We were at the same college in Cambridge.'

'See! That's what I said!' gloated Mike. 'Richard can look after him. Chuck is free to go and do what he pleases once we're shot of him. He's not under arrest or anything. He'll have to look after himself as far as I'm concerned, once we give him over to Richard. If he takes my advice, though, he won't come back to the Philippines.'

'But what about what he knows of all the goings-on here? Won't that damage your relationship with Marcos?' I asked.

'I doubt that very much. What he writes won't ever be published here and, as you may have guessed from the local press, it won't even get reported. They don't care about anything other than what the First Lady is up to. The headline in today's *Manila Times* was 'FL Flies in from France'. It's a crazy place. Marcos can do what he likes, pretty much with impunity. These days, we're more interested in what other people try and do in the Philippines. Like the Chinese. If Chuck had anything going in that direction, we'd keep him for ourselves. We know all we need to know and more about Marcos. You're right about one thing though – if we wanted Chuck, we could hole him up at the Clark base for ever.'

I still wasn't happy. I thought I'd tackle my fears head on.

'What's your role at the US Embassy, Mike?'

'I'm in the commercial section, trade relations, that type of thing.'

'You're not CIA then?'

'You expect me to answer that?'

'You just have.'

'Are you MI6?'

I couldn't help but burst out laughing.

'Good Lord, no.'

'How do I know?'

'How do I know you're not CIA?'

'You don't. You have to take my word for it and see what happens to either confirm or deny your suspicions.'

'Let me put it another way. It's said that Marcos started off his political career with help from wealthy backers *and* the CIA. Before that, the CIA are supposed to have been active in the Philippines in counterinsurgency and they'd helped put down a rebellion or two, and then used that model in Vietnam and elsewhere.'

Mike turned his head and looked directly at me.

'Where are we going with this exactly?'

Nick turned round, giving me a quizzical look, and I could see Ramon's eyes flick to mine in his rear-view mirror. All three awaited my reply.

'The US needs stability in the Philippines and the CIA has been active in supporting Marcos to fight the threat of nationalist, communist or Muslim insurgency. This is seen as a bolster against the spread of communism in South East Asia in particular. Heck, Marcos committed Filipino troops in the Vietnam War.'

'Your point being?'

'Why are you interested in helping Chuck when US policy has been to support Marcos at all costs?'

'Simply because, we aren't all for Marcos. Your analysis is out of date. Jimmy Carter had started supporting opposition groups because we knew the Philippines needed to be a more stable democracy. I've written a paper to the State Department, outlining the corruption and crony capitalism that's rife under Marcos, which makes the regime unstable at a time when we need a stable democratic ally to prevent the spread of communism, as well as helping to keep our critical strategic military bases in operation. There's no succession to Marcos in place and the guy's not in great health. That worries us. We don't see him as part of the transition process whether by death, retirement or forcible removal. But you didn't hear it from me. Satisfied?'

We all nodded and I mumbled a yes.

'And, what's more,' Mike added, 'I had a Filipino nanny and my personal sympathies are all with the people.'

'OK! OK! I get all that, but is that official policy?'

'I can see you are deeply suspicious. How about this? Your government, through your old college chum Richard Hart, wants us to extract Chuck because they see him as a UK asset. We can't officially touch him without there being a major diplomatic incident. You should worry more about MI6 than the CIA. We're the good guys. What we've all got to make sure of now, is that we keep our involvement unknown to anybody associated with Marcos and his gang. I'm not happy Mr Besky won't be spotted in Hidden Valley or might already have been, or that there won't be a nice reception committee waiting for us. How's that? Satisfied now?'

'Thanks, yes, sorry,' I mumbled further.

# 6

I WOULD NEVER HAVE RECOGNISED CHUCK. Bearded, straggly haired and unkempt, in a battered tropical suit with pockets everywhere, he looked much more like some revolutionary who'd been hiding out up-country for quite a while, than Che Guevara ever did in his famous poster shot, but maybe *he'd* taken his barber with him.

Nick and I'd gone in first to the restaurant, as arranged, leaving the others at the vehicles, the jeep following ours having parked a little distance from our car, to make us look less like a convoy.

We looked around for him and couldn't see him and, turning to look again, we noticed our grizzly friend coming through the doorway. He'd followed us in and must have been looking out for us to arrive.

We tried to say hello, but he was straight away on the offensive.

'What the hell are all those other guys here for? They look like CIA to me. Promise me you'll keep them here whilst I make a run for it.'

'Chuck, sit down for a moment. Everything is safe,' Nick started to say. 'Let me introduce myself, I'm ... '

'I know who you are,' said Chuck. 'He's Rich because he's my friend and I know him and, as you're with him, you're Nick. Good to meet you at last and thanks for coming. I'm edgy is all.'

We sat him down and bought three buffet tickets as we figured he'd need to eat more than we did and we knew we were ravenous. When we had our food – a choice of 'the freshest' (although we were miles from the sea) 'tropical seafood broiled, grilled or steamed, all with rice' – we explained what we'd done and what seemed the best plan.

The one thing we didn't do later was tell Mike that Chuck had told us he'd hidden his report in a toilet cistern, or that he wanted us to get a copy of it to the Filipino opposition groups that were in touch with Ninoy Aquino, one of their leaders, who was still living in the US. As Chuck put it, that report would provide Aquino with a lot more to say on his tub-thumping speaking tours of the States, and help him to build opposition to Marcos and undermine the legitimacy of the Marcos regime at home.

Nick asked him how this could be the case as it was well known that Imelda herself had given Aquino two conditions when they let him go to the US for heart surgery; one being that he must return and the second being that he would not speak ill of them whilst he was away. Chuck explained that Ninoy had said, more or less, that 'a pact with the devil is no pact at all' and, therefore, had felt free to speak out. Ferdinand and Imelda were not happy with that. Not one little bit.

Chuck had been adamant that he did not, repeat not, want the report to fall into the hands of the CIA, where it would either be buried or doctored or used to incriminate him with Marcos. We tried to say he could be wrong about that, but he wasn't having any of it.

'I'm American and I *know* you can't trust the CIA.'

'Mike hasn't admitted he's CIA,' I tried to reassure him.

'Naturally he'll deny he is,' Chuck replied, 'but pardon my cynicism born of years, literally, in the field. They can't help themselves but make a mess of things. Look at the Congo, look at ... never mind, this is wasting time.'

We'd assured Chuck we'd get the report out of the country, somehow, and to Hong Kong where he could be reunited with it. We'd also Minox the pages to give us a copy, just in case.

When he was calm, Nick went out and brought in Moreno and, of course, the report was the first thing

Mike asked for and he looked disbelieving at all of us when Chuck said he'd lost it when he'd had to leave his hotel in a hurry after getting a tip off from a porter that some Marcos goons were hanging around.

However, once Mike was satisfied that Chuck was going to play ball after all, and was happy with the rules, a game plan was agreed.

In the end, Chuck went off with Mike quite happily, although I did wonder if I'd ever see him again.

All we had to do now was retrieve the report, drive back to Manila and hope we hadn't been missed, or that our cover story had been blown. What could go wrong?

We secured the report without any hitch, but then came the first, slight, inconvenience.

The car wouldn't start and Ramon had the bonnet up and what seemed like half the kitchen staff standing staring at it offering advice. Tools were brought and Ramon and his mechanics started prodding and poking the oily engine without inspiring any confidence.

Nick and I decided to take a look at the Hidden Valley Springs. He was supposed to be showing me the sights after all. We made off, following the signs, to the pools and the hidden valley. It was a worthwhile chance to talk to Nick and walk along the tropical trail, amongst vast and magnificent trees and dense green vegetation, and to see tourists enjoying the warm pool and the lovers' pool. It gave us some sense of normality. We could talk in a matter-of-fact way about handling Chuck's report as if we were experienced old hands in espionage and subterfuge. For a start, we knew that not leaving as soon as possible made us more vulnerable, and if there was any risk of us being in danger, we'd need a convenient tree to hide the report.

On the other hand, if we made it out of the valley with the report, it was agreed that we would conceal it in the door panel of Ramon's car and leave it with Ramon and Ramiro who would take a Minox to film it, with Nick training Ramon in how to use the camera. The film would be brought to Hong Kong by Nick, as he was less likely than I was to be searched. He had, he told me, been given a special card to show at Manila airport at departure or on arrival because, he'd assumed, he would one day be asked to carry sensitive stuff in and out of the country for the Marcos accountant without being stopped. It gave him almost complete freedom at the airport and he'd tested it out on a recent trip to Singapore; once he'd shown it, he was waved through on his way out and on his way back in.

We reluctantly felt that it was not worth the risk of copying the report any other way as to be caught with a copy could have fatal consequences.

Ramiro, it came as news to me, did in fact know some of Aquino's supporters and would be asked by Nick to get the report to them. They would then get it, God knows how, to the man himself.

'It's a jungle out there,' I ventured.

'It's a jungle in here,' Nick gestured around us.

We found a quiet spot to sit and Nick took the report out of his lightweight rucksack. We carefully unwrapped it and passed page after page between us. It ran to a dozen closely written pages.

We learnt that Marcos had: taken over the national electricity industry by threats of the death penalty against the owner's son on a trumped-up charge of plotting his assassination; taken over the sugar industry through presidential decrees to acquire the planting, milling, marketing and shipping rights and topped that off with exploiting the workers by scrapping wage protection; taken over control of the three other main agricultural sectors of coconuts, tobacco and bananas; dominated the logging, paper, meat, oil, insurance, shipping, airlines, beer, cigarettes, textiles, hotels, casinos, newspapers, radio and TV areas; created his own corrupt banking system to handle his unlimited cash; and used a foreign-owned yacht to smuggle gold, rare species and historical artefacts out of the Philippines.

When we'd finished, I told Nick that I finally appreciated my old school motto, *Inter Sylvas Quaerere Verum* – to seek the truth amongst the groves.

'That's exactly what we've got in our hands out here in the middle of the trees in this valley where the truth is no longer hidden,' I said.

'Don't go all poetic on me now. This stuff is very scary and I don't want it in our hands for a minute longer than necessary. Let's get to the car, pronto.'

We made our way back to find Ramon sitting, smoking in the car with the engine running, but sited a hundred yards from where he'd been parked. Impressed, we asked the cause of the engine trouble and, after an animated explanation, he eventually told us the battery was flat for some reason and he'd been given a push start to get the engine going. Some technical problem. Some mechanic. I hoped he could use a screwdriver. He could, just about.

In we got and off we went, stopping with the engine running, after a short distance, only to allow Ramon to unscrew his door panel, put the report behind it and screw it back up again. He managed it with only a few visible scratches on the fabric around some of the screws, but enough that a moderately awake official would spot on a cursory glance inside the car. We just had to hope we weren't stopped and subjected to a search.

The return trip was strangely hypnotic with the rich lushness of the countryside contrasting with the poverty of the homes we drove past and our heads full of the oppressive heat and the overwhelming fear of being found out.

Back in the city, the second and more major inconvenience was when I strolled back into the Manila Hotel to be greeted by the concierge and that nice man I'd met at the Filipino tax office, the unmistakeable Marcos lookalike.

Or perhaps it was Marcos himself, come to join me for dinner to welcome me to his Philippines?

\*        \*        \*

'We've been worried about you,' the concierge said, in mock concern, shaking my hand. ' You did not show at the Pagsanjan Falls Hotel – I'd phoned them to make sure they looked after you.' Yes, I bet you did. And to tell them to watch my every move.

'Sorry it was a last-minute change of plan. Our driver said it was an easier drive to the Hidden Valley, although between you and me, we think it was because he was getting a kickback from the restaurant. Look at the size of our bill.'

I handed over the official receipt that showed two guests. We'd cleverly made sure that Nick had paid for his own. That way, we would have some proof of there being only two of us.

'You say "we",' said the slappy chappy. 'Who were you with?'

'My old school friend, Nick. He wanted to be my tour guide and we had a nice day not thinking or talking about work, just two old friends who don't see each other very often, talking about life and death and the meaning of it all, with me being shown your beautiful country.'

They didn't like that. I followed up with, 'What's your name?' to Marcos II. 'If we're going to keep meeting, I'd like to know.'

The concierge looked shocked at the question and I expected another backhand to the face. All I got was, 'I know your name. That's enough. For the moment your friendship with Mr Dale gives you some protection. Him, we trust. For now. But you! You are being watched.'

I turned to go, but No-Name viciously grabbed me by the arm and menacingly asked me, 'Do you know where Chuck Besky is?'

I tried and failed to pull my arm out of his grip.

'I don't, but I know someone with that very unusual and memorable name died here in Manila. American wasn't he? Do you know who killed him yet?'

Then in a threatening tone he said, 'We are warning all Westerners to be careful. We don't know where the killer will strike again.'

He pushed my arm away and asked when I was leaving the Philippines.

'I think I'll bring my flight forward. I'm going to Singapore for a few days, if that's OK ?' I seemed to be getting out of places sooner and sooner. Maybe, with any luck, I'd eventually not even arrive.

'An earlier flight is a very good idea after what you've done today,' he said, turning to the concierge, 'can you arrange it for tomorrow for Mr Rowlands?'

He paused for a second and then followed up with, ' We think you are a spy for the British government and you are trying to recruit agents, but I asked about you in Hong Kong and one of our contacts was prepared to speak for you. He said you were a harmless publisher. "Low grade" I think he said. For what it's worth, he's right. But you will need to be very careful if you ever return to our country.'

With that he turned on the stacked heel of his very black, very patent, very pointy shoe. I wondered if he and Imelda swapped notes on footwear?

Preoccupied with that thought, I hadn't even pressed him for his name.

\*       \*       \*

I had to stifle a laugh as I walked away and went to my room. Me. A spy? Why was it that people who were secretive and corrupt thought everybody else was as bent as they were? It was too ridiculous for words. I went to my room, booked in for a last night dinner and rang Nick to say I was leaving ahead of schedule. We arranged that, as soon as I knew my flight time, he would come and pick me up and drive me to the airport.

Hardly a successful visit, but I had a lavish dinner to give myself a good send off, followed by several nightcaps in the Après disco in the hotel. Having slept surprisingly soundly, I was wakened by room service bringing me my order of *pandesal* bread and coffee, delicious dipping the one into the other, with a plate of papaya.

On the tray was a Philippine Airlines ticket to Singapore departing at 13.30 and arriving at 17.30 and a note telling me that my previous ticket was cancelled.

I rang and told Nick.

After a walk, another people-watching coffee in the lobby and then packing, I had a call from reception to say Mr Dale had arrived and did I need a porter? No, I didn't need a hand with my bags, I could manage, thanks. One bag and one carry-on were sufficiently lightweight for an international spy of my calibre to handle.

After much laughter at my new man-of-mystery persona that had rendered me *non grata*, we realised that it put Nick in some danger. He'd have to watch himself and talk very carefully with his contact at the palace, to make sure his positive vetting had not gone negative. He'd have to make sure he wasn't being tailed, not just by Marcos men, but also by the CIA. We still didn't trust Mike Moreno.

We agreed to meet in Hong Kong, once I'd arrived back there from Singapore. As luck would have it, he'd been asked by the palace that morning to go to Hong Kong, at some point, on a financial mission he didn't know the details of yet, but could only guess probably involved carrying a suitcase of cash. He'd bring the report and the spare Minox. After all, now I was a spy, he told me that I was going to need it even more. Cue more laughter.

Nick asked me who I was going to be meeting in Singapore and yawned at how mundane it sounded especially the ex-tax inspector from Liverpool who wrote for me and knew a lot about tax regimes in South East Asia.

'You have to admit it, Nick,' I said, 'it's a hell of a cover I've got!'

More laughter, until he stopped to let me and my baggage out of his car. I waved goodbye cheerily, but part of me was rather concerned, not for my safety, but his.

## PART THREE
# SINGAPORE

*If you want to keep a secret, you must
also hide it from yourself.*

GEORGE ORWELL

# 7

RODNEY BOLT WAS A larger-than-life character in every way, from the top of his big, bald head, down his tattooed arms and to his outsize butcher's hands. The fact that one of those meat hooks could hold a very sharp pencil to calculate intricate accounting and tax planning computations was a miracle of function over form.

He was, in every sense, a pirate of the South China Seas, full of stories of the riches plundered from Hong Kong, Indonesia, Borneo, Malaysia and Singapore being hidden away in distant ports or buried on remote tax haven islands. Listen to him talk and you would swear that he alone possessed the treasure map and the knowledge, not only of where the loot was buried, but also of the savvy needed to 'parlay' with the tax authorities of

overseas jurisdictions, given his status as 'formerly one of
Her Majesty's Inspectors of Taxes'. His confidence, surely,
would convince even the most cynical of revenue officers
that his clients weren't brigands at all, but privateers,
with the seal of legal authority legitimising their acts.

I'd met him first when he was speaking at a tax
planning conference where he'd grabbed the attention of
the audience with a vivid description of the risks of doing
business in Indonesia because of its company ownership
rules; you had no choice but to set up what he called
an Ali Baba company in Jakarta, whereby you took in
local partners who, in the middle of the night, would rise
up and steal the company from you. His tax avoidance
advice for some countries was just that – avoid them
at all costs. His other pearl at the time was that 'to get
involved in tax planning, you've really got to first make a
profit.' How could I not have signed him up as the author
of *An Insider's Guide to Tax Planning in the Far East*.

We were sitting poolside at the Tanglin Club on
Stevens Road. It was *the* leading expats club on the
island and not far from my hotel, the Marco Polo, which
actually *was* on Tanglin Road.

Rodney was in his XXL swimming trunks at a round
table by the club's vast pool. After telling me about the
history of the club (something about it either being
named after the local species of tanglin tree, the type
under which Buddha was born, or after the words 'tang

ling', Chinese for the 'eastern side of a small hill'), he told
me that if I wanted to see him during my visit, I'd find
him there every day at five o'clock and he'd be delighted
if I'd join him for a swim and a chat followed by a drink.
Eh? Breakfast meetings were all the rage in London and
New York, but pool meetings? That was a first.

Fortunately, he'd just had his swim and was settling
into a Sundowner, a cocktail he said he'd found when he
was in South Africa – he was forever place-name dropping.
He urged me to join him in a 'large one', so I did, and,
sipping away, he held forth in that transatlantic Liverpud-
lian drawl of his that made him sound as if Ringo Starr
had downed sticks and become a financial advisor.

He told me about arcane tax avoidance schemes
involving Cases I and II of Schedule D, whatever that
meant, and told me about the fun of being taxed on
the remittance basis and never actually being resident
anywhere in the world.

'Being on a yacht and sailing the seven seas like Craig
McMasters then,' I ventured, which was a good shout, as
Rodney spluttered into his drink, momentarily thrown
off-kilter.

'Do you know him?' he asked.

'Not really. I met him briefly in Hong Kong.'

'Watch out for him. He's a marked man in several
jurisdictions and he owes me money.'

'Whatever for?'

'Advice, mainly. But I gave him loads of introductions to key government and private practice experts out here and he promised me a hefty commission. He was looking for speakers the same way you're looking for authors, but no contracts and no money were ever forthcoming. Nobody was paid. He's got a lot of people's backs up. And he sails off without a care in the world, but it won't last. It'll catch up with him one day. Don't go the same way as him.'

'No chance of that! I think being honest and straightforward is much easier, if a little timid. Anyway, I can't sail. Put those together and I couldn't possibly do what Craig, or Tufty as they call him, is supposed to do on the side.'

'Oh, the smuggling rumours?'

'Are they true?'

'Let's put it this way. I know for a fact that he's done the trip from Hong Kong to Manila quite a few times, because he boasted about it to an ex-navy pal of mine who works in a shipyard in Hong Kong.'

'Wow. What do you think he's up to?'

'That I don't know for sure. But have you ever come across Jimmy Chan?'

Even better shout!

Now it was my turn to half swallow, half spit my second Sundowner and I couldn't speak for a moment.

Rodney, pleased with the effect he'd had, followed up with, 'I can see you have. Boy, have we got a lot to talk about this evening. Let's order some food and I'll get changed out of this swimming gear.'

*     *     *

When Rodney returned, it was just as the Chinese steamboat he'd ordered for us was being put on our table. He'd insisted that that's what we'd both have.

'It's like a Chinese version of fondue,' he'd said to tempt me. 'We cook up raw chicken, vegetables and noodles at the table. That way, we don't get disturbed by the, er, *very* attentive staff. It's a good dish to have here because you get to cook it yourself. No disrespect to the chefs.'

When he returned and sat down he took up his large linen napkin and tucked it behind the top button of his short-sleeve blue linen shirt like an extravagant cartoon gourmet, before turning to me.

'I trust *you* all right. You've been pretty straight with me and paid for what you've commissioned. Anyway, I like you. You remind me of me.'

'Thanks. I'll take that as a compliment.'

'I might say a few things this evening which you didn't hear from me, if you understand me. The fact that we'll then both have that knowledge will bond us together in some kind of secret society of fiscal freemasons.'

'That's a good way of looking at it. We know it and we'll keep it to ourselves.'

'Share it only with like-minded folk.'

Whilst we set about cooking at the table and eating, Rodney told me bits of his life story.

He'd been a docker and a Royal Marine before going into the Inland Revenue in the 1950s. What a combination! You'd certainly answer his questions at an interview into your tax affairs.

He grew restless as a civil servant and, when he was told his next tax district after Liverpool would be Merthyr Tydfil, he'd resigned and started working for a shipping company out of the Liver Building.

'I specialised in the PanLibHonCo flags-of-convenience dodges.'

'What's that when it's at home?'

'When it's not at home, you mean. It's a racket for sure, but it was a perfectly legal way of using the overseas jurisdictions of Panama, Liberia, Honduras and Costa Rica, where you'd register merchant shipping in one of those countries to avoid financial or regulatory restrictions that applied in an owner's own country. That gave me an insight into that world of financial manipulation and I realised I could use different offshore territories to have the same impact in reducing tax bills for clients. I just set up on my own as a tax planner, with a few shipping owners as my first clients. Once I'd realised that people with real wealth were just like giant tankers roaming the world laden with container loads of cash and I could "register" them anywhere that had a low tax regime, I knew I was on to a winner.'

'Were you in at the birth of tax avoidance then?'

'Hardly, but it was growing fast, and I gave it a leg-up. There were a few of us then specialising in different aspects and we swapped and referred clients to each other. One guy did things for rock stars and creative types like inventors and authors, which usually meant sending them overseas for a tax holiday. High tax rates in the UK meant we were never without punters willing to take a chance to shelter their earnings.'

'How did you end up in the Far East?'

'That's easy to explain. I had a spell in the Netherland Antilles, on Curaçao, working on one case, and that got me involved with big companies in the pharmaceutical areas, with interests in the US. For some of the biggest, I did a "recce" in Hong Kong and Singapore and spotted more opportunities. I met my wife in Hong Kong and, because she was ostracised by her family for getting involved with me, we thought Singapore the more civilised option as a base to live in. I like it here. I like the fact that it's clean and everything works.'

'Isn't it a bit "Big Brother" with the ban on chewing gum, jaywalking and long hair on men?'

'As you can see, the ban on long hair holds no threat to me and the other stuff is perfectly sensible. Some of the other things about living here are more worrying, like the fact that the Chinese, as you'd expect, see themselves as superior to everyone else, mainly the Indians and Malays. The Chinese hold the economic power in Singapore, and in Malaysia if it comes to it, and that's fine with me and my wife, but I don't like it as a set-up. We send our son to school in England and in a few years we'll go back and live there when I retire from this sordid game. I couldn't live here for ever. It's a soulless and sterile place and a complete contrast to Hong Kong where, for example, despite all their "No Spitting" signs, they can't stop that old Chinese habit. I couldn't live there permanently either – too many people chasing after dollars and completely cut-throat.'

'Does that bring us back to Jimmy?'

'Neatly. But how do you know him?'

'Just because he prints a lot of stuff for Langleys and he is, or acts as though he is, a bit of a Hong Kong kingpin.'

'He is that, and a whole lot more. What do you know of him and what opinion have you formed?'

'I take it he's not a friend of yours?'

'No, but he's a distant relative of my wife's and let's say our paths have crossed. We both completely loathe him.

You can have no fear in talking openly and critically of him with me.'

'For a start, he frightens me. He thinks I'm a useless and very small cog in Langleys and to me, he seems to have fingers in many, many pies – big fingers and big pies at that. A contact of mine in the Hong Kong Revenue, and another in Military Intelligence, have warned me about my dealings with him. What he's up to seems to be bordering on the illegal and he's even turned up as having something to do with Marcos in the Philippines.'

'It seems like you already know enough to be a risk to him. That puts you in a dangerous place.'

'He doesn't know I know anything about him, judging by how he treats me. I'd like to think he sees me as harmless and only interested in my job, with no knowledge about the way his world works and no imagination as to how you can exploit your way to wealth and power. Even Langleys haven't shared with me what they must know about him. I'm just a pawn to him and a gofer for them.'

'I'd like to talk about your work and what brings you to Singapore. It must be more than wanting to see me.'

'Actually, it would be a relief to talk about publishing. I seem to have got caught up in things that really shouldn't concern me and I'm a bit fed up of talking about Jimmy and even Marcos. After all, what can I do about either of them and why should I even care?'

'That's a different question, but let's have a change of topic.' Rodney lowered his voice to a whisper and waved his hand and half smiled at somebody over my shoulder. Still sotto voce, he carried on: 'That suits me as, don't look now, but the guys who've just sat down at the next table are three accountants that I know for a fact are on a retainer from the Filipino government. They're with another fella I don't know. We'd better watch what we say. Come for a swim with me tomorrow. Nobody can hear us talking in the pool and we can trade tales and lengths to our hearts' content and to the benefit of our health.'

Resuming his normal booming voice, he asked me, 'Now, tell me what you're up to in Singapore.'

So, I told him about my plans at finding new printers, new authors and even about my thinking about setting up on my own, publishing a few special reports on tax planning and maybe some periodicals, which is where he would come in. All Rodney was interested in was whether there would be any money in it for him, as he had his son's school fees to think about and, maybe, a royalty stream would help him in his retirement.

Actually, he was really helpful in my thinking about publishing in my own right and wanted me to meet another friend of his, Miguel Bentoz, the son of a Paraguayan diplomat who had wound up in Singapore and worked as a journalist and editor.

'He'd be a good pair of eyes and ears and even legs on the ground. He often has to travel in the region, knows the score and, what's more, he already has an entrée with government press officers and local bigwigs. He's a real hard worker and very personable and, once you get past the bow-tie façade, he has a wicked sense of humour and could easily charm a few reluctant authors to pen a few lines, and a few tax authorities to license official texts to reproduce.'

'He sounds too good to be true and, if I've learnt one thing in business, it's *always* to look a gift horse in the mouth.'

'Look, just meet him for yourself and make up your own mind. You can always give him a trial – see how you could work together. No skin off my nose if you can't. I like him, that's all, and you can't keep popping over here from the UK, even if you wanted to. Local control of events is crucial to setting up business overseas in my experience. Don't make the mistake of thinking that absentee entrepreneurship would work for you any more than it does for anybody else.'

Rodney went on to virtually draft my first Far East publishing list and I was warming to the idea of getting some financial backing and going it alone. I'd have to make a detailed note of all that when I got back to the hotel. Langleys would have to be told, of course, but the relief of not having to deal with Jimmy on their behalf would be worth the trauma of resigning and striking out on my own with a start-up company.

I felt relieved to be talking about me and my plans and was liking the idea of this Miguel Bentoz, even if it only meant I'd never have to go to the Philippines again.

*          *          *

I pitched up again the following day, poolside at the Tanglin Club at the appointed hour. Rodney was sitting there in his trunks, smoking a cheroot this time. He looked for all the world like the Merlion symbol of Singapore, with a lion's head and the body of a fish. I took my time to savour that, but when he noticed me, standing by the door to the terrace in my swimwear, and modestly holding my towel, he started to laugh uproariously at my appearance for I looked like a walking Neapolitan ice-cream: chocolate-brown hair, strawberry-pink front and vanilla-white back. Why so ludicrous?

I'd fallen asleep on a sun lounger earlier that day when I'd gone by the Marco Polo's circular pool after break-fast to waste some time before a lunch meeting with a chap from the British Council. It was overcast, you see. I assumed I wouldn't actually be bothered by the sun. Mistake! Singapore is only eighty-eight miles from the Equator – I'd since checked! That's why I'd got burnt. Oh, and bitten by some little white, midge-type insects. I was in a right mess and Rodney couldn't hide his delight at my embarrassed anguish.

The hotel had been very good about it, giving me some Tiger Balm ointment, but the smell only added to my discomfort.

'Have some tea, Rich, and tell me all about your day,' Rodney greeted me, and, still smiling, poured me a cup.

'As you can see, I got burnt.'

'Not a day of heavy meetings then?'

'Only one, with a British Council guy at Raffles which turned out more interesting than expected.'

'You don't mean with Eric Old?'

'Yes. Him. You obviously know him.'

'I've only met him a few times, usually at formal government receptions or some expat social event.'

'I met him years ago, in Cambridge, at a recruitment evening at the British Council building in Portugal Place and we used to meet for a drink at The Baron of Beef, the pub virtually next door to his office.'

'Does he *ever* do any work? When I first met him, while he was hosting a tour out here of a ghastly Derek Nimmo production at one of the hotels on Orchard Road, his one Council story was that his best posting was in Khartoum, where he used to have his breakfast bacon and eggs flown up from Nairobi. It's a strange organisation if a chap like Eric Old can thrive in it, if you ask me.'

'It certainly is that. He once told me about his first boss, who'd advised him to put whatever came into his in-tray straight into his out-tray, and that he'd be amazed at how little of it ever came back.'

'We used to do that in the Revenue – must be part of some Civil Service training course.'

'Sounds like something out of *Yes Minister* to me.'

'What on earth was interesting about meeting him?'

'The interesting bit was not actually him exactly, although he did promise to help me with a grant, or some such, to help me employ Miguel Bentoz, if I went ahead and took him on. Turns out he's met him and thinks highly of him. I'd like to take you up on the offer to introduce us and get that ball rolling.'

'Good. At least he's got some judgement. But look, cut to the interesting bit.'

'We were meeting at Raffles and when I walked in he was sitting at the Long Bar with a chap I'd met in Hong Kong called Kenneth Minter. Do you know him?'

'No, I don't. Should I?'

'Maybe, but, after today, I'm not sure. They both clearly had had a couple of stiff Singapore Slings by the time I got there at noon. They were insisting on a liquid lunch, which I managed to avoid by telling them I was still a bit too jet-lagged to drink much and they didn't press me. The conversation was the interesting bit. You see, as I've said, I'd met with Kenneth Minter in Hong Kong. He seemed pleased to see me and said he had been going to try and find out where I was staying, as he knew I was in Singapore. This had saved him the effort. Turns out we'd both known Eric for years without our paths ever having crossed.'

'What scoops did they serve up to make it interesting? Sounds like a typical ex-pat, inebriated, waste-of-time lunch session to me.'

I told Rodney that by the time I'd headed off to go back to the hotel before coming to meet him, Kenneth had told me the two of them had met when Eric had recruited him to do some work for the Council 'flying the flag and giving a little push to UK interests' in the conference world. Eric had provided him with some inside contacts in various countries into the bargain. In return, Kenneth had done some fact-finding. They both wondered if I was interested in doing the same. Turns out that Kenneth was happy to be doing something for Queen and Country.'

'Careful, Rich,' counselled Rodney. It all sounds like a slippery slope to me. Remember Greville Wynne? You don't want to get involved in all that.'

'Have no fear! I've already got people in the Philippines *thinking* I'm a spy and *that* was unpleasant enough. Why on earth would I want to get into that world for real?'

'The classic reasons, according to the FBI, are money, ideology, compromise or ego. Of MICE and Men! Which one of those vulnerabilities would get *you*, Rich?'

'Not sure, but I think Kenneth was probably "got" for a slap-up lunch at the Savile Club and a chance to talk to someone who would listen to his stories.'

'There must be more to it than that. Money is the most usual motivation, but your man Eric preys on middle-aged businessmen who are frustrated in their work, or have some issue like alcoholism or homosexuality. One thing you can bet on is that people with nothing to hide don't usually become spies, even in an amateur capacity. Greville Wynne's character weaknesses were certainly exploited to the full and he ended up with a ludicrously inflated idea of his own importance. What does that tell you about Minter?'

'Ego then? I quite liked him when I first met him, but I can see he is prone to gossip and likes to cast himself as a man of mystery. He seems to talk too much and too openly to be a real spy.'

'Or is he, and are they, testing you? Have you thought about that?'

'They did get more and more interested in my publishing plans, even more so at my travelling around and recruiting local authors and correspondents, so, yes, you could be right.'

'Watch them, and don't get Miguel involved with them, for his sake, and yours.'

'OK, message received. But a couple of other interesting snippets came up. Kenneth knows Tufty McMasters. It was him who first used that nickname for Craig to me. However, he doesn't really know Jimmy Chan, I don't think, other than, when it came up before, he knew the name as someone who'd tipped Tufty off about me competing with him.'

'Even more reason to keep them all at arm's length if you ask me.'

'God, I'm getting heartily sick of all the intrigue and I want to draw a line under it and get going on the publishing.'

'Let's do that. Presumptuous I know, but I've arranged to have lunch with Miguel tomorrow at the Goodwood Park Hotel, which, like this place, is not that far from where you're staying. Let's have a publishing day tomorrow. But first, let's have that swim.'

It turned out that Rodney had a few things to get off his chest and he felt better doing that in the pool where we couldn't be overheard. Swimming up and down the length of the pool, we did a heads-up breaststroke, like Chairman Mao Zedong and his bodyguards in the Yangtze, and we talked and talked, with the main exercise being that taken by the face muscles trying to sustain breathing and speaking at the same time; the swimming strokes were confined solely to keeping the conversation afloat.

Rodney said, 'I want you to have the full SP on Jimmy. Once I've told you, I want to draw a line under it, then rub that line out and never talk about it again.'

Naturally, I agreed, because although he'd piqued my curiosity, I was beginning to wish I'd never met Mr Chan.

It turned out that from business and distant family connections, as well as some old friends, Rodney was something of an unofficial biographer to Jimmy.

'I've compiled a dossier,' he explained, 'of the more outrageous financial dealings, listing bank accounts, company names and contact details, which I'm going to give you. This stuff will only really mean anything to someone who knows what I'm now telling you, so you'd better remember it. I've got no use for the ruddy dossier itself any more, and I don't particularly want it in my possession a moment longer.'

I tried to protest that I didn't want to know any more than I already knew and that I wouldn't know what to do with yet another secret document entrusted to me, but I swallowed some water at that point and my coughing prevented me putting an end to the revelations.

As I spluttered, Rodney carried on. 'I don't feel safe knowing what I know and having the dossier puts me and, worse still, my wife, in some danger.'

He warned me, 'If Jimmy gets hold of it, he'd know straight away who it came from. I want you to get it into the hands of the authorities in Hong Kong as an anonymous document. You can tell them what I'm telling you, can't you, without revealing the source? That way they'll be able to check for themselves on the named companies and individuals and it'll look like it's just their investigation and not necessarily the result of a tip-off.'

Rodney swore me to secrecy about where the information originated. The big man was scared. What was I to do but appease him by saying I'd do as he asked? And feel a bit scared myself. I assured him I wouldn't pass information on to anyone else other than my contact in Hong Kong. Can you imagine if I told Minter? What was it Oscar W said? – "I'm very good at keeping secrets, it's the people I tell them to that aren't".

'I see it as a final act,' he told me, explaining why he wanted to get it all off his chest. 'A lifetime in tax avoidance has left a bitter taste. I've ended up compromising all my real principles. How can I have sacrificed my ideals to the cause of saving money for super-rich scuzzy gits?' he said in his best scouse. 'I know too much about too many people and I want to get back to being the person I felt I used to be.'

I supposed he meant that having been a gamekeeper turned poacher, he wanted now to be a poacher turned gamekeeper.

I couldn't really argue with any of it, as I felt more than a bit breathless at that point and I comforted myself by thinking that it would be perfectly harmless to swim back and forth taking his confession and, when I got back to Hong Kong, simply sicking his dossier on to Simon at the Hong Kong Revenue and letting him decide what the hell to do with it.

*Private Eye* would have had a field day with what Rodney proceeded to tell me and by the end, I was trembling good and proper, as much from what I then knew, as from the effect of spending such a long time in the water.

'Jimmy's parents,' he told me, 'were prosperous traders in China, who, during the Cultural Revolution, were sent to a remote and poor mining town, having first been financially ruined. Jimmy never forgot that humiliation and hated his parents for meekly "taking the iron rice bowl".'

Rodney explained that this expression referred to those compliantly putting up with being forced to be ordinary workers and given only meagre healthcare, pension and housing.

'Jimmy boasted that his father had moved gold between East Africa, the Philippines, Hong Kong and China, and until his disgrace had carried on the family tradition of import/export which had been practised by his grandparents and great-grandparents based in Shanghai.'

Continuing the family history, Rodney could seemingly talk and swim without drawing breath as I struggled to keep up.

'Robbed of their family wealth, Jimmy and his brothers set out to get it back. That's what motivates him. In coming from nothing,' Rodney observed, 'Jimmy behaved as if he'd got nothing to lose. When you rise from obscurity, you don't care if you risk sinking without trace. That's what makes Jimmy so dangerous. He escaped, with relatives, from the mainland, and they eventually got into Hong Kong as illegal immigrants. Some were deported but Jimmy and the brothers managed to stay on, becoming utterly ruthless in exploiting the system and anybody they came across.

'One brother inevitably became a triad member, and got Jimmy in to the gang which preyed on the various Chinese communities of Hong Kong. Through their tong, they were in illegal gambling, narcotics, vice and protection rackets. The violence they used was notorious and it gave them their hold over their victims. Jimmy was, from the start, astute in handling the money side of things, but you have to remember he wasn't averse to savage brutality himself.

'That's where he really started out, completely on the wrong side of the law, but triad secrecy, with breaches punishable by death, means nothing is known for certain.'

As I swam it was difficult to think of Jimmy as this out-and-out criminal, but without any proof, I tried to comfort myself that it was all supposedly and allegedly!

Rodney went on. 'Jimmy got hold of his first printing works as a forfeit when the boss defaulted on protection payments. Rather than burn the place down, Jimmy cleverly took over the business at the same time as its previous owner mysteriously disappeared. Surprise, surprise, Jimmy claimed to be the vanished proprietor's cousin and told the workforce that, at his own personal cost, he would step in to save the factory and the jobs. What a good bloke!

'This is the clever bit, though. Jimmy knew that the warehouse for the printing works had its own godown by the harbour. That's why the decision to run the business proved to be Jimmy's masterstroke. He knew he could use the warehouse, not just for books and magazines, but also for no end of crooked schemes and nefarious practices.

'One was the smuggling of rare and other endangered animals for the traditional Chinese medicine trade, for example Asian black bears and brown bears from China plus powdered rhino horn from Africa, via the Philippines.

'He made a lot of money from that, but really started coining it when he got involved in the lucrative trade of sending heroin from the warehouse in Hong Kong to

New York, hidden in stuffed animals. Destined for the vicious Flying Dragons gang in New York, Jimmy set up that route for a cousin of his who was high up in the gang and he himself spent quite a bit of time in America.'

So that explained his weird accent.

'Jimmy by then,' according to Rodney, 'had become the leopard that can't change its spots and cheated on everybody from his customers and his business partners to his three wives. He double-crossed friends with the same lack of conscience he treated his enemies.

Length after length, Rodney ploughed on with his strokes and his narrative.

'Astute with figures, creative with any commercial dealings, Jimmy got used to using "yin-yang" contracts in his business dealings: one recording a low figure for declaration to the tax authorities and the other showing the much higher, genuine amount of the arrangement.'

'Why anyone would want to do business with Jimmy, unless they *had* to is beyond me?' Rodney asked. 'What on earth do you think he has on Langleys, that they carry on using him?'

'I don't know, Rodney,' I spluttered.

Of course I didn't know and could only surmise. I knew that most of the senior directors came in and out of Hong Kong regularly for board meetings of Langleys Asia Limited. God only knows what they got up to whilst they were there. It seemed obvious to me that Jimmy would have plenty of opportunities, knowing him, to get them into his pocket. It made me even more determined, in my own mind, to get the hell out of the company and plough my own furrow.

Betraying his profession, Rodney couldn't help but tell me of his admiration for Jimmy's bookkeeping and his eye for detail. The irony of him caring about keeping records whilst engaging in fraudulent activities, made us chuckle in the telling. 'Jimmy's accounting was meticulous,' Rodney put it, ' because even crooks have to keep books.'

'Did you see his accounts then, Rodney?' I managed to ask.

'I'm ashamed to say I did, when I mistakenly first got involved with Jimmy through a mutual friend, who was very respectable and who lived in the same block. He'd been one of the last British Consular staff in Shanghai to flee in 1941, only to end up incarcerated by the Japanese when they took over Hong Kong. As a result he was a bit of a guru to people like Jimmy as he knew important people in the colony and on the mainland. He acted as a consultant to the Chan businesses and I felt that, if he thought Jimmy was kosher as a client, then that was good enough for me.'

'How does your wife fit into all this?'

'At that point, when I was doing some advisory work for Chan, I wasn't married, and it was only after I'd met and married her that my wife spoke of her misgivings about me working for Jimmy. She hadn't told me until then that her side of the family didn't see eye to eye with Jimmy's. That's one of the reasons we left Hong Kong, but the main one was me realising just what I was getting myself into. I'd always seen tax planning as an intellectual exercise, a kind of cryptic crossword where nobody gets hurt.'

'Aren't you going to incriminate yourself by telling me all this and handing over the dossier?'

'Oh, don't worry about that. Nothing is traceable back to me from what I've written unless it's put together with what I'm telling you. For a start, I only gave Jimmy verbal advice. I put nothing in writing to him and I didn't put any of the schemes into play myself. I'll say this for Jimmy, he puts his mouth where his money is, even if he doesn't put his money where his mouth is. That's how he ended up not paying me all that I thought I should have got. "Nothing is in writing," he'd say to me. "You've done little for me. A bit of advice? I've paid for that! All the rest, the difficult stuff, I've done all by myself".'

'Look, what sort of schemes are we talking about?'

'The main ones were for the Philippines and, indirectly, Marcos, which is one of the reasons I feel badly about what I've done.'

'This is getting me deeper and deeper into areas I feel distinctly uncomfortable about. Do you have to tell me?'

'Not much more, but before I tell you about tax stuff for Jimmy himself, I've got to tell you about what I call the Marcos Model. It looks now like a kleptocrat's charter, a blueprint for state corruption, and I shudder to think how many other banana republics will follow suit, presuming Jimmy spreads his wings.'

'Crikey, Rodney, just what did you tell him to do?'

'For a start, I outlined for Jimmy the set-up by which Marcos could rig auctions of company shares to take over key industry sectors. I scoped out a loans-for-shares scheme that meant money flowed into the Marcos coffers, with the money then routed to a safe-haven place like Jersey, looking like it was money to protect the country's foreign reserves, but was really a slush fund for Marcos and his cronies. I showed Jimmy how transfer pricing and related-party transactions could be used to hide the reality. I explained how the end of exchange controls could be used to their advantage and showed why the Marcos bean counters should have reliable and desirable destinations to keep the cash and why that was better than keeping it in pesos. I told them how to set up a passports-for-cash system for wealthy Chinese from Hong Kong and from the mainland, and even outlined how to use money laundering tricks to get dirty money moving around the world.'

'Christ, Rodney, why did you tell him all that?'

'Money. Ideology. Compromise. Ego. Remember MICE? I had them all. I was greedy, I felt at the time that people should be allowed to do what they liked with their own money.'

'Surely not if it was obtained dishonestly?'

'I didn't make the distinction. Money was money. Protecting it was the intellectual exercise, pure and simple, and that was my ideology.'

'Then what about the compromise bit?'

'That was a rather unfortunate episode and a regrettable stain on my character. Jimmy lured me into a classic honey-trap, filmed me with a prostitute and basically blackmailed me into giving more and more advice. I'm not proud of that. Eventually, I came clean and told my wife which irritated Jimmy as he thought he'd lost his hold on me. Of course, he could never tell the authorities about my role in his affairs as that would incriminate him.'

'The ego bit, Rodney. Don't tell me. You were flattered by the attention your tax knowledge generated.'

'Look, I feel bad enough about it. I didn't stop to think about the repercussions of what I was doing. Not many advisors do. The client is king, remember, and, in a corrupt world, you can easily form the distorted view that everybody is at it. And perhaps they are, or would be if they had the wealth and the opportunity. More recently I've changed my position on all that. For a start, it's clear to me that the more money most rich people accumulate, the less well off they are; those who are fabulously wealthy seem doomed never to enjoy it. I've stuck to fairly legit tax advice for the past few years. That's why I'm having to try and boost my income by writing for people like you. I earn less, but sleep more. I can honestly say that, apart from Jimmy and what he got up to in the Philippines, my work has not been, technically, law-breaking.'

'That's what they all say. I can remember reading about the guy who set up constitutions for various tax haven islands. I'm sure that was a sound legal test of his intellect, but morally, I couldn't really guess what he was thinking. And how many auditors say they act within the law even if that means turning a blind eye and saying, Nelson-style, "I see no shits"?'

'All right, all right. Anyway, it's all in the dossier. Company names, registration details, everything – the use of bearer bonds, the debts created between shell companies and enforced by crooked judges so that dirty money can flow and get "laundered" in the process, the financial centres to use as conduits or the ones to use as sinks, and especially how to use not-for-profit foundations in Vaduz, Lichtenstein for minimum tax and maximum secrecy.'

He told me of many other tax-saving strategies and various ways he'd seen dirty money being taken out of certain jurisdictions and laundered into others, ending up in legitimate investment assets and businesses.

'While on the subject,' I asked him, 'where does Jimmy keep most of his money?'

'He was too canny to tell me, but, to give you a clue, he took down from me details of certain banks in the British Virgin Islands and he was keen to know if I knew anyone in a law firm in Panama. That was all for the cash. One thing I do know is that just like they do a lot in organised crime, which still operates the gold standard incidentally, he kept a lot of gold and he used a trick he said he'd learnt from Marcos.'

'What on earth was that?'

'Gold blocks covered in lead, used as bricks to build internal walls at his home and then plastered all over. In Marcos's case, Imelda had redesigned some rooms and the "bricks" had been removed and dumped in the grounds to be removed as rubbish. Ferdinand hit the roof when he found out and all the "bricks" had to be found again and piled up neatly. The trouble is, I don't know which of Jimmy's properties houses the gold. I was convinced that gold smuggling was something Jimmy did for Marcos.'

'Rodney, you are a walking, sorry, swimming compendium of corruption, but how do you know for sure that Jimmy swung all this into operation on the scale you seem to envisage?'

'I don't, but something tells me he would do it without any qualms at all. And, what's worse, that he'll do whatever he needs to do to make sure nobody finds out and tries to stop him.'

At this point, I felt mentally and physically exhausted and said as much to Rodney. When I suggested we get out and have a whisky he must have felt the same because he agreed straight away, with, 'Yes, let's do that'.

Actually we had a club sandwich each and more than a couple of whiskies before I left the Tanglin Club, having fixed a time to meet for lunch the following day.

I staggered back to my hotel room for some jasmine tea and a relatively early night.

# 8

I NEEDN'T HAVE BOTHERED as I had a middle-of-the-night call from the London office – morning time for them, but they'd deliberately ignored the time difference – asking me what the hell I was doing in Singapore anyway? Where was my report on my activities in Hong Kong and the Philippines? Why was Jimmy still hopping mad with me and complaining that I was looking to print anywhere and everywhere else but with him?

I hadn't switched the aircon on, which meant that the room had been unbearably hot. The mini-bar mineral water barely wet my whistle as, having been woken, I sat ruminating about Rodney and what I was going to do with what I knew and the wretched dossier he was going to give me.

Is Rodney as bad as Jimmy? How about him telling me that rich crooked Asians he knew had put money into buying or even building hotels to launder it. I must ask him which hotels, I thought. My head was swirling with the whisky and with his tales of sham companies in Ireland and captive insurance companies in Bermuda. I kept remembering all the other things he told me and started jotting them down, in case I forgot and he hadn't included them in his report.

The fact that Jimmy had two main homes, one ordinary one for his wife and family and one swanky one for his mistress. The fact he used names like Chao and Chong as well as Chan, but Jimmy as a constant. Why? The fact that he could move freely in and out of mainland China despite having fled from there. What were his connections? Was Rodney's ego so big that he really thought he'd given Marcos, through Jimmy, the complete kleptocrat's kit of how to ruin your country, whilst enriching your family and cronies?

I looked out of the window of my room high above Singapore and, as in Hong Kong, the cynic in me felt again that, except for its low tax regime and all that, wouldn't this place just be a swamp?

I'd finally dozed off and woke mid-morning feeling surprisingly bright. I must drink more whisky, but with fewer tax experts.

\*　　　\*　　　\*

Unlike the night before, when I'd lurched along Orchard Road back to my hotel and its pavements had been busy and bustling with groups of elegant trans women presumably walking to join other Bugis Street ladies, daytime Orchard Road was full of rather desperate-looking shoppers, me included.

I ventured into Lucky Plaza, a shopping mall on several floors, and strolled around it rather aimlessly without buying anything other than some music tapes. The several floors of small shops sold everything any consumer would ever want, seemingly cheaper than you could buy it elsewhere. Was it genuine or fake? It didn't seem to matter.

Having picked up a few bootleg cassettes, I quickly got bored and decided to head back up Orchard Road and over to the Goodwood Park Hotel, dreading the thought of more food and more drink.

Not wanting to frighten the local police into arresting me, having already been on the receiving end of their stares at my not even very long hair, I waited patiently at a crossing.

As the lights changed and the throng started moving, I was jostled and pushed viciously from behind and, stumbling, I half fell, bumping into other pedestrians, who reacted badly towards me because I was waving my arms about frantically, trying to stop myself falling over. I realised too late that my attaché case, one of the two I'd bought in Hong Kong, had been snatched from under my arm.

I looked ahead of me and, as I tried to regain my balance, saw it disappearing, being carried by a jogger. I'd seen a blur of yellow trainers as I'd lost my footing and when I finally stopped and was alone in the middle of the road, I tried to look at the traffic policeman on duty on the crossing and, in supplication, raised my hands rather pathetically and tried to shout 'Stop thief!' He saw me all right. How do I know? Because with one hand he put a whistle to his lips and blew, whilst, with the other, he waved his baton, wildly gesticulating for me to get my arse across the road or else. He didn't have a clue what I was saying, or what had just happened.

Damage limitation. In a moment I'd done an inventory in my head.

What had been taken? My expensive leather folder for a start. Think. Passport? No, that was back in the room safe along with most of my money and plane tickets. What was it they'd taken? I couldn't think. Sod it. A pad, a map and some notes I'd scribbled over breakfast of the questions I should put to Miguel Bentoz, certainly. What else? Think! Maybe nothing. And I even had the duplicate of the smart leather folder. No worries then.

But who was the thief? A random opportunist or had it been a targeted steal?

I ran the rest of the way across the road and tried to look along the wide and crowded pavement. At that moment, the throng seemed to part in an almost biblical fashion and there, about fifty yards away, just breaking into a run, I caught a glimpse of the face of my assailant, the only person in exercise gear. He chose that moment to look back, straight at me.

I was too stunned to react. He'd turned his head away quickly, then vanished. I'm not even sure he realised I'd recognised him as my mugger and, what's more, had identified him as the fourth man on the table at the Tanglin Club the previous night.

And I'd seen those yellow trainers before ... where? ... come on ... at the hotel! ... in the lobby! ... this morning!

Now I knew who'd robbed me. I'd better think what he'd taken and I'd better remember fast.

I went cold as I thought that maybe my middle-of-the-night notes about Rodney and various musings about Marcos could be in the case. Were they? I wouldn't know for sure until I got back to the hotel later. Now what?

The Goodwood Park Hotel wasn't much of a walk, once I'd crossed Orchard Road. All I had to do was walk up Scotts Road and there it was, with its Grand Tower sitting in all its colonial majesty, virtually on the other side of the road from the Tanglin Club. Rodney didn't like to stray too far, obviously.

By the time I got there, I'd remembered that I'd written some names on a sheet that was with my papers, in the spoof style that Kenneth Minter had advised in Hong Kong. They were meant as something to laugh about with Rodney and Miguel. I had only listed the fictional names like Harold Holt, Michael Bancroft, Bertie Ball, Willie Tang and Charles Benyon and I'd planned to see if Rodney could work out who I meant, although I did wonder if Rodney would find that funny now.

*         *         *

The lunch was a non-event as far as enjoyable eating went. I'd no sooner sat down in the large plush restaurant at the hotel, said hello to Rodney and been introduced to Miguel – incidentally incongruously dressed in a suit and bow tie as promised, a stand-out look in Singapore, I can tell you, but never mind – and told them about my mugging, when Rodney went into full panic mode.

Worst-case scenario, this puts us all in grave danger if there's information they can get from what they've taken, was the gist of what he said. We'd have to use his contacts to try and remove the threat was what I think he was saying.

He ordered us all, in his usual 'You'll have what I'm eating' manner, their speciality chilli crab and, whilst that was happening, he outlined what we'd better do. I felt distinctly queasy.

Miguel thought it was all very exciting and clearly relished getting involved. His life must be unbearably dull, I thought, if this sort of stuff is enticing rather than off-putting. I wondered how long that would last, but whilst it did, well, he can stand in for me from now on, and, I think, I more or less said that to him, as he beamed and rubbed his hands in eager anticipation.

The food came and went, and Rodney came and went even more often than the attentive waiting staff. He made a few phone calls, or, as he put it, 'it's time to pull a few strings'. First pirate and now puppeteer.

I kept thinking of the Frank Sinatra song, 'I've been a puppet, a poet, a pauper, a pirate, a pawn and a king'. That about summed Rodney up in all his guises, but I'm still wondering how he managed to get these people in authority in Singapore to do what he got them to do that afternoon.

The long and short of it, according to what Rodney learnt from his calls, was that the guy who mugged me, and who'd been at the Tanglin Club dinner with the three others in the party that Rodney knew, was based in Manila as local representative of their firm. Rodney knew one of the others, the senior partner, and must have had some kind of hold over him. Rodney had asked the unknown's name, as if in passing when he'd telephoned, and he'd apologised for not going over and speaking to them all when he was with me the night before. Rodney was then able to tell us that the name of the mugger was Tan Siow Mong.

Tan Siow Mong, he'd been told, was an accountant with the same firm but in the Philippines and handled the local relationship with the senior finance people working for Marcos, and that he was going back there later that day. Clearly he took his accounting work commendably seriously and went to extreme lengths to get hold of any relevant papers. That's what you call a thorough audit.

Rodney had formed the impression that the Singapore firm were probably ignorant of Tan Siow Mong's freelancing banditry. That meant he could be working for Jimmy, which would be typical of Mr Chan, or, perhaps, was more in cahoots with the Marcos men in Manila than the Singaporeans realised.

After a nerve-settling whisky, Rodney then rang a high-level contact in the Singapore police who he said he'd helped out a few times with various anti-money-laundering operations and they'd done good turns for each other ever since.

Whilst he was away making his calls, I filled Miguel in on what had happened to me in Hong Kong and Manila, all of which he found worryingly fascinating.

The result of the various further calls made by Rodney, one seemingly leading on to another, was that we found out that Mr Tan Siow Mong had checked out of the Marco Polo and, according to the concierge, had a car collecting him to go to the airport in an hour's time. The police, Rodney had been assured in another call, would ensure that his hand luggage would be searched by airport security after check-in and as he was going airside. Any papers in English and the leather case would be confiscated on some pretext or other.

Meanwhile, his checked luggage would not be loaded onto his flight but removed and would then be available to view. It would later be placed on the next available flight to Manila. That would give us a chance to have a look at it and maybe Tan Siow Mong would just think his hold luggage had gone missing and turned up late, more so if nothing turned out to be in his hand luggage and the routine security check ended up looking like just that and no more.

I was fairly spooked by this point and said I'd go back to the hotel to check exactly what was missing, but Rodney insisted we finish our lunch and have coffee and talk about publishing with Miguel. How cool, calm and collected. Not me!

We sat and talked about how Miguel could work for me both with Langleys and if I went on my own. He was happy either way and showed a real grasp for what it would entail. Added to that, he was articulate and personable and really looked forward to the travel involved, not least because it would mean he'd no longer be confined to his cockroach-infested apartment in Singapore, which was so bad, he told us, that any nightly visit to the bathroom was a toe-curling, foot-crunching experience, which the landlord refused to do anything about. He hoped a regular salary would enable him to move somewhere better, maybe with fewer cockroaches.

Once Rodney had taken a call informing him of the good news that Tan Siow Mong had checked in and no leather case or papers in English had been found in his hand luggage, we set off in a taxi, first for my hotel and then to go on to the airport where we would be able to inspect his hold baggage, which had been diverted and was ready for our viewing.

A quick look in my room confirmed that, indeed, my notes on Rodney's revelations had gone. Bugger!

Fortunately, it didn't look like my room had been searched, even though housekeeping had carefully given it a service since I'd last been in it that morning.

We drove out to Changi Airport along the wide boulevards with their colourful central reservations full of the whites, pinks and yellows of oleander, crepe myrtle, bougainvillea, cat's claw ivy and a whole range of other tropical plants and flowers.

Once he'd told us the names of the shrubs on the way, Rodney changed tack and then went into the full Blue Badge Guide-style routine that you might half expect from an ex-Royal Marine. The theme switched from floral colour to Changi and POWs. 'What the bloody hell would *they* have made of the airport?' was Rodney's refrain.

We were met by airport security, as promised, at the airport's main arrivals entrance. They had clearly been properly alerted of our visit, and whisked us, like VIPs, through to a room that was starkly furnished with bare tables and a few chairs. Once inside, you could look out through one-way glass at all the travellers. Slightly sinister and disturbing. How suspicious most travellers look, was all I could think.

The Samsonite-style suitcase sitting open on the main table in the room was, interesting, shall we say. In it, we found my leather folder.

'Well done on the facial recognition after all,' Rodney patted me on the shoulder. 'At least you got the right mugger. When they didn't find anything in his hand luggage, I thought you might have been wrong about who it might be.'

'One thing I am good at is remembering faces,' I said in a slightly offended tone and, bridling a bit, I carried on. 'I could tell you, for example, of instances where I've seen somebody in the street in London and been able to recall seeing them in a restaurant or on a train or whatever and remembering virtually on which day and date I'd seen them. I know, I know,' I continued after their expressed admiration, 'it's uncanny. I should have gone into the police or something and put the skill to some use. Most of the time I just annoy the people I'm with by saying, "I've seen that person before". "Big deal" is the usual response I get.'

'It's a special talent. Today's proved that.'

'What are we going to do now? Remove my folder and send Tan Siow Mong's luggage on its way?'

'Good Lord, no,' Rodney replied. 'We're going to assess if he's looked at it first and then think of what we're going to do to cover our tracks. Make it look like he hasn't been rumbled.'

We examined the papers. We decided the top one, my spoof names, could stay as he'd probably read it anyway and removing it would be a probable give away. One thing for sure: it did not seem funny, or clever, on seeing it again.

Rodney was convinced that Tan Siow Mong would not have read the rest of the papers: 'He's had no time for a start. I think he's just a pick-up and drop guy. The partner I spoke to when I asked about him said he would be of no interest to me because his spoken English was not that good.'

That being the case, Miguel came up with the idea of removing the notes of my meeting with Rodney, which

I'd rather stupidly put in the folder, and replacing them with something else. At first I'd been reluctant, because I knew it would take a bit of thought and a little while to complete.

But I sat down and, on my usual plain paper, made notes of some of the publishing ideas discussed with Rodney and, separately, with Nick. I kept to boring sounding titles and a mix of real and fictitious potential authors. I was particularly proud of a financial summary of budgeted turnover, gross profit and profit for a few years ahead.

This took about an hour and, when the swap of papers was complete and the leather attaché case put back, the luggage was removed by airport security to be fed into the system to go onto the next Manila flight. Tan Siow Mong would have a fraught time when he found it missing and an anxious wait until it turned up. Hopefully the relief of being reunited with it and seeing it seemingly intact would prevent any doubts and fears he might have from taking over and causing him to be suspicious.

We were about to leave and be ushered through the other door into the arrivals side, when I froze.

Through the big one-way window, queuing at the first passport control desk, I recognised the Lane Crawford bag man who'd first tailed me that first night in Hong Kong.

'What's the matter, Rich, you look like you've seen a ghost?' Rodney remarked as he saw me stop dead. He followed suit, hanging back with me, and leaving the security guard stranded at the half-open door looking back at us, mystified.

When the guard had closed the exit door, I said to Rodney, 'That guy standing in line at passport control, the second one back, he works for Jimmy. He followed me one evening in Hong Kong. He was carrying a local store's branded carrier bag. That's why I christened him Lane Crawford.'

'Have you met and remembered everybody?' Miguel laughed.

'This could be significant,' said Rodney and he asked the security guard if he'd mind popping out to the desk and finding out just who the man I was pointing at through the one-way glass actually was, and, if possible, where he was staying. The guard went out to do just that, relishing the chance to assert the authority that he could see was wasted on us. We saw him as the scene unfolded in front of our eyes, but safely from behind the glass where we could not be seen.

'We need a name for him. Then I can get my police contact to keep tabs on him and we won't have to keep calling him Lane Crawford,' said Rodney, rather seriously, no doubt trying to sound professional in front of the other security staff in the room.

'I rather like the name,' said Miguel, 'it fits in with Rich's spoof name fetish. He'll always be Lane Crawford to me. It suits him in an ironic kind of way even though he looks more like a Bruce Lee if we had to choose a better nickname.'

'Whatever we do, he can't see us leave. I don't want him to spot me again and follow me around everywhere I go,' I found myself whispering.

We all stood watching the exchange taking place outside our window. Neither our man, nor Lane Crawford, looked concerned and the conversation seemed to be relaxed. They could each handle themselves without panicking, that was clear, and eventually both smiled as Singapore's latest visitor was allowed through passport control to proceed with his journey.

'Maybe he's on some other kind of business for Jimmy. It's not all about you, you know,' Rodney tried to reassure me. 'Let's see what our man has been able to find out. Here he comes now.'

'I'm finding these one-way glass windows spooky and I'll be glad to get out of here. Looking at departures of muggers like Tan Siow Mong on one side and the arrivals of probable assassins like Lane Crawford on the other is enough to put me off travel permanently,' I replied.

Security looked pleased with himself. 'Your man is Ting Tack Chee, here on business. Staying at the Shangri-La Hotel. He's in Singapore for four days.'

'Did you ask him what business he was in?'

'Of course, Mr Bolt. What do you take me for? If you'll listen, I'll tell you what he is up to in Singapore.'

He paused to allow Rodney to apologise and, having asserted himself, carried on. 'He's arranging the sale of rare Chinese historical artefacts for his company and hoping to buy others he's seen listed for sale. He's very knowledgeable about the auction houses here. Here's his card.'

We took it in turns to read 'Ting Tack Chee, Director, Chan Antiques (Hong Kong) Ltd' with an address in Hong Kong that meant nothing to me. We could check that later.

'That company name could refer to Jimmy Chan,' Rodney said which drew nothing from the security guard as the name obviously hadn't meant anything to him.

'What sort of things can Jimmy be selling?' asked Miguel, of nobody in particular.

'He was very polite and helpful,' replied the official. 'He told me he's selling an ancient porcelain "chicken cup", two very old porcelain vases, a Tibetan silk tapestry from the Ming era, an ancient mandala made of coral, gold and turquoise and a chimera in *cloissoné* enamel. This kind of stuff is worth a fortune. I know about these things because it's been my speciality on the customs side. I asked him to show me his certificates of provenance. He told me the *objets* and the documents were with the shippers and the auction house. It all sounds legal. I welcomed him to Singapore and I don't think he was suspicious in any way. I would not want such an important visitor inconvenienced in any way by unnecessary intrusions.'

'Yes, but how does Jimmy Chan get hold of these things to sell? That should be your question,' Rodney pointed out. 'He knows that millions of antiquities disappeared from China after 1840. Getting them back is a bit of a mission for him and a clever way for him to be patriotic and boastful at the same time when he curries favour with Beijing.'

'We know all about that and the looting that went on in the Century of Humiliation,' came the stern response. 'China and all Chinese want them back. Who can blame this Jimmy Chan you talk about?'

Looking directly at each of us in turn, he continued, 'The British were the worst of them all. If there's a touch of bitterness about it from us Chinese, who cares?'

I think that change of tone meant we were ready to be escorted from the premises and, with the coast clear of Lane Crawford, sorry, Ting Tack Chee, that's exactly what happened.

When we were in the taxi, Rodney, clearly miffed to have been spoken to in that way by the security guard, was rather exercised in his reaction and you could tell that by the way he, still seething, set out a bit of a history lesson.

'That's the trouble with the Chinese. They hate the British and almost everybody else. In art terms, they haven't recovered from the sacking of Beijing's Old Summer Palace in 1860, when it was plundered of virtually everything. I know for a fact that they've got intelligence people, as part of a treasure-hunting team, trying to trace it all. Jimmy might be involved in that, come to think of it, because our man said Lane Crawford was looking at lots to buy as well as sell. This squad of plundered-booty seekers are trying to track down things like the twelve bronze heads representing the animals of the Chinese zodiac that were removed from the gardens of the palace. And it's not like the British at the time didn't know what they'd done. Even the first Pekingese dog the troops brought back and gave to Queen Victoria was brazenly named Looty! I mean, I ask you.'

'But do you really think that's why Ting Tack Chee is here? Because of an art auction?' I asked Rodney, if only to get him back on track and dealing with my fears rather than the legacy of colonialism.

'Quite possibly. Tan Siow Mong looks more like he's a Manila man and not directly involved with Jimmy, which is good for us all. We might get away with our little bit of subterfuge with your attaché case.'

'Subterfuge? It's more like Spy vs Spy from *Mad* magazine.'

'Glad you're finding it funny!'

'I'm not, but it would be more chilling if it didn't seem so ludicrous. What *are* we doing?'

'Taking it all too seriously,' Miguel said. 'Listening to all this, it's easy to forget that all that has happened is that Rich has fallen foul of Jimmy in Hong Kong and was thought to be behaving oddly in Manila. Nothing for anyone to get worked up about.'

'You're already forgetting I've been mugged, which is pretty unusual and a bit disturbing to the say the least, either by a Marcos goon, which may put Nick in the frame for worse treatment, or it could be that Tan Siow Mong is a Chan man which is probably more serious.'

'If he is working for Marcos, your papers now show an innocent publisher going about his business. You and Nick are in the clear there,' Miguel replied.

'But I am an innocent publisher!'

'Not if they all put two and two together,' Rodney said. 'And I still think that Ting Tack Chee's arrival is more than a mere coincidence, even though, as he clearly doesn't seem to know about Tan Siow Mong being here, it looks like it isn't.'

We rambled on with our theories until we arrived at an elegant single-storey colonial bungalow, just off Orchard Road, where the taxi drew up.

'This is my home,' Rodney said, gesturing out of the car window towards an elegant old wooden house on stilts that had an open-sided, covered verandah running around it.

'Wow,' I couldn't help but exclaim. 'I bet there aren't many of these left.'

'There aren't, but despite it making a change from all the high-rise monstrosities, this is due to be demolished when the lease ends in a couple of years. I'm lucky to be able to enjoy it. Of course, the locals think I'm mad and eccentric for not wanting to live in a nice modern flat.'

We paid the taxi driver and carried on into the house. Miguel joined in and sounded off about 'disappearing Singapore' and 'everything being flattened in the cause of progress'.

'Pretty soon,' he said, 'there'll be nothing of the old stuff left. They don't realise that tourists want to see the old Singapore, but Lee Kuan Yew and his lot can't wait to rub it all out and put a fresh stamp of progress on the place.'

We walked into the palm-filled garden in front of the pretty house and went up the wooden verandah steps and straight in. As Rodney's wife was obviously out – he'd called out first and got no reply – he strolled around the house, clearly checking the rooms. When he came back into the rattan-furnished living room, he gave me a large envelope, telling me, 'This is the paper I mentioned the other night at the Tanglin, I suggest you post it off to your friend in Hong Kong as soon as you get back to the hotel. He offered us a drink, but in a not very convincing way and, when he mentioned that we were within easy walking distance of the Marco Polo, I took the hint.

'Don't worry about making anything for us. I'll take Miguel off, if he's free, and we can see if we can remember all the publishing ideas we didn't actually give to Tan Siow Mong and try and set out a real, doable plan that we can get our teeth into.'

Rodney offered no resistance to that and we left, with me looking around at the elegant home he had created for himself, which looked extremely comfortable if you could forget about its incredibly hot and humid atmosphere. The Marco Polo's air-conditioning was beckoning, with its cheongsam-wearing waitresses offering a more enticing prospect than a brew made and served by Mr Bolt in his best crumpled linen suit.

# 9

THE EVENING WAS INTERESTING, FROM the moment we got to the Marco Polo from Rodney's – and reception had agreed to post the envelope I'd been given to Simon – until I got back to my room much, much later.

Miguel and I had discussed the kind of job he could do if he was working for me, either with Langleys or in our new venture. We agreed that he could start anyway on a trial few months and we talked salary and general terms. It seemed sensible to show him the local offices of Langleys out in Jurong and we arranged to do that the next day.

Our pleasant chat in the lobby bar was, however, disturbed by Kenneth Minter and Eric Old, loudly saying hello to a large, rather bulky man, who was obviously, by the sound of him, an American and whom we hadn't noticed before, sitting in the far corner talking with a smart-looking Chinese man, a businessman we assumed by the look of him.

Inevitably, as soon as Kenneth saw us, he was over and insisting we both join them.

'You must meet Bill Brumby and his partner Tong Lim – they run a book distribution and direct mail marketing company – they could be very useful to you.' He wasn't wrong about that.

Our tea abandoned, cocktails took over with the blustery Bill trying to tell us what tipple to drink – 'you can't go wrong with a Gin Martini' – but then ordering us large versions of whatever we wanted and arguing with the others as to where we should go for food, which, he insisted, had to be hawker food from Gluttons Corner. That figures!

Miguel and I just went along with them, relieved to be able to concentrate on publishing industry chat. Tong Lim and Miguel seemed to be talking turkey about mutually beneficial business opportunities and that seemed to please Bill as much as it did me. Kenneth kept nudging me in an I-told-you-so manner.

Bill and Eric spent the evening planning a Singapore publishing exhibition and it all seemed for a while like it was an evening at the Frankfurt Book Fair, but with a Far Eastern twist: too much to drink, too much mutual back scratching, too many empty promises, too few realistic timetables, much slagging off of industry competitors, very little agreed action, and no responsibility for outcomes.

Kenneth and I, left to our own devices conversation-wise, caught up a bit on Hong Kong gossip and I realised he counted me as part of his semi-secret world, merely because I seemed to know a few people in it that he either revered or feared.

I tried to pump him for more info on Tufty McMasters and he tried to pump me for what I knew about Rodney. We were both wary of giving too much away, but I did hear that Manila and Sydney were likely ports of call in the coming year for Tufty and *NonDom*, his aptly named yacht.

Kenneth, cleverly, revealed only a few nuggets at a time, and I twigged that he was trading with me. Up to a point, I learnt a bit more about how Jimmy used the *NonDom* in what was obviously a smuggling operation, but I could see that what I knew about the Marcos connection would be breakthrough stuff for whoever Kenneth was reporting back to.

For my part, I tried to imply Rodney was only an authority on tax planning and didn't have any dealings at the moment with anyone else I knew apart from me. That was factually correct.

Kenneth, who clearly knew more about Jimmy than he'd let on, was testing me when he said he'd heard that Rodney had fallen out with Jimmy and that they'd been close at one time. I don't know if he bought my story that it was because there was a family rift over his wife who was a third cousin, twice removed, or something, to Jimmy, and that all that was in the past.

I managed to steer the conversation back to my publishing ambitions and that meant that, by the end, we were all talking about how successful or not a new venture in professional publishing would be. All of them wanted some involvement or another, but I kept thinking that with Rodney involved, we formed a very strange bunch. I saw us launching ourselves like a band of free-booting, publishing pirates on an unsuspecting world.

I should have realised that for us to go on to the Shangri-La Hotel for a nightcap was a mistake, but I didn't put two and two together until we were seated in its large lounge area and served. It seemed logical, as Bill was staying there, so we went along for the ride. It was only when Bill had ordered brandies all round and had got up to go over to the bar to say hello to someone he said he knew from Hong Kong – and that person had turned to face him – that it dawned on me.

Bill knew Lane Crawford. This could be difficult. I could see Miguel looking sideways at me. His face-spotting skills were switched on too.

Fortunately, Bill came back on his own, but the eyes following from the bar noticed me. They gave me a straight, steely stare, before being turned back to the barman.

He recognises me just as I do him. That means Jimmy will soon know the company I've been keeping.

'The guy is meeting a friend, or else he would have joined us.'

'Who is he?' I innocently asked.

'He works as a bagman – I stifled a giggle – for a big shot in Hong Kong that we try and avoid, but can't. Some Americans I know have figured out how to make money out here through some deals they've done with him, and now they're trying to do business with his boss.'

At that point, a nervous Miguel made his excuses and got up to leave. It was getting late. I stood and walked to see him out and we agreed it was better to keep quiet about what we knew of Ting Tack Chee and his boss Mr Chan.

'I'll try and find out a bit more from Bill, but how did you get on with Tong Lim?' I asked Miguel as we walked through the lobby to the front entrance.

'They could be very useful to us, provided they aren't crooked too. Lim runs the business and he poked fun at Bill who he kept calling 'our flunt man', which confused me until I realised what he was talking about.

We arranged to meet at the Marco Polo for breakfast and I went back to join our party, noticing Ting Tack Chee with two elderly men who looked like ancient Chinese art experts, but could easily have been acupuncturists specialising in poison-tipped needles or who knows what else.

I discovered that Bill travelled around just as much as Kenneth and Eric did. They seemed to know an awful lot about each other and their paths crossed often throughout the countries of the region. I gathered that Bill had been in the US army at some point in this part of the world and had just stayed on out East, working as an agent. At the mention of that word, I couldn't help but ask a direct question.

'You're an agent. Would that be an agent in the secret service sense of the word?' I asked.

'Jesus, no! An agent for international publishers! I worked in Washington DC for an outfit that did government contract publishing before the call up for Korea. I went back into publishing and decided to stay after the war ended. I've been here ever since and started the direct mail business out here. I also handle marketing and distribution for most major publishers, or rather Lim here handles it.'

He was a man who loved to talk to men who loved to talk, and he did, telling us about his travelling and his local contacts throughout the Far East.

Eric gave me knowing winks from time to time and, on my other side, Kenneth kept nudging me, both at the same points in the conversation. Remarks from Bill like 'meeting with my people up in Bangkok', 'assets on the ground in Jakarta' and 'what about a book tour up to Beijing' all drew winks and nudges.

I think I got the point: Bill Brumby was not as bumbly as his name implied. The CIA was now in book distribution, it seemed. You certainly can't judge a book by its cover.

*        *        *

I sat in departures at Changi, admiring its fountains, yes, but whilst Singaporeans could only see it as the future of aviation, it hadn't lost its prison-camp aura for me. The queues and the herding of passengers echoed its former incarnation, but instead of emaciated men lining up for some watery chow, it was the well-fed taking to the air and escaping Singapore.

After much testing, I spurned my usual Aramis and bought some 'Kissymyarsy' eau de cologne and then a bottle of J&B in duty free. I sat, smelling like a perfumery counter, waiting for the gate to come up for my flight to Hong Kong on Singapore Airlines. No wonder nobody sat anywhere near me.

I was playing one of the knock-off tapes I'd purchased at Lucky Plaza, Jimmy Buffet's *Changes in Latitudes, Changes in Attitudes*. It was perfect airport lounge music, a fitting backing track for the travellers milling around, most of them fat international businessmen with weighty overhanging guts which gave each of them an outline of the map of Africa. The noise from my leaky headphones must have put them off me too, because I continued to sit in splendid isolation, alone with my music and my thoughts.

The day had been mixed. After an early breakfast, I'd introduced Miguel to the local Langleys lot and there'd been the usual standoff, and some resentment that he might be taken on as a locally based appointment that they hadn't had a hand in. They were placated by the fact he would only be working for me and not getting in their way or taking work from them. The usual difficulties, in other words. Fortunately, the local MD, normally based up in KL, was a decent cove and he and Miguel hit it off. I could tell any teething troubles would be quickly dealt with. A tour and a coffee rounded off a useful exercise and I let Miguel know in the taxi back that I'd confirm his role once it had been agreed by London, if I stayed with Langleys. If I didn't, then the decision would be just down to me.

Miguel and I went our separate ways after I said I'd be in further touch, once his appointment went final.

We'd already agreed a list of authors and publishers he needed to contact to set the ball rolling and until they came on board, he'd have to help market our existing titles through Bill and Tong Lim, getting hold of their standard contract for us to have a read through.

I'd spent a sandwich lunch, checking out of my room and sending telexes to the office. They had a whizzy new fax machine, but as my boss couldn't even work a cassette player – and we were also meant to be an audio publisher these days – it wasn't worth risking that form of communication. He'd have been happier if I'd sent a telegram.

I'd made a few calls whilst I still had my room, with a fast checkout pre-arranged.

Nick in Manila was finding things a bit tricky and, since I'd left, he had been subjected to closer scrutiny with surveillance on him increased in the street which even extended to him being supervised when he worked on papers at the Malacañang Palace. He put it down to a fit of the jitters at some higher level, as the accountants themselves that he worked with treated him just the same. He'd met Tan Siow Mong a few times, it turned out and, at first, didn't believe my mugging story, but said it fitted with the way he himself had been watched, with his briefcase being searched when he entered and left the palace. He was clearly relieved to know that no suspicious information about him or me was making its way to Manila with my mugger. That might take some of the heat off him. He told me that Tan Siow Mong – a thieving accountant to me – was a decent bloke, well known in the local accountancy world and with a wife and family. Obviously he'd only been carrying out orders. 'That's still outrageous,' I'd said and got the reply, 'Not by Filipino standards, it's not.'

In another call, Simon in Hong Kong had been alerted to the imminent arrival of a package from me, with no details other than what he could read in the papers enclosed until I got there and could feed him some background. No, I couldn't tell him where they came from and I said, with all the firmness I could muster, that once I'd given him a full verbal report, I didn't want to have anything more to do with the matters raised or the people involved.

I'd then gone to see Rodney at the Tanglin Club for an early cup of tea, thereby avoiding his swimming ritual. I'd stopped there on my way to the airport. I filled him in on the night before, including seeing Ting Tack Chee again. It was no surprise that that bit of news did nothing to help cheer him up, for he already seemed to be set in a very maudlin mood, maybe even a philosophical one, because, in an even more avuncular fashion than usual, he was keen to give me advice on money and women.

'*Cherchez l'argent* is what I've always done in any deals I've been involved in or any businesses I've looked at.

Watch out for Bill Brumble and all of them, especially Jimmy.'

'I thought it was *cherchez la femme* in most crime novels?'

'They're wrong about that. Take it from me. If you can't trust women, believe me, you can trust anyone with their eyes fixed on money even less. No, follow the money every time. And ask yourself *cui bono*, who benefits?'

'That's disappointing. I was hoping to follow a few women, but that hasn't happened.'

'I thought you were divorced. Haven't you had enough? What do they say about second-time arounders, "The triumph of hope over experience". Anyhow, if you do get involved, avoid the secretive ones.'

'Why's that?'

'Because the secretive in this world invariably have something to hide.'

'Rodney, you old cynic, what's happened to your romantic side?'

'What you have to realise, Rich, is that you never really know anyone, in a friendship or in a relationship. You can be let down and you can get it wrong. Don't make assumptions about people and how they'll behave, otherwise you'll get caught out. Think that they're all out to get you and then you'll be pleasantly surprised if they don't turn out to be like that, but assume they're all decent folk and you'll constantly be disappointed.'

'Rodney, I think you need a pick-me-up instead of this tea.'

'But that's just it. For every pick-me-up you buy, people let you down. Don't trust anyone is what I'm saying. Question the facts, look behind the words, study people's deeds and actions carefully. Oh, and *always* read the small print.'

I'd tried to tell him that once I'd seen my friends in officialdom in Hong Kong, I was going to concentrate on publishing, which was complicated enough without getting caught up in anything else. I'd seen enough already to know that there were too many murky areas and I was going to try and steer clear of the kind of dodgy customers and shady dealings I'd already come across.

That's what I focused on sitting at Changi airport, especially when I was further imprisoned there by a delay in the flight.

My plan of campaign was straightforward, in theory. First, to be polite to Jimmy and give him the Langleys work he'd been expecting. Simple as. Second, to brief Simon and forget all about it. Third, Chuck Besky. Not quite so simple. I'd forgotten about him. Still, not my problem. Unless he needed anything from me, don't get drawn in. Fourth, Nick and his threatened trip to Hong Kong: treat it like meeting an old friend and contributor. Urge him to watch his back and leave the problems of the Philippines to others who could actually make a difference. Fifth, draft *two* publishing plans, one for staying with Langleys and one for going it alone. Sixth, try and relax and have a bit of fun in Hong Kong. I told myself to keep those six goals in mind and mentally tick them off.

Now, seventh, board the plane and hope you don't sit next to a talkative passenger.

*       *       *

I could only hope that the other six goals were more achievable.

The flight, comfortable in business, courtesy of the overly generous Langleys travelling expenses rules, was taken up with stories of 'my glorious career' by a chatty executive – 'Hi, I'm Jeff Parker. I guess you're stuck with me for the duration' – made more talkative by his consumption of a couple of Gimlets and a healthy(!) intake of Mâcon Villages Pinot Chardonnay A/C 1980 and Château La Jaubertie Bergerac A/C 1979.

I was mentally making notes, as if I were a food reviewer, whilst he talked all the way through our Hors d'Oeuvre de Luxe, my Lobster Thermidor (he had Roast Goose with Peanuts), both with Buttered Long Beans, Boletus with Fines Herbes and Anna Potatoes, followed by Chestnut Bavarois and, for him, several black coffees and Cognacs, XO-Otard.

I suppose I should have listened more carefully, but Rodney's words echoed in my mind and all I heard was a boastful, patronising, boring, full-of-himself, verbal diarrhoea-ist recounting his days of endless business travel throughout Asia.

I didn't believe much of what he said, as I put Rodney's advice into practice. I should have read more between the lines, because he was telling me that he worked as Far Eastern managing director – he said that's what he was, but I had him down as an international salesman plain and simple – of a large British company, which he described, in an obviously rehearsed, jokey way, as selling 'the Mercedes of aircraft engines'.

Mostly he spoke about having a girl in every port, or a port in every girl, I can't remember which, but the only thing that stuck in my mind was his view of the constant bribes he found himself handing out. 'It's not bribery,' he said, 'it's extortion! We have to pay what's demanded just to stay in the game. From Jakarta to Beijing, engines don't sell themselves, you know, however brilliant a salesman you are. The wheels have to be oiled, so to speak.'

It went on and on in that vein until he finally asked me what I did. Unfortunately, his eyes lit up when I told him about my government contract work.

'Why didn't you say so? I'm looking for consultancy roles on the side.' I bet you are!

'What sort of subjects could you speak about?'

'Try this for a programme: Defence Contracting in Asia, an Insider's Guide.'

'Sounds good. What would it cover?'

'Just that, of course. I'd review Indonesia, Malaysia, China, Singapore and the Philippines and I could cover others like Cambodia, Laos, Vietnam and even throw in Brunei; me and the Sultan go back a long way.'

'Wouldn't that sort of thing conflict with what you do for your company? How would they feel about you sharing trade secrets with possible competitors?'

'I wouldn't do that, would I? I wasn't born yesterday. I'd keep to defence contracting in general, go into a bit of detail country by country and only spice it up with a few war stories of my own, from my experience. Anyway, most of our competitors know what we're up to, as we're all spying on each other all the time, and, when we're not doing that, we're meeting up at defence contracting or aircraft shows all over the world as drinking buddies. No, what I'd hope is that I'd get a lot of government officials attending, for them to see how others do it and, therefore, I might get to forge some new relationships and oil a few more wheels for my own company. I could then charge in and steal a few more contracts.'

It carried on in that vein, more or less throughout the whole flight, and I had to take his card – 'Jeffrey Parker, Head of International Aeronautical Sales' – when we finally landed and parted company, but, sadly, not before he'd found out where I was staying. He said that he'd love to meet up for a drink, to take 'our most interesting and fruitful conversation further'.

Great!

But, I supposed I'd have to take our discussions further, because it made sense to make use of him and what he'd told me about going in and out of China; how I should rush to get in first with publishing opportunities as the 'whole place is opening up for the West, and it's as if gold has been discovered in the hills, to go by the companies that are flocking there to try and do business'. That did strike a chord, for Langleys and for me.

*No man ever steps in the same river twice, for it's not
the same river and he's not the same man.*

HERACLITUS

# 10

WHEN I GOT BACK TO The Mandarin after my flight to Hong Kong from Singapore, the first people I bumped straight into in the lobby were the weak-chinned, balding CEO of Langleys, dressed in his crumpled safari suit, the tall bespectacled finance director, in his trade-mark blue shiny accountant's suit (and tie!) and the smooth, suave, international marketing director, casual in his regimental blazer. They looked about as British as you can get. If I'd had to cast them in a film, they would have been played by the actors Miles Malleson, Michael Caine and Richard Todd respectively. They were about to go into the Captain's Bar with ... Jimmy Chan, who would have had to portray himself, a role he was born to play.

It was, apart from a grinning Jimmy, a frosty welcome back, with my firm's top executives looking at me as if I really was the one shit-shovelling minion they'd hoped never to have to deal with at close quarters. How nice to be put firmly back in my place with their own style of motivational leadership.

Eschewing the normal greetings you'd expect on bumping into colleagues in some far-flung outpost, they acknowledged me with an 'Ah, it's you!' and were straight into telling me that *they* were taking over negotiations with Jimmy, who was standing right next to them, inching forward, beaming at me and giving me a small hand-wave greeting ... I was therefore free, to go off and concentrate on getting on with my own area of the firm's publishing. Basically, get out of our way and don't bother us.

Added to which, they proudly informed me, Jimmy had now offered Langleys an introduction to some high-ranking mainland Chinese officials – just as Jeffrey Parker on the plane had said – who were handing out publishing contracts.

No doubt it would be trebles all round.

Having been told, only out of embarrassment I figured, that they'd catch up with me in a day or so as they had a busy schedule of meetings of their own, I'd checked in, gone up to my room (no harbour view this time, thanks Jimmy) and phoned my immediate boss in London to try and find out what was going on.

Being told that I'd – surprise, surprise – cocked things up with Jimmy and this had meant that the CEO had felt he had no option but to fly out to patch things up, was bad enough. But worse, he told me that Jimmy had told them of some big China deals – that I should have gleaned from him in my meetings – and which Spreadworths were pitching hard to get, even sending *their* big cheese Nigel Bland out to Hong Kong to follow them up. I'd known that of course as I'd seen him at Bottoms Up, but news of Bland's involvement had been a red rag to a bull as far as our CEO was concerned.

Spreadworths, we'd been told by Jimmy, saw the same potential opportunity in China government publishing that Pergamon Press and Maxwell had grasped in scientific research materials in Europe from the 1950s onwards. Me saying it was obvious that Jimmy was playing us all off against each other, and that he would be the main beneficiary, fell on deaf ears. Thanks to Deng Xiaoping and the opening up of his country, the scramble for Chinese publishing rights was underway. I'd jeopardised Langleys' chances as far as my boss was concerned and I was told to buck up my ideas.

I'd better think fast about jumping before I was pushed, was my conclusion.

I tried to share my fears about Jimmy's 'integrity' with my boss in the same conversation, but was cut short and told to wind things up, not just with the telephone call but my trip generally, and head back to the UK.

I'd then telephoned Simon Perkins and arranged to meet him and, if he could arrange it, Will Tomkins, inviting them for a lateish bite to eat and a nightcap at the hotel. Simon seemed pleased to hear from me.

After I'd unpacked, freshened up and enjoyed a room-boy delivered pot of jasmine tea, I went down to the lobby. Thinking I'd have a stroll out in the open-if-not-fresh air, hoping that the bustle of the city would pep me up, I saw Jimmy and the Langleys lot leaving and then, sauntering past them and towards reception, smiling at everyone, including the departing Jimmy, came the Aussie trio. I must find out what they know about Jimmy.

Once they'd spotted me, it was straight into the Captain's Bar to sit up at the bar itself with them insisting on getting the drinks in. Dom Pérignon it was then, charged to their offshore fund account, no doubt.

They were celebrating another successful tax deal, they informed me, and, unfortunately, they then proceeded to try and explain it. Routing licensing fees due to a nameless pharmaceutical giant through Vanuatu from a Bermuda-based holding company that had its licensee company based in West Germany and paid its fees through a joint-venture company in the Netherlands, or something like that. They even drew me a little diagram on a napkin, but I was really none the wiser.

Still, they seemed pleased enough to see me and managed to ask what I'd been doing. I tried to tell them the main outline, but spiced-up of course and anonymous, and I majored on run-ins with the CIA, Marcos gangsters and Chinese hitmen. They looked dubious and even *I* felt like a bit of a Walter Mitty. I moved on to ask them about Jimmy. All I got was 'if we told you, we'd have to kill you', which I took as more of a send-up of my adventures, but, probably, in truth, they were as interested in my stories as I was in the intricacies of their latest tax avoidance schemes. That night, they were intent on getting slaughtered and getting me roped in as their straight man on a night out on the town.

Thankfully, I had my arrangement with Simon and Will to honour. Off they went, but not before loudly challenging me to join them on their daily jogs. 'Every morning, rain or shine, six-thirty sharp, we do route two of the hotel's jogging trail. Come with us, you Pommie Sheila, or we'll give you a big breakfast.' Laddish laughter all round from the lairy lawyers and a how-could-I-not-rise-to-the-challenge response from me.

Simon and Will had turned up soon after and once we'd ordered a bottle of expensive white Burgundy, they were happy to stay at the hotel, order a bar food snack, and keep the corner table we'd bagged for ourselves. Simon turned to face inwards as he'd spotted quite a few wealthy local businessmen dotted about, who probably would like to spike his drink to return the favour of him having skewered some of their tax dodges and false accounting tricks over the years.

I'd started to try and tell them briefly what had happened in Manila and Singapore, but quickly got cut short by them both, each making gagging, keep-it-zipped and throat-cutting gestures to get me to shut up.

Simon and I did manage to arrange to meet at his office the following morning and Will, after disappearing to make a phone call, came back and said he'd fixed for me to meet up with him and Dickie Hart the next afternoon for what he called 'a proper debrief in the light of what you've said'.

I'd been meaning to arrange to see my diplomat friend anyway, not only for old times' sake, but because I thought he might be useful to me, partly because of what had been happening wherever I went. Clearly, Will felt the same.

I tried to whisper a 'What's happened to Chuck?' and got the same mime-show from Will to silence me. I understood straight away why I should be more careful about what I said, as out of the corner of my eye I'd seen, staring at us from the bar, an intense looking thug who reminded me of Lane Crawford/Ting Tack Chee, who was fortunately still in Singapore, wasn't he? I wondered who else might be eavesdropping our conversation. I'd forgotten the place's reputation as the spring of gossip where Chinese whispers would begin their flow.

The others were as perturbed as I was when I told them in hushed tones how Lane Crawford had turned up in Singapore. Will remarked in passing that it was unusual that a *gweilo* like me could pick out particular Chinese faces as readily as I could, especially once Simon had confirmed the face at the bar was the dead spit of the guy who had followed us on our first night in Hong Kong.

We must have looked guilty of something the way we sat huddled together discussing him and when our club sandwiches arrived, we'd tucked in more or less in silence and called it a night.

When I got up to my room, there was a message in an envelope which reception had pushed under my door. It was from, talk of the devil, Chuck, who'd heard from Nick Dale in Manila (How did Nick know? From Miguel, perhaps?) that I was back in Hong Kong. He was going to call by for breakfast at eight o'clock. Great! Can't go jogging!

\*     \*     \*

How strange that next day was.

I'd been alarmed by an early call from Miguel in Manila telling me he'd just heard that Rodney had had a serious heart attack and wasn't expected to pull through. He said he himself didn't have much else to report and said he'd do that later. He wanted to get off the phone double quick, that was obvious. Was he fearful he was being bugged?

I dozed on and off after that, but luckily I'd set my alarm for a fall-back seven-thirty and I leapt up and managed a 'shit, shave, shower and shampoo' in record time. Barely just dressed, Chuck arrived on time and telephoned me from reception bang on eight. As requested by me, he came up to my room, and we ordered breakfast off the room service menu. He insisted on putting the radio on and kept pointing at his ears. I finally twigged. He thinks the room might be bugged. Jesus, why was the whole world spooked?

He was in a venomous mood, critical of Mike Moreno and the Americans and equally of the British, with total contempt for Dickie Hart.

'Not one of them is interested in what I've found out about Marcos and what's going on in the Philippines. Everyone is scared shitless of challenging the status quo. They're all more concerned about a power vacuum letting in the Chinese than they are about the exploitation of a country, its people and its resources. "It's Alright Ma (I'm Only Bleeding)". What does anybody care about any more?'

He carried on his diatribe in that vein and seemed to have forgotten completely about his initial fear of being bugged. In fact, almost as if he was playing to an imaginary gallery, he gave me an articulate dismantling of Western foreign policy.

'Don't you realise that after 1975 the Yanks knew Pol Pot was a genocidal tyrant, but they supported him anyway because he was fighting the Vietnamese ... and Reagan's giving Stinger missiles to the Mujahideen in Afghanistan, despite Gorbachev warning him about the dangers of courting Islamic fundamentalists. The Americans can't see further than the certainty of fighting the next communist. They care more about propping up Marcos at all costs, never mind the real human price of doing so.'

He carried on ferociously and I asked him where it now placed him. 'What are you going to do next? You can't go back to the Philippines. The Yanks would probably just like you to go away. You say the Brits are trying to close you down too, fobbing you off by assuring you they'll investigate all your allegations thoroughly and make representations through established diplomatic channels.'

'Bullshit! Bollocks! They're all pillocks! And they're the bastards that still rule the world. I'm going public. I've got to. Somebody has to show a bit of courage and conviction. And that's me. I've seen that journalist guy

Martin Rochester and he's doing a piece about how I was public enemy numero uno in the Philippines because I was investigating corruption in just about everything. He'll be telling how it's the Filipinos paying the price, whilst the world just stands aside and condones the outrages. It's time the world woke up to what's going on, it really is.'

'Is that wise, Chuck? It doesn't sound sensible to me.'

'Sensible? Who needs sensible? Sensible doesn't change the world. I thought you were on my side. What have you done with my report? What's Nick done?'

It was now my turn to start miming shut-the-fuck-up actions and I jumped up and turned the radio up to full blast.

'Christ, Chuck, if you really think we're being bugged, you've just given away quite a lot.'

'You're a fucking scaredy-cat, dumb-ass like the rest of them,' he said. 'You don't believe in anything anymore. What happened to the socialist principles you had when you were at university, or was that just an act?'

'Hey! Aren't you going to thank me for getting you out of the Philippines. Without me and Nick, who risked a hell of a lot and who actually still has to live there, you'd have been a sitting duck. Certainly you wouldn't be here now insulting me as if I was Marcos himself.'

'Thank you for plonking me in the custody of the CIA, who graciously tried to assure me that they knew what was going on, and had a grand plan that I would only be fucking up by making a song and dance about conditions under Marcos. Didn't I know that it was a complicated world and that if we wanted change and Western values to hold sway, we had to play nuanced politics, or some such crap?'

'But how did you get to Hong Kong?'

'Your guy Mike Moreno the Fourteenth, or some such stupid bloody name, played the good cop and kept threatening me with his boss, Bill Brumby, who he said was as mean as hell and wanted me holed up for good.'

'Bill Brumby? Are you sure? Why would he give you his name?'

'I don't know if he exists. Who cares? They were trying to scare me.'

'Oh, he exists all right. I've met him, masquerading as a simple book distribution specialist. Actually, he seemed like a nice guy.'

'Rich, you are getting worse and worse at judging people. Nice people are the ones to be most suspicious of. Charm and bonhomie cover deceit and duplicity. Nobody is ever that nice.'

'What happened to get you here?'

'At the airbase, Pope Moreno the Twenty-third kept mentioning getting hold of an Air America pilot, which I twigged eventually is their shorthand for CIA transport. The Brits in Hong Kong wanted me, and the Americans seemed happy to see the back of me. All they did was warn me of "consequences for me *and* my family" – get *that* as a veiled threat – if I went public with any of my stuff, and that I had to have confidence in them. Marcos was part of their plan and he wouldn't be around for much longer. I was told I should hold fire.'

'So, how has it been in Hong Kong?'

'Worse. Dickie Hart is as bland as they come. Despite me telling him all I'd found out in the Philippines, and incidentally, he kept taking copious notes, he still said he wanted my report. Speaking of which, where the hell is it?'

By this time the music was so loud, I couldn't really hear myself think.

'Safe, but let's talk later.'

'That's right, fob me off. You're all the same. Rich, I'm disappointed in you. I thought you'd want all this out in the open.'

'Nick is going to be bringing your report somehow to Hong Kong and he was going to try and get a copy of it to the opposition groups in the Philippines. Now you're out of the Philippines, you can tell your story yourself. Knowing you, you can remember every word of your report anyway. What more can I do?'

'Carry on poncing about in the publishing world for all I care.'

With that, he stood up, and marched out of the room.

\*       \*       \*

After that session with Chuck, it was a relief to see good old dependable Simon. I'd taken a taxi with my usual daft precautions and, despite all the work piled up on his desk – brown, orange and green files, all yay-thick, doubtless with tax returns and computations inside them, Simon exuded quiet calm and resolve.

I gave him a bit more detail of what had happened in Manila and Singapore and inevitably we were focused on talking about Jimmy.

He had some papers out in front of him, and spotting an envelope positioned to one side, I could see it was the one I'd sent from Singapore with Rodney's dossier.

'These papers are dynamite, Rich, and I've only just started reading them. You're certain no one else knows about them?'

'Actually, there's been a development. The anonymous writer has had a heart attack and the way my day is going, I'm beginning to wonder if it isn't a bit suspicious, especially as Jimmy's bagman, Lane Crawford, was in Singapore when I left.'

'A heart attack? When? And that's a terrible bagman joke. Just tell me about the heart attack.'

'I heard about it in what seemed like the middle of the night, but Miguel, the chap I mentioned to you last night – the journalist who is doing some work for me – didn't feel able to tell me any more over the phone. Seriously, Simon, are phones and hotel rooms bugged that often out here? Are we being recorded now, for instance?'

'No, we aren't, but yes, they are. And if you go to mainland China, everything is bugged. The Philippines? Maybe. The Mandarin? Doubtful, but you never know. Is Mr Anonymous dead?'

'I don't think so, but he's in a critical condition. I hope he pulls through.'

'Not half as much as I do. I'd like him to turn Queen's evidence on a whole load of stuff. The Revenue in a dozen or more countries could clean up on the basis of what I've got in front of me, but we'd need him to give us personally testified evidence. We could guarantee confidentiality, but we need him to be a real person.'

'And not dead, presumably?'

'Exactly!'

I was able to regurgitate all, I think, of the background detail Rodney had fed me about Jimmy, which left Simon slack-jawed and open-mouthed, furiously writing notes on foolscap paper in front of him.

Then, by way of light relief, I filled Simon in with more detail of my publishing plans and how I'd decided to hand in my notice. In the middle of my spiel he went over to his bookcase – glass-fronted as befitted his grade – and took out a copy of one of our journals. By the way he started smiling, I realised, he'd worked out who Mr

Anonymous was, by reference to the authors and correspondents printed as part of the masthead.

'OK, OK, Simon. Don't look smug. I can tell you've worked out who you think my source is. But you're wrong. He doesn't write for me.'

'Alright, Rich, if you say so ... '

'Come off it, Simon.'

'I'm not on it. But promise me this. You will tell me if our tome of the unknown tax warrior's author dies from his heart attack, won't you?'

We could only smile at each other.

'What should I watch out for when I meet up with Dickie Hart this afternoon?'

'Once you tell him what's been going on, he'll doubtless try and rope you into providing information for him, especially now that Will is involved.'

'What on earth could they really want from me? I'm not cut out for that kind of cloak and dagger stuff.'

'That's what they probably find appealing. The fact that, honestly, no disrespect, you're the last person I'd think of being caught up in their undercover world.'

'Haven't you got to believe in something to get dragged in?'

'Or need the money, or the kudos, if you don't want the honour of serving your country.'

'Look, Simon, I had a very unpleasant breakfast with Chuck Besky this morning and basically he told me that

I was a complete tosser who didn't believe in anything. I think he sees me as someone who'd rather make money than make a difference.'

'That's true, isn't it, and not necessarily anything to be ashamed of in any case.'

'That's OK for you to say. You do what you do, because you believe in what you do.'

'What? Raising taxes for governments to misuse?'

'Isn't it better for elected governments to misuse the wealth of the country, rather than greedy fat cats and crooks who misappropriate it and squander it on conspicuous consumption or squirrel it away in forgotten nominee accounts in shady tax havens?'

'Nice of you to sum up my career for me. And I thought I just happened to be good at a job I fell into after university.'

'And, you can respect your bosses as well, can't you?'

'I suppose so. They're a decent bunch and none that I know take bribes, but, of course, I might be being naïve.'

'I can't respect mine. I bumped into them yesterday because they've come over to Hong Kong, probably to sack me. The CEO is an old- school publisher, even down to the tatty safari suit he obviously jumps into whenever he's travelling 'to the colonies', as he no doubt sees them, including Hong Kong. He and Jimmy have got to have something on each other. They go back a long way and they're as thick as thieves in every sense. And they've got a lot in common. For a start, they both cheat on their wives and I'm sure they'd think nothing of cheating on everybody else.'

'Why don't you leave Langleys then? You've spoken about it often enough. Just do it. What have you got to lose?'

'That's true. I'm not married anymore. No dependents. Even if it all goes pear-shaped, it doesn't really matter.'

'Anyway, that's enough career advice from me, can you now get out of my office and let me get on with some work?'

'Sure.'

'Let me know how you get on with Dickie and Will and, of course, let me know how Rodney Bolt is doing.'

He'd winked at me and smiled as he'd said Rodney's name. That was a well-kept secret. I'm not very good at this game. 'OK, OK. You win. I'll give you a call,' I said as I was leaving.

# 11

I WENT BACK TO THE hotel and ordered a caesar salad in my room, but the chef had over-egged it with the anchovies. As soon as I'd eaten it, I regretted it and felt uncomfortable, not a good preparation for my afternoon session on Government Hill.

Swigging desperately at a very gassy Perrier didn't help, but I rang Rodney's home number in Singapore and spoke to his wife, who'd only just got in from the hospital.

Rodney was in a critical condition and it had all been a terrible shock – no history of heart problems and a relatively healthy lifestyle. He hadn't been under any real stress, she thought. He'd got back from the Tanglin Club and seemed pretty much as normal, but had started to feel very unwell and didn't want anything to eat, just a lie down, before finally collapsing when he got up a little later from the bed. Emergency services had responded quickly and he'd been rushed to hospital.

'What did he do during the day?' I asked.

'The usual! It was a perfectly normal day. He'd dealt with his mail, finished writing a report for one client and said he was meeting a potential new one for lunch at the Tanglin Club, staying on for a swim before coming home.'

'Who was the new client?'

'I don't know.'

'Can you find out? Look at his diary maybe.'

'Why? Do you think that could have something to do with it? I don't like to look at his diary. He'd go mad if he knew.'

'I think we're beyond that now. It might tell us something. Even if it was a cause of some stress, perhaps.'

'I'll get it then, but it might take a few minutes. Can you hold on?'

'Of course! Thanks.'

New client. Not really strange, although he had been telling me he was winding down. Suspicious. Probably not, but ...

'It's blank. Just says "Tanglin Club. 12.30 pm".'

'Is that suspicious?'

'I don't think so. Rodney worried about being on time and forgetting appointments, but he always seemed to know who he was meeting.'

'Are there any notes from the meeting?'

'I've got his briefcase here. I'll take a look ... ah, here ... a pad of lined paper ... he's scribbled some things ... it's headed "New client meeting: Stanley Ho, gold dealer, based in Bangkok and Antwerp" and then it goes on with words like, "HNWI in the millions", what does that mean?'

'That's high net worth individual, that's all. What else?'

' "Homes in Geneva, Bangkok, Manila and Hong Kong" and then it says in underlined capitals, "CLAIMS NOT TO KNOW JIMMY CHAN". That is suspicious, isn't it?'

'Because any gold dealer in Hong Kong would know Jimmy?'

'Exactly! Even I know that.'

'What else does it say?'

' "Gave him the usual wealth preservation suggestions, but in addition told him I could not act for him, as I was winding down for retirement and could recommend him some possible suitable advisors".'

'Is there a business card in there?'

After some more briefcase rummaging, she replied, 'Yes, here it is, double-sided for English and Chinese. All it gives is the name of Stanley Ho, followed by the name of his business, Ho Trading Company Limited and an address in Bangkok.'

'What do you make of that?'

It had set some alarm bells ringing in her head.

'Sounds like Jimmy sent him. The card is probably worthless. His real name is probably not even Stanley Ho. Something must have been said for Rodney to be suspicious and not take him on. I know Rodney, if he thought he could get a fee for some advice, he'd have done it.'

'I think you should tell the police.'

'I can't without talking to Rodney.'

'The man could still be in the country. The Tanglin Club staff might give a description.'

'When Rodney pulls through, I'll talk to him about it.'

'And if he doesn't?'

'I'm not thinking like that, but if he doesn't make it, I'll go to the police, even if it's too late.'

'Can you check with the hospital and get them to test if he was given anything to eat or drink that could have triggered his heart attack? Say you're suspicious.'

'Then they'll call the police.'

'Look, yes, they might, but it could be important and it could help his treatment. Will you promise me you will? Straight away, please.'

'Yes. Very well. I'll go back there this afternoon. But while you're on the phone, I did think that someone had been into the house whilst I was at the hospital, but I can't see anything's missing.'

'Any sign of someone searching through Rodney's office?'

'Not really, no. Look, I'm being silly. It's probably the cleaner. She comes in at odd times. I noticed our bedroom door was closed, when I always leave it open. The cleaner's the only one who closes it. Probably it's something and nothing.'

Now I was really curious. What might have happened? And why now? What was Jimmy worried about? Rodney's dossier? Did he know about it? Was it all a coincidence? Was Lane Crawford involved? Or was it the cleaner?

I rang Simon and put him in the picture, swearing him to secrecy over the identity of the source of his new revelatory papers and the uncertain fate of the author.

\*  \*  \*

I was a bit early for my meeting at two-thirty that was going to be in the main wing of the Central Government Offices in Lower Albert Road, on Government Hill, not that far from the Foreign Correspondents' Club. A lot had happened since *that* night out.

Deciding I might as well walk it, to waste some time and try and shake off post-lunch blues, off I went, slowly and quite happily, with a mission of trying to lower the average speed of everyone else bustling alongside me. I hadn't gone that far from the hotel when, over my shoulder, a smartly dressed man in a suit and wearing a turban caught my eye.

'Good day to you, sir,' he said in an exaggeratedly polite fashion. 'It is going to be a wonderful day for you.'

'Thanks,' I said, walking on.

He was now in step, by my side.

'No, I mean it. You have an open and honest face and a warm smile.'

I now tried to walk a little faster, but he kept pace with me. Opening a small notebook in his hand, he wrote a couple of things down, whilst walking, that I couldn't see and he turned the page over.

'Is your favourite colour red or blue?'

'Red, I suppose,' was me trying to say something and get it over with.

'What then is your favourite number? One to twelve and not six or ten.'

'Five!'

'See this piece of paper?' he said holding open the notebook, 'without ever meeting you, I wrote down those two answers. You will have good luck today and for the rest of your life.'

'Thanks,' I mumbled, embarrassed as hell, trying to turn away from him and cross the road. 'Just who are you and what do you want?'

'Direct and open and to the point. That is why you will go far. I am an Indian mystic and I am trying to get back to my yogi who I haven't seen for the best part of a full year. Will you make a donation to my travel expenses, please?'

A beggar in other words! Do I look that much of a mug? I suppose I must. Still, he had kind of cheered me up.

I offered him a ten-dollar note, but he looked at it, most insulted.

'Something more than that, I think, would be appropriate. Fifty would be a better minimum.'

'Get lost,' I said, realising I'd been had. I pocketed my ten dollars and, seeing a gap in the traffic, stepped smartly into the road and power-walked across the street.

He waved at me as he walked away. I'd found the encounter a bit unsettling and the caesar salad made an unwelcome return visit to the back of my throat. God, I was too gullible to travel.

*     *     *

Simon had told me to take my passport to get through some basic security at the government offices, but as soon as I arrived at the door, I was met by a young British foreign office junior – no doubt a first from Oxford, an ambassador for a father and on the fast-track – who'd greeted me by name and ushered me up the nearest stairway and along a stark corridor, where busy-looking people seemingly raced along clutching files, as if they were all late for very important meetings or maybe tea with the Mad Hatter.

A knock on an unnamed door generated a bellowed, 'Come'. In we walked, to be greeted by Dickie Hart and Will Tomkins, both friendly and welcoming.

'Hello, namesake,' Dickie stepped forward to shake my hand. 'You know Will, of course.'

It was weird to see Dickie Hart again, looking smart and groomed, as I was amused to think back to first meeting him over a game of table football in the JCR at Maldwyn College, Cambridge. His ultra-curly black hair had been long then, whereas now it was short, giving him, with his black-framed specs, the look of a Maurice Saatchi, slick in his adman's pin-striped suit. Very much the FO high-flyer, in fact.

'Grab a seat, Rich, and tell me what you've been up to on your travels.'

I did both.

If I went into too much detail about Marcos and Chuck, Dickie cut me short with 'Yes, yes, yes, we know all that from the horse's mouth,' and if I tried to specu-late about just what Jimmy and Tufty and Mike Moreno or Bill Brumby were up to, I was bluntly told to 'Keep to the facts, Rich, if you don't mind.' When I speculated that Jimmy might have been behind the heart attack of one of my authors, I was gently assured that I was 'being fanciful', even though I could tell that Will seemed amazed by each revelation.

What Dickie seemed most interested in were my publishing plans, having asked me directly to explain to him exactly what my job entailed, after he'd asked me why I was 'swanning around in South East Asia'.

I must have told him three times about how my international journals operated and what plans I had for new ones. He chuckled at the problems I was having at Langleys and 'you're for the chop, my friend' became a catchphrase he repeated as each episode that pitched me against Jimmy was explained to him. He seemed to be more amused than concerned by my references to Jimmy.

In the end, I got a bit fed up, I suppose. I looked at him and then Will, who had been almost silent throughout, apart from a few raised eyebrows and the occasional questioning prompts during my recounting, and I couldn't help myself asking them a direct question.

'Look, why am I telling you all this? You can't be that interested in the exploits of a failing publisher and so far, you're not exactly saying any of the information is going to be of any real interest or even of use to you. You're not even taking seriously what I'm saying about Jimmy. We could have just had a drink and a catch-up. I feel just like Chuck said *he* felt and I'm beginning to see what he meant when he said that nobody really cares. Just what is your agenda? And that's a question for both of you.'

'Fair enough,' replied Dickie looking at Will, who nodded in agreement, 'let's order some tea and have a nice little chat. I'll go and do that and Will, if you could join me for a mo, there are a couple of things I'd like to have your take on, if I may, before we answer Rich's very reasonable question.'

\*       \*       \*

Whilst they were out of the room, tea duly arrived on a trolley, delivered by an old Chinese filing clerk in a tan cotton warehouse coat. He was, for all the world, just the perfect figurehead for the Civil Service, home from home, in Hong Kong. As I was thanking him, I could see him craning his neck around to try and read some of the names of the files on Dickie's desk, but, when the door opened, he instantly rewound his neck and was quickly back to pushing his trolley out as fast as he could.

Looking at what the plate of biscuits represented – that there is some corner of a foreign field that is forever digestive – it all seemed parochial rather than international. No wonder the Chinese were walking all over us in the negotiations for 1997.

'What did you think of the Indian mystic you met in the street?' Will asked me out of the blue.

'How ... ? Don't tell me, he's one of yours.'

'That's right. He'd tailed you from your hotel. He engaged with you. He could have killed you, easily.'

'Great. Now you tell me.'

'At least you didn't part with any money, you old skinflint,' added Dickie smilingly.

'What am I being tested for? Stupidity?'

'No, it's something we routinely demonstrate to all our recruits, before we teach them counter-surveillance techniques,' Will stated.

'Wait a minute. What do you mean "recruits"? I'm not one. I haven't agreed to join anything.'

'Yes and no,' Dickie butted in. 'You see, we're interested in you as a publisher, primarily as that gives you carte blanche to go virtually anywhere. You want to start up in business on your own. We can fund it. Enough to take on a few staff and you can do your own recruiting, although we might have the odd hand in that. Check people out. Maybe suggest some. For example, we'd have to vet this Miguel Bentoz bloke you mentioned in your opening patter.'

'Hold on, what are you talking about here?'

'Simple' ... 'Yes simple'. Dickie and Will were taking it in turns to answer my latest question. 'We'll finance your publishing start-up and in return, you can supply information' ... 'Just like you've done to Simon on the tax and financial side' ... 'And just like you've finessed with Chuck'.

'What's the point of it all? You should hear Chuck on that subject.'

'Chuck is …,' whatever Chuck was, Dickie had thought better of saying it. 'Chuck is Chuck,' was all he could come up with.

Will stepped in with, 'Look, Chuck is an idealist and that's not the world we inhabit. He wants instant results and that's not going to happen.'

'I'm an information gatherer who's not meant to have any opinions. Is that it?'

'You have a useful cover. You can travel. You have a legitimate business that will be yours. You'll own it. You can build it up. You can take the profits,' Dickie outlined and then Will filled in.

'You'll work with us in different countries building up a new network of contacts. You'll be discreet. You won't go anywhere, or into anything, all guns blazing like Chuck. You won't try and draw attention to yourself.'

'It's a bit late for that, isn't it? I'm *persona non grata* with Langleys, Jimmy thinks I'm a twit, some Marcos goons have marked my card and, for all I know, Singapore security have got my number. Can't you find some other publisher to do it all for you?'

'We know you. We have a relationship. We think we can trust you. We can trust you, Rich, can't we?' Dickie asked.

'I want to get out of Langleys, the sooner the better. I'd love to resign right now, as a matter of fact. I think I could develop a publishing business and if it means dishing the dirt on people like Jimmy then I could believe in that.'

'What about sifting information about companies operating in the defence world – you could do some more seminars and publishing in that area, couldn't you, letting us know who you're dealing with and doing some research for us?' Will suggested.

'I don't know the first thing about the kind of activities you're on about.'

'You wouldn't need to. You'd stay a publisher operating a legitimate business and go about your work as normal. It's just that you would facilitate us operating within your organisation, using your company as a cloak. Incidentally, we should at this point get you to sign the Official Secrets Act, if that's OK?'

They pushed a single yellowish-coloured sheet across to me.

'I've already signed it when I was in the Civil Service.'

'Yes, I'd forgotten that about you,' said Dickie, 'still, you'd better sign it again, if you don't mind.'

I couldn't be bothered to argue, but I felt strongly enough to say, 'There's no way I'm going to be working directly for you, that's not on. Anyway, I know nothing about that world of surveillance, Moscow rules, telephone tapping and all that jazz.'

Will couldn't help himself. 'You seem quite well informed, from what you've just said. Anyway, we're intelligence officers of now, not fifty years ago. It's more important to be able to read a set of accounts than it is to handle a Walther PPK. And, unlike Smiley and co, we work on trusting people – not on everyone betraying everyone else.'

'You know what I mean,' I countered weakly, 'I've already felt out of my depth in the events that have happened of late.' Then I remembered something, which bucked me up a bit.

'I'm curious. Did your Indian mystic spot I was being followed, not just by him, but by another guy, whose face I couldn't quite see ... I couldn't actually be completely sure he was following me, come to think of it. Anyway, did he spot anyone suspicious and, if he did, does he know who that was?'

Will leapt up at that point and raced out of the room saying, 'I'll check that out, right away.'

Meanwhile Dickie pointed out reassuringly, 'Don't worry, we'd train you in some of the basics, but we're not actually going to make you fully operational. We're more interested in any new firm you set up being used from time to time as a vehicle, a bit of a front, if you will. It would fit with Bill Brumby's book distribution outfit and I gather you've met Bill. We like the sound of this Miguel chap and, if he checks out, then he could work for you and us, and you and he might be able to nurture your own sources for us.'

Will came barging back in. 'Yes, I'm pleased to say he did spot him and he knows his name. Let's see if *you* do. We know you're good with remembering faces,' Will said.

'Don't tell me who told you that. Kenneth or Eric. They're obviously your puppets too.'

'Associates, you might say,' said Dickie, 'or assets, you could call them, I guess. But yes, they were as impressed by your apparent spotting ability as Will was. It's a rare skill and a valuable one, especially if it isn't confined to fellow Caucasians. Kenneth and Eric are old hands in picking up on potential. Incidentally, they'd both be useful to you. Maybe you could take them on as consultants. That'd be a good wheeze and mutually beneficial, don't you think?'

'Great idea,' replied Will as he pulled some pictures out of an envelope. 'Here's a little test,' he said, handing me two photos, 'to check your legendary spotting skills, Rich. Which of these is Jimmy and which is his brother?'

I looked at them. Different hairstyles; one with glasses, one without. One very smartly and ostentatiously dressed, like an early version of David Tang, and the other, just dressed as Jimmy.

'They're both Jimmy.'

'Good. Now who are these men?' he asked, giving me four more photos.

'This one is Ting Tack Chee, otherwise known to me as Jimmy's bagman, Lane Crawford. This one is Tan Siow

Ming. This one is Tong Lim. And this one looks a bit like Lane Crawford, but it's not him and although I think I saw him at the hotel bar, I don't know who he is,' I unhesitatingly replied, even impressing myself.

'Nice. Neat work on the faces and the names. Puzzled how we seem to know the same people as you do?'

'Yes, it does seem a bit odd.'

'Not really, you see we're interested in the same people as you are. They are of relevance to us, I should say, and I think they are for you too,' Will informed me.

'He's a born spotter,' said Dickie, 'Ken and Eric were right about this special talent of yours.'

'Yes: any face, any place, any time and I seem to be able to recall it with a name, if I know it. I'm used to seeing a face, say in the street, and enjoy saying to myself, "He was on the 7.54 two weeks ago buying a pork pie, a coffee and twenty Embassy". That sort of thing.'

'Ken and Eric weren't wrong. Our people rarely are, they're all top-notch,' boasted Dickie. 'Please say you'll think of throwing your cap into the ring with us.'

'Oh, God. I don't know. I'll have to think about it.'

'Don't take too long. Say tomorrow? You can report back here at the same time if that's OK and try and give me a figure for our initial investment which will go straight into an account we can open in your name in Hong Kong, no questions asked by the manager.'

'I suppose so. Incidentally,' I said, directing my question at Will, 'who did the mystic say was following me?'

'Ting Tack Chee's brother, Billy Ting. He was the chap in the photo you couldn't name but you did spot the family likeness. It seems like Jimmy is keeping tabs on you right enough. We'll have to show you how to lose a tail – "dry cleaning" we call it. And, we'll have to have a word with Jimmy, won't we, Dickie?' Will said rather pointedly.

Dickie couldn't have been more dismissive. 'Don't you start, Will. You're nearly as bad as Rich here, seeing conspiracy everywhere. Jimmy is looking after his own interests and he's perfectly friendly to us.'

This drew puzzled looks from Will and me.

With that, the junior was summoned to escort me off the premises. As I left, the Indian mystic was following me from across the road, but minus his turban this time – see there's no fooling me – keeping watch on me no doubt, and, I hoped, checking to see if anyone else was.

Nevertheless, I was looking around me all the time, checking reflections in shop windows, trying to see which faces stood out from those who passed me and those behind me and especially noticing anyone who paused at the same time as I did. I must have done my shoelaces up three or four times and walked in and out of numerous shops, crossing the roads behind cars and doing all the rest of what I thought was 'dry cleaning' on the walk back to the hotel.

But then I caught sight of what must have been Billy Ting, tying his shoelace – quite deliberately – across the road, where I could see him smiling at me.

Good point, Mr Ting, well made. At least he had a sense of humour, unlike his brother, Ting Tack Chee.

\*        \*        \*

When I got back to my room, I'd had another note pushed under the door. I opened it as I cradled the phone, ordering more tea to wash away the taste of the government-issue cup that had been quite disgusting, almost deliberately, perhaps. However, its strength, if not its taste had cured any remaining digestive discomfort from my lunch.

My note was a cheerful one. The Aussies were off to Club 97 and one of them had written 'You're expected there at nine pm to join us', whilst another of them had added 'Get yourself there! It's on Lan Kwai Fong, in case you don't know'.

I didn't know where it was, but, of course, I'd heard of it. On my famous junk trip, Davina and her gang were raving about this nightclub whose very name was cocking a snook at the so-called end of Hong Kong. 'Club 97! What a brilliantly "up yours" name for a nightclub,' one of them had said. 'Who cares what's going to happen, we can always "party, party" there, right the way to the bitter end,' Davina had said rather forlornly.

I'd have to go, wouldn't I? Why not? It might be good to let my hair down. I rang Davina straight away, and yes, her gang would all be there later. Fixed. Lan Kwai Fong, here we come.

I thought about ordering room service, but I lay on the bed. I must have dozed off, because, when I awoke, it was already eight-thirty, and I barely had time to freshen up and change, before heading off to Club 97.

During my twilight forty winks, I'd had some strange dreams, drifting back to Cambridge days – brought to mind, no doubt, by seeing Dickie Hart again.

What should I do about him and his offer? Provided I owned the shares, what would I have to lose exactly? So what, if they funded the start-up and covered some of the salaries and expenses, that could work to my advantage, couldn't it? And my philosophy thus far in life had been 'outwardly conforming, inwardly free', which had become my mantra. Keep your head down and your nose clean and remain true to yourself. I could still do that. And if I was really honest with myself, there was some element of excitement to all this. But, not only would I have the problems of trying to keep a business profitable, I'd be serving two masters. Would that be difficult or not? Maybe if the demands from Dickie and co got too much, I could plead pressure of keeping my publishing viable, playing one off against the other. A servant of two masters can end up being his own boss, can't he?

When I was ready, I went downstairs and the concierge drew on a map the walking route I should take to Club 97, marking with a cross its position on Lan Kwai Fong, all of a ten-minute walk away.

I tried to keep my wits about me in case I was being followed and anyway, I knew I needed to get a fix on directions to get back again, especially if I'd had a drink or two, which would now be on an empty stomach as I'd slept and missed my chance of any food.

Chater Street, Pedder Street, Des Voeux Road, Theatre Lane, D'Aguilar – I recited to myself as I made my way on foot through the busy streets on what was an incredibly humid night, even for Hong Kong. Oh forget it, I thought, and screw the map, I'll just ask where The Mandarin is if I get lost on the way back. The Aussies'll know it at any rate. They can get themselves home no matter how much alcohol they've consumed.

'Quiet' and 'secluded' were just two of the adjectives that you couldn't apply to Club 97. The name in neon outside in the narrow street, and the frenetic atmosphere inside, combined to emphasise the last days of the Raj ambience. Music – loud enough to cover the noisiest Chuck Besky outburst and interfere permanently with any 'bugs' and your own eardrums – made conversation a challenge. It was air-kissing, drinking and dancing until breaks in the music and then a frantic shouting match to converse with the people you were with.

The Aussies were already there, drink in hand and ready for the night ahead, but, hello, standing next to them was Will and another group of four or five blokes getting equally warmed up.

As I had to pass him first, I greeted Will, who introduced his 'friends' as visiting members of a touring ex-army cricketing team. They seemed to be as up for a night on the tiles as the Aussies.

Will's companions might as well have been wearing MI6 t-shirts, and I had no doubts they were in the same line of work as he was, but I let that one pass.

Introducing the two groups to each other was just meant to be. I did that and, following up the intros with the words 'You can always discuss 1981' and 'Botham's Ashes', the blue touchpaper was lit. Adding 'Jammy Poms versus Aussie wimps' started the sledging off.

Will looked relieved that his 'charges' had new friends and he quickly said his goodbyes and sloped off home, whilst I just slipped over unnoticed to join Davina, her husband Laurence and a bunch of her glam friends, who looked quite at home in a corner.

'Rich, I knew you'd find your way here. After all it's *the* place to come to and, in Hong Kong, you've got to see and be seen in all the smart places,' she said, 'unless you want to mix with fat businessmen from all over the world and their prostitutes from all over the Far East, in which case you'd be better off over in Kowloon.' Much laughter from the group.

I loudly made jokey small talk with them all for a while, but then went over to where Katy and Clive, the advertising pair I'd met on the junk, were talking with the most gorgeous woman I'd seen for quite a while with black hair in a bob, an exquisite face and wide-awake eyes. Exotic was a word I wouldn't be using, but she was slinky all right and her loose but clingy silk dress (how's that even possible?) promised a body that would be fun to fool around with.

Katy and Clive introduced her as Elizabeth, their new assistant, who was working with them on a big video-training film contract they'd won with Cathay Pacific. Clearly the pair of them had patched up their differences temporarily, or perhaps had had to out of business necessity, but they were both in a jolly and expansive mood.

'You two are both single,' encouraged Katy, 'you should have a dance.' With that, David Bowie's 'China Girl' started up, as if the DJ was doing the music for a rom-com film and, as it would have been rude not to after Katy's cajolings, Elizabeth and I headed off to the tiny dance floor.

I thought there was some real chemistry between us and when we could talk in any lulls in the music, each of us tried to learn more about each other's background and work. She'd spent time in New York and wanted to live there more than anything, or, at a pinch, in London. That might work, but hey that's getting ahead of myself, I'd only just met her.

She wanted to know the people I knew in Hong Kong and what my plans were in business. I made the mistake of telling her more than I should, I suppose, but how was I to know?

Earlier than I would have liked, but later than I realised, she said she had to go as she had an early start filming, but she refused my offers to see her home and we returned to Katy and Clive, who announced that they were leaving with her. Knowing grins and winks from the pair of them and a gentle kiss goodbye from Elizabeth left me in high spirits that matched the slightly obscene number of drinks I'd consumed over the course of the evening.

The Aussies and the MI6 touring cricket team had disappeared by then and the only faces I recognised by the bar were Davina and Laurence who, now deserted by their friends, were as tipsy as I was.

'You two make a lovely couple,' Davina playfully remarked as I joined them. 'I thought for sure you'd be leaving together until spoilsport Katy jumped in. She can't bear anybody else starting a new relationship, because it's what she desperately wants to have herself.'

'Davina, that's not true,' said Laurence, 'they've been saying all evening that it was going to be awful to drag her away from you, but she was bunking with them tonight. They're all up at sparrow fart tomorrow, sorry, *this* morning, to catch an early flight for the videos they're working on.'

'I hope you've arranged to see her again,' Davina fished.

'I think so,' I replied, 'although we left it that she would contact me at the hotel when she was free from this project, whenever that might be.'

'Oooh! How exciting! I hope it leads to something,' Davina smilingly remarked.

'You do know who she is?' asked Laurence.

'I only got the name "Elizabeth", but no contact details,' I said, 'although I did give her my full name and hotel details. I guess, if I don't hear from her, I'll have to get in touch with her via Katy or Clive.'

'We thought you'd know who she was. She's a Chan. Elizabeth Chan. You know, Jimmy Chan's niece or something, maybe even his daughter,' Laurence stated in a matter-of-fact way.

Shit. Damn. Blast. What did that mean? Was it a trap? Was I vain enough to think it wasn't? No, I wasn't.

Laurence twisted the knife. 'I'm sure you know, but Jimmy has a frightful reputation in Hong Kong and he'd never let a member of his family have a *gweilo* boyfriend.

Pity, but I think you were barking up the wrong tree there, my friend.'

'Laurence, you are a spoilsport,' said Davina, 'they can have some fun, can't they?'

That seemed to be the moment to leave and off I went, alone. Dejected, I rambled slowly back to the hotel. It was pretty late so, fortunately, any self-respecting 'tails' had gone home to bed and the only people lurching around the streets were expats like me, all the worse for wear. I felt sorry for myself and, when it started to rain, heavily, my night was complete.

I had a bath back at the hotel and arranged an early alarm call. I knew I couldn't get out of the jogging commitment again and realised I wouldn't wake up without intervention. A few hours' kip would have to do.

Route two, I think they'd said and I quickly looked at the hotel jogging map: 'Route 2, out of the Chater Road exit of the hotel and up Ice House Street to Garden Road, past the Peak Tram, to Upper Albert Road and the Zoological and Botanical Gardens.'

What a fool, I haven't had a run in ages. It might kill me.

I fell asleep dreaming of Elizabeth Chan.

# 12

I'D HAD SOME TIME TO work out what had happened to me since my early morning jog. Route two, toute rue, toot-a-rooty, root-toot. Talk about brain jumble.

My head still hurt like hell and I'd been in this hospital in a private room, half way up the hillside on the island side of Hong Kong – to judge by the view of Victoria Harbour from my bed – for a couple of days that I knew about, and another day or so before that, from what I'd been told.

I'd fractured my skull – unironically a 'hairline fracture' – or had it done for me is, perhaps, more accurate to say, having been 'sapped' whilst out jogging.

Lying there, I was able to work slowly through and remember all the events leading up to my 'unfortunate random assault' since coming round from the concus-sion. There was no real memory loss, thankfully.

The last thing I could hazily remember was the night I'd met Elizabeth Chan in Club 97, but she hadn't been to visit and I wouldn't be going there again in a hurry. I tried to put that out of my mind. Jimmy Chan, damn him.

Maybe it's like food poisoning, where you can suddenly picture what you'd eaten that caused you to feel ill, as in 'it was the prawns, ugh,' as whenever I had a sudden sharp pain in my head as I was lying there, all I could picture was Elizabeth Chan, the beautiful creature. Surely she wasn't the cause?

Of the incident itself on that fateful morning, I had no recall whatsoever, but with some effort and persistence, I'd managed to reconstruct a diary of what had happened to me over the previous days and weeks. My brain was actually working and all I'd lost was the incident, which the doctors and nurses had said was perfectly normal.

I was beginning to be able to think straighter, without it making my headache worse, and the routine of injec-tions and painkillers was being eased and my mind seemed to be clearing.

I'd felt weak at that point, but regular walks along the corridors and up and down the stairs had definitely made me feel more like myself – 'strong enough to have you out of here in no time' as the nurses told me.

At various intervals I'd had a few visitors.

Will had called in, with the local police in tow, and I was told that I'd had a lucky escape. They'd outlined the known facts for me.

Gavin Gordon, my Aussie friend who'd originated in Glasgow and, therefore, was as hard as nails, had 'saved' me by noticing two men who'd jogged behind me from the hotel. He'd left later than the other two Aussies, much as I'd done, and he'd thought nothing of the other two runners just ahead of him and behind me, doing the same jogging trail from the hotel. He'd been impressed with their fitness, especially when they'd sped up considerably as I'd entered the Botanical Gardens.

When they'd caught up with me, one of them had almost run straight into me and, as he did so, he'd hit me on the head from behind with what looked like a hand-held running weight. To Gavin, they had looked like they were then going to go in for the kill as I'd gone down like a sack of potatoes. They were about to start kicking me, but Gavin, who'd sped up trying to catch up with me himself, shouted loudly and ferociously whilst running pell-mell at them and they had paused and panicked.

The other two Aussies, hearing the din and seeing what seemed to be happening, had stopped when they'd heard the commotion and started running towards them across the park, yelling.

Seeing they were outnumbered, the two attackers had turned tail and fled, racing out of the gardens at full speed. One of the Aussies, although they were all knackered by then, had followed them for a bit until he'd lost them in the already crowded streets.

'It was Jimmy,' I'd said to Will and the police. 'It must be.'

'I don't think so,' Will had said. 'In all honesty, I don't think you're that important to him.'

What had changed Will's tune about Jimmy from the first time we'd met?

'Charming! But what about all the things that keep happening, like Rodney's heart attack and all the other incidents that have happened to me? You've got to admit that my life seems to be in danger. Jimmy's the common denominator.'

'Yes, you may be right, but the Aussies say the men attacking you were Filipinos, not Chinese, and that's just not Jimmy's M.O., never, ever. He only uses Chinese thugs to do his dirty work.'

'But surely Gavin has given you a description?'

'That's what makes it worse, the Aussies can't seem to give us anything but the broadest details, other than "they looked like typical Filipinos". Without a proper description of the men, we've got nothing to work on. And, for the record, we haven't got any Filipino hitmen that we know of in Hong Kong, not one. That means we've got precious few leads to follow up. But we're on the case and we'll keep you posted.'

They'd been ushered out by a nurse when it was time for my meds, but they seemed only too happy to be able to leave when they did, to get away from me and my conspiracy theories.

Each time the nurse left my room, I drifted in and out of sleep and even though I was trying to think about work and the risks I seemed to be taking, whatever drugs I was on, and the whack on the head, combined to take me into my past. Everything mixed together in crazy dreams as if my subconscious was trying to make sense of the wild things that were happening wherever I went.

Not only that, but the dream factory was seemingly trying to make sense of my life, in retrospect – the only way it does have some kind of sensible structure. The dreams put it all into some kind of pattern: meeting Dickie Hart and Eric Old in Cambridge; my Director of Studies, subsequently exposed as a spymaster, trying to get me to learn Russian; the skinny-dipping – illicitly – in Corpus Christi's Leckhampton pool late in the evening and yes, there, diving in the full muff-fabulous buff was Marie-Louise Audran, now the French vice-consul (and probably with the French secret service herself).

I'd half forgotten that had happened. What was it saying? Was all this meant to be?

In another post-meds fitful sleep, the shape-forming power of dreams placed a traumatically faithless marriage as merely a stepping-stone across the turbulent river of relationships and there on the other side was Elizabeth Chan, swaying provocatively.

Will I ever learn?

Not only that, but in sleepy reminiscence, it was easy, looking back in my drugged state, to see my tedious first job as opening the door to all of this and realise that my mad first boss had taught me, unintentionally, to pay lip-service only to subservience and to keep my mind as my own and free from the trammels imposed by employee status.

On another occasion, a really exciting, real-life visitor showed me what truly caring employers I was lucky enough to have. Langleys had 'helpfully' sent someone from the personnel department of their local office to see me, to tell me that they'd be paying for my private hospital costs. She only seemed interested in how long I was likely to be in for, evidently more anxious about the likely cost of my stay than my recovery during it. At least the hospital would be billing them direct, if what she'd told me was true, which was something. Nice of the CEO himself to call in to check on the welfare of a key member of his team.

Simon came on by and seemed most amused that I hadn't resigned from Langleys yet. 'That's a good thing then, because it's saved you a bob or two,' he rejoiced on my behalf when I told them they were paying for my hospitalisation. 'Don't resign until your treatment and hotel bills have been settled,' was his only piece of advice. Never mind my near-death escape, as long as my hospital bill got paid. He'd then told me to threaten to sue Langleys for damages for personal injury and mental trauma sustained in the course of my employment. 'You might get a lump sum out of them to shut you up. And that'd be tax free.' Ever the taxman, my caring friend.

I tried to share my Chan-gang scenario with him, but even he was sceptical, or maybe he was trying not to alarm me.

'Elizabeth Chan, this beautiful femme fatale who has entered your story, what exactly did you do to her that would mean a hit squad were after you?' was his only question when I'd told him about my night-before-the-morning-after experience at Club 97.

I think, in fairness, he was pretending to see the humour in everything that was happening to me, but I could tell he was as rattled as I was rapidly becoming. I told him my Jimmy theory had been poo-pooed by Will and the Hong Kong police, because of the Filipino angle. We ran through it all, from me being followed and mugged and now attacked, through the events in the Philippines and Singapore, to the latest piece of business with Rodney. He just told me to write up a report and give it to Will or

Dickie, or lodge it with someone as a kind of insurance in case the worst happened. Very reassuring.

I even thought, at one point, that he was more concerned about Rodney's welfare than mine, as he was urging me to telephone Singapore to get the latest news of his expert witness.

However, that turned out to be a prelude to him telling me that he'd been following up some of the things that Rodney had set out in his dossier, in particular concerning Tufty McMasters.

He'd decided to issue some protective tax assessments covering Tufty's activities in Hong Kong and serve them on him aboard his boat. 'Get this,' he said, 'I've actually been along this morning to serve the papers myself.'

Despite my protests that I couldn't care less about all that any more, as it didn't help me at all, he persisted with his bureaucratic report until something suddenly dawned on him. 'Listen, listen, I've just realised something important. Guess what? The crew aboard the *NonDom* are all Filipino! How about that?'

'Simon, you've got to get onto Will and the police now ...'

'I know, I know ...'

And off he went, rushing like he'd just solved the crime of the century.

*       *       *

Back at the hotel, after a day in its civilised surroundings – basically not being in a hospital – I was at last feeling OK, not exactly ready to take on all-comers, perhaps, but functioning well enough.

I'd got over the disappointment of hearing the news from Simon that Will had followed up his lead, but had discovered that Tufty's yacht had sailed out of Hong Kong just before he'd got to where it had been berthed – suspicious, no? – and had logged Manila as its destination with the harbourmaster – intriguing, yes? The crew's names written on the yacht's manifest were completely indecipherable – malice aforethought?

I'd caught up with a few people on the phone and had even had a quiet drink that evening with the Aussies, which I didn't think was going to be possible before they left for Sydney.

Gavin whispered to me when the other two had gone to the loo. 'In the strictest confidence, and only because of everything that's happened to you and your feelings about Jimmy and all that, I feel I must tell you a few things. A lot of Jimmy's wealth is in funds in Panama, which *we* set up for him, putting everything in his wife's name. Now, Jimmy finds that he can't get divorced from his wife, at least, not until she's transferred everything back over to him which she's refused to do. His current mistress is furious, but it's stalemate. What's more, and even Jimmy doesn't know this, his wife has made a new will. I've found out that this new will, unlike the old one, leaves nothing to Jimmy. I dread to think what will happen when Jimmy finds out, especially if anything happens to his wife before he does and manages to change things.'

Gavin, who had originally left England for Australia, fed up with the snobbery in the legal profession towards a working-class boy from Glasgow trying to make his way as a barrister, still, it seemed, had a moral compass, despite spending his time devising tax schemes for the super-rich and not worrying about how they'd got their wealth. 'Not a word about this to anyone,' he'd counselled, 'keep it as information to use only if you have to.'

Full of thinking whether and how that gem of intelligence might be of any use to me, I'd said goodbye to the Aussies soon after that revelation and had had an early night.

During the following day I again stayed in my room, and, with tea and food, courtesy of room service, appearing at intervals and with paperwork constantly in front of me, I'd made some calls.

First up was Dickie Hart. I told him that I would probably be taking up his suggestion to resign from Langleys in the next few days and that we needed to agree the financial side of things, but I enjoyed filling him in about my new contact – Jeffrey Parker from the plane – who'd been in touch and had given me the chance to go into China with him. He'd left a note for me to that effect recommending that I take him up on his offer, which would mean I could follow up on some publishing opportunities.

I could tell that Dickie had nearly dropped the phone at that point and he said he was aware of Parker and his access to China (that hardly shocked me) and in view of that and any planned trip, he, Dickie, would 'have to see that you, my dear Rich, are properly briefed'. He'd asked, 'When are you going?'

'As soon as Jeffrey gets a visa sorted out for me,' I'd said, which had earned the response from him of, 'I'd better get over to see you pronto.'

Next up was Nick Dale, in Manila, to tell him I was now out of hospital – Simon had kept him posted – and to warn him to look out for the *NonDom* in Manila and report back any sighting of it, or Tufty, to me. Pressure on him, he told me, was increasing all the time and he was constantly being followed and monitored. He knew his phone, bizarrely, was not being tapped, because Mike Moreno had told him so. But someone was always with him now when he was working in the palace and they were giving him less and less direct access to papers and asking him to give advice in more general terms without him seeing confidential stuff.

They'd recently wanted him to write up a detailed résumé of facts, advice and action, which he thought was an odd request and, as a direct consequence, he'd started making an escape plan. He'd asked me about Chuck, but other than repeat my shouty morning exchange, I didn't have any news to give him. He said I should seek him out and that I'd better warn him that he really was in Manila's bad books now. A lot of people were talking about what should be done to him and not in a pleasant way. I told him that, as far as I knew, Chuck was still under the wing of Dickie Hart and co here in Hong Kong whilst he behaved himself. There was not much more I could do, even if I knew what to do, or indeed, if he'd actually let me do anything.

Nick had no explanation as to why Filipinos, possibly from Tufty's yacht, would want to attack me, unless they somehow thought I was Chuck. I hadn't even thought of that. My name hadn't come up with any of the people Nick dealt with. They'd obviously written me off as somebody not worth bothering about, perhaps because of my mugging in Singapore having not produced anything that could be used against me. I still wondered what Jimmy's role was in my attack.

Worryingly, Nick's escape plan (given that he didn't have much in Manila by way of possessions and most of his money was, yes, offshore – 'why not practise what you preach', was his excuse) was to flit to Hong Kong and take things from there.

He told me that he'd met up with Miguel in Manila, who'd basically been following up potential authors and getting nowhere. Nick had told him not to use my name and to trade on his freelance press status, but this had backfired because nobody wanted to talk to the press, unless it was the local Marcos-owned rags. Miguel had left for Singapore, Nick informed me, but was said to be planning on heading for Hong Kong. All my chickens coming home to roost, I thought.

Finally, I called Miguel, to hear that after drawing a blank in Manila seeking out contributors and authors, he'd done some useful background research for a free-lance piece he was working on. He was now back in Singapore, where he'd found Rodney still in hospital, but recovering. Yes, he'd try and make sure his wife followed up on her suspicions, but we'd agreed that was unlikely now Rodney was on the mend. No, the medical staff had not mentioned the possibility of it being a drug-induced heart attack.

Rodney had told his wife that his new client, Stanley Ho, was a fraud. He'd said Ho had told him he didn't know Jimmy, which was odd enough, but he'd also said he'd been recommended to use Rodney but wouldn't reveal who by, which was odder still.

Miguel was reserved in his response to my confirmed job offer and the new developments I hinted at, but he said he'd give it a try on a freelance basis to 'suck it and see'. He'd been commissioned anyway to write an article on Hong Kong for *The Straits Times*. He'd be heading on up to HK in the next few days and we could talk about everything then.

*     *     *

No sooner had I got off the phone with Miguel than there was a knock at my door, which I answered of course, only to see Dickie standing there.

How did he know my room number? I hadn't given it to him. Was the hotel lax about who they let up to a guest's room? Or could his name and position get him in anywhere, anytime?

He came bounding in and started talking straight away. At least *he* seemed to be confident the room wasn't bugged. Or was it bugged, but on his behalf, and it didn't matter?

'We're making arrangements to open you a bank account. I'm cleared to give you two hundred and fifty thousand Hong Kong dollars, with an overdraft of a further five hundred thou. That should get you started. We'll expect a financial budget, decent accounts and regular financial reports. We've a tame firm of auditors who can do the necessary, but I think you're pretty clued up on that side of things, aren't you?'

'Yes. I'll need to form a company and get shares issued.'

'One of our associated firms of lawyers will do that. Call my assistant to get an appointment fixed up for you.

And, in order for us to release the funds, you can sign an NDA with us at the same time as you're dealing with the company formation matters. You'd better resign asap, don't you think?' he'd said. 'Let's just proceed as if you already have. Now let's get on with this China thing.'

'I don't know much about it yet.'

'Get onto the blower right now with this Jeffrey Parker fellow.'

'Now?'

'Yes, now.'

'And say what, exactly?'

'Where are you going in China? Who are you seeing? That kind of thing.'

I'd phoned Jeffrey, as instructed, who, once he'd said 'you're a bit keen aren't you' had told me that we were going to be off to Shenzhen to meet some Mandarin from high up in the party.'

I was half repeating what Jeffrey was saying and receiving whispered prompts from Dickie.

'What's his name?' urged Dickie in a whisper. I'd asked Jeffrey that question.

'Khoo Ah Au, if that means anything at all to you, which I very much doubt. He wants to publish a series of books of government statistics.'

'Really? That sounds interesting.'

'Softly, softly. That's the way to win their trust and who knows where it might lead. Khoo Ah Au is one of their key commercial bods and, incidentally, a rising star. If you can win him over, you'd be in pole position to pick up all kinds of official publications. Maxwell is after the deal and is going to be one of the bidders.'

'Why would they listen to me?'

'You can tell a good story about your publishing pedigree and you're not already a greedy capitalist pig. Anyway, his uncle and I have done some mega aeronautical deals and they trust me.'

'Wow. That sounds terrific.'

'Let me get hold of the visa and as soon as I have it, we can arrange the trip. Who are you with?' Jeffrey then almost shouted down the phone. 'It sounds like you've got someone with you your end.'

Dickie heard that and shook his head.

'No-one,' I lied, 'I was repeating things to myself whilst I made notes and the room service boy kept fussing around.'

'OK. Glad you're keen. Let's do lunch tomorrow, if you can make it. At the Hong Kong Club. Your concierge can direct you. Say one-thirty?'

'Yes, that should be fine. See you there.'

I repeated various bits of the conversation to Dickie, and, thinking that he'd probably heard most of it anyway, I didn't deviate.

'Khoo is a real coup,' he couldn't resist saying, 'he really is. Rising star. Likely Supreme Leader material.

Westernised to a degree. We'd like to get in with him. Not half!'

'I might not get the deal. Don't count your chickens,' I tried to say, restrainingly.

'Don't be negative, Rich. Jeffrey is right. Softly, softly. What's important is building a dialogue. Give Eric a ring, see if he can suggest some freebies you can dangle in front of them.'

'Dickie, that is patronising in the extreme. And very nineteenth century, if I may say so. I can't think of anything worse than offering him bibliographical baubles from the British Council. That'll put them off. No, I'll think about it. Let's see what happens and if I can actually come up with anything that they might find commercially worthwhile.'

'All right, all right, you're the publishing expert, but remember Jimmy's got Langleys and Spreadworths all gunning for this type of contract and they won't like it if they find you're sticking your nose in. And we don't want Maxwell to get the contract and get in with the Chinese. Remember, not a word about my involvement, especially to Jimmy.'

'Dickie, what do you take me for, exactly?'

He ignored that and continued with, 'And not a word to Jeffrey. *Entre nous*, we did try to recruit him once, but he was having none of it, which means he either works for somebody else already, or he's got that many private arrangements going on that he's happy doing his own thing.'

'Wouldn't his company have something to say if he got involved with you?'

'Not a bit! We use some of their people in Africa and South America already. There's a clear precedent. No, Jeffrey is a bit of a rogue male and does his own thing. The fact he's taken you under his wing is impressive. Nurture that relationship. It can only be a good sign. And, when you meet the Chinese, you'll have to mind your p's and q's and kowtow like mad. You know, kneel and touch the ground with your forehead in worship or submission as part of Chinese custom to try and win their favour, meta-phorically speaking, of course. It'll be good if you get an excuse to go in and out of China and meet key people there. Good for you and your business and, needless to say, very good for me and mine too.'

Ignoring for the moment his advice on protocol – I'd be better off taking my cue from Jeffrey on how to behave with the Chinese – I tried to press Dickie about Jimmy and how crooked we now knew he was and how he might have had a hand in an assassination attempt on Rodney in Singapore. I asked what he was going to do about it, but he just kept stalling me, I felt, by saying that any financial chicanery of Jimmy's wasn't something his department was looking into. It was more of interest to Simon and possibly Will and the Hong Kong police, which I found puzzling.

He was equally dismissive about Chuck and what he'd discovered in Manila and nor was he at all interested in Tufty McMasters, his boat, or the 'alleged' Filipino connection.

'You seem a bit preoccupied about corruption, money laundering, tax evasion, the links between organised crime and business, and whether Jimmy and Craig are smugglers or drug runners. It's not your job to sort them out.'

He then told me in five different ways 'to leave it to the police and the proper authorities'. Strange though it was, I dismissed it at the time as being just a jobbing civil servant not willing to stray from his brief.

At that point, the phone rang and it was the CEO of Langleys wanting to meet me the following morning for breakfast – 'to see how you're coming along after your nasty jogging accident and if you're well enough to get back to the UK' was how he tactlessly put it.

'You'd better practise your resignation speech this evening,' were Dickie's parting words, 'and do try not to focus too much on Jimmy. He and your boss are like *that*,' he said, forcibly interlocking the index fingers of both hands. But what exactly did that mean?

# 13

BREAKFAST WITH THE BOSS.

First, how did I look? Smart, yes: a clean shirt, a tie and a jacket. Why should I care? I didn't particularly, but I thought it worth looking as if I was able to operate at a reasonably sophisticated level and knew how to dress for a meeting with a senior executive, even if I did know that he'd be dressed like the district commissioner in some forgotten outpost of the empire.

However, my appearance was rather spoilt by a nasty-looking burst blood vessel in my right eye. It made me look like a drunken oaf with a hangover dressed up for a court appearance after a night in the cells.

What had caused that to happen to my eye overnight? Stress?

In truth I'd had a lazy evening in my room, punctuated again by room service, a drink or two from the mini-bar and by stints at the desk, trying to make some notes on what I should say the following morning. Hardly stressful at all!

Perhaps the strain of the past weeks was getting to me and the pressure was proving too much. Something had to give. My eye!

That morning, I went downstairs to the restaurant early, to beat the boss to breakfast. I picked up the *South China Morning Post* from the pile on the desk at the entrance.

I spotted, straight away, a lead article by 'Martin Rochester, Reporter At Large', as he was bylined. The headline captured it all, 'Government corruption in the Philippines – the evidence is damning'.

I was taken to a table for two, but I was shaking to such an extent that I thought maybe my other eye would pop any moment.

I ordered a black filter coffee and read the piece, which all but named Chuck as the origin for the story. How's that for protecting your source, Mr Rochester. Or was it only because I knew Chuck and the whole background that I could see through it to the horse's mouth? For heaven's sake, I'd been the one to put them in touch with each other, originally, even suggesting Martin might do a feature, but it was his decision to get after the story.

And I knew Chuck was up for it and wanted the exposé to appear, to drive international outrage. It was hardly my fault. Still ...

Would anyone but me, and maybe Dickie, Simon and Will in Hong Kong, know about Chuck's role in this? What implications would there be for Nick in the Philippines? Would the authorities there see the article and know it was Chuck behind it? Would they link Chuck with Nick and put two and two together?

I didn't have long to find out.

My boss, Ferdy Graeme, came storming in.

'Have you seen this?' he said, waving his copy of the paper. 'It's a disgrace. It's all hearsay. Jimmy says it's come from some chap called Chuck Besky, an American, would you believe, who thinks he knows the Philippines inside out. Jimmy said it's all sour grapes because he was kicked out of the place. He should be hauled over the coals for this. We've got business interests in the Philippines, you know. What will this do to the value of those?'

'What, Langleys have business interests in the Philippines?'

'Not Langleys as such, but I have, in a personal capacity, a language school for which Langleys supplies all the books. But never mind all that now. Jimmy is incandescent and he says Besky is a known associate of yours. Is he?'

'First of all, you don't know it's Chuck supplying all this information. Rochester wouldn't rely on one source, he's a top investigative journalist, for heaven's sake. He'll have checked this out very carefully and verified it with lots of different people on the ground in the Philippines. It might not be Chuck behind this.'

'Of course it is. What do you take me for? A schmuck?'

'Well, yes, I do, as a matter of fact,' I, perhaps, foolishly, replied. 'You believe whatever Jimmy tells you, for a start.'

'I beg your pardon?'

'Look, I think it best if I just resign. That's what I was intending to do anyway. I'd even written out a little speech, but in the circumstances, I think I'll just give you my letter of resignation.'

I passed an envelope over to Ferdy who picked it up, opened it, and read my resignation, neatly written out on the very smart Mandarin Oriental paper, provided to me as a guest with my name typed in at the bottom and embossed at the top with the hotel's iconic logo, a beautifully simple red fan. The shit had certainly hit that.

He took my resignation a bit too well.

'This better be with immediate effect. I'll let personnel know and they can pay you up to today, including any outstanding expenses, provided you don't try on anything silly. It's for the best that you go as of today as I don't want Langleys associated a moment longer with you and your anarchist friends.'

'Mr Graeme. Anarchy has nothing to do with this. What Marcos is doing to the Philippines is a disgrace. It will all come out in the end, believe me, and I'd rather be on the side that Martin Rochester is on, as an honest crusading journalist, than on the side of corruption where anyone who supports Marcos could be said to be.'

'Are you implying that Jimmy and I are corrupt just because we think an article like this is irresponsible and ill-considered? You're new out here in the Far East. You don't know how it all works. You don't know what on earth you're talking about.'

'I bow to your enlightenment then, and, yes, my resignation is with immediate effect. That way I don't have to endure a moment longer in your company or with your company. Let me just add to my letter a codicil that we have agreed the date I leave the company as being today.'

I'd gone too far, I knew, but I reached over to a speechless Ferdy and took the letter, opening it out and appending the additional relevant words. I then got up and departed saying, 'Thanks, Mr Graeme, for the experience of working at Langleys.'

He was scowling, holding my letter, as I left and still staring stunned at the newspaper. I hoped Chuck knew what he was doing when he'd ignored all the advice he'd been given and gone ahead with cooperating with Martin Rochester. Where the hell would this lead?

*    *    *

I went back to my room and rang Nick in Manila. He'd been shocked to hear that Chuck had decided to go public and was irritated that we'd had no advance notice. He hadn't heard anything about the article from anybody else until my call, although he felt it was already sure to be known officially through the usual diplomatic channels. He was relaxed that the Filipino authorities would not be that quick off the mark and confident that they wouldn't link him with Chuck. He said he'd speak to Mike Moreno in case he needed help to arrange transport to Hong Kong. As a precaution, he thought he might book a flight within the next few days and, meanwhile, pack a bag and even stay at a hotel for a night or two.

'You should get the hell out of there, smartish, Nick, as you could be seriously compromised,' I said.

'I can't leave straight away, Rich, as I'm working on a very interesting bank audit with an international banker who's had certain suspicions, shall we say, of what certain people have been up to.'

He assured me he would be careful.

I then spoke to Miguel who was concerned, as Nick had been, when I told him the news. 'I'll bring my plans forward and make my way to Hong Kong as soon as I can. Does the article finger you in some way?' he asked, 'because if it does, it might implicate me.'

I tried to reassure him and repeated Nick's reaction, but I think I failed because he said, 'This only serves to cast doubt on our working arrangements.'

I tried to play things down.

'There's nothing clear to tie me to what Chuck has just done. Yes, sure, I know him, as do lots and lots of people both here, in the Philippines and elsewhere. In fact though, I've barely seen him in Hong Kong if anybody's been keeping tabs. He's got plenty of friends and contacts here other than me, you know. We can't all come under suspicion. That's the same with any journalist's sources. How can an aggrieved party jump to the conclusion that all associates of a suspected adversary have a hand in what might feature in the press?'

I realised that, in what I'd said, I was trying to reassure myself as much as Miguel, but, I felt he'd been placated. I'd know the score for sure only when he got to Hong Kong in the next few days

I think that was when I realised that events were moving beyond my control and I reverted to first principles: if wracked with doubt, anxiety and uncertainty, do something you can concentrate on to the exclusion of all else. That's why some go sailing; you can't think of anything else but staying afloat. That's when I start working. I sat and planned out some titles I could develop with Jeffrey Parker and could discuss with him at lunch, which would take me into doing more international defence seminars and specialist in-depth published reports. I thought maybe a defence procurement newsletter would work rather well if I could persuade the MOD to play ball.

However, my encounter with Ferdy Graeme kept haunting me and, although I'd have liked to have a word on the phone with my immediate boss, I thought I'd better telex him with the news, in view of the time difference.

Fortunately, I still had plenty of cash and a large batch of travellers cheques as an advance of expenses, which I realised I'd better do something with whilst I could. I took them straight downstairs with my passport to the cashier's desk, where I exchanged them for Hong Kong dollars. That'll make a nice final expenses claim, especially as I already now had the cash in my possession.

Returning to my room, I'd tried to phone Chuck, but with no joy. I'd then played around with thinking about how I could get a business started without relying on finance from Dickie. I didn't like the sound of signing an agreement with him. What would it say? If it were secret, what would happen if I broke its terms? What legal process would be involved? Maybe none. If it didn't work out, perhaps they'd simply liquidate their investment – i.e., me!

\*     \*     \*

I was a bit early for lunch. Because of that, I set off to walk to the Hong Kong Club, which was in temporary accommodation, according to the concierge, on the twenty-fifth floor in World Wide House on Des Voeux Road. My guidebook had told me it had started as a taipans' club for the eight heads of the various Hongs, way back in 1846. Hardly surprising then, that it had a smart dress code, which, thanks to me having seen Ferdy earlier, I passed without a single eyebrow being raised.

Jeffrey was there to greet me and sign me in, and he said he'd thought I'd like to see the place, even though it wasn't the same now that its old Victorian premises had been demolished in 1981. It was having to make do with much less grand surroundings, until its new home was built. The desecration of the wonderful old building had been, he told me, yet another example of Hong Kong not caring a hoot about its origins.

'Nobody in Hong Kong gives a damn about the history of the place apart from a few people dismissed as cranks. Only the British see it as British. The Chinese, even the ones resident here or born here, certainly don't think of it as British, or as having any cultural heritage other than their own. And, more important than any of that cultural baggage, here in Hong Kong it's the pursuit of money at all costs. Who cares about heritage and local character? Sweep it all aside to make way for the future. I hardly ever use the club anymore. You can see why.'

As we were shown into the dining room, the supposed nice view was spoilt for me. I could see another reason for not using the place. There, sitting in the window, was Martin Rochester, who waved at me as I sat down.

'Who's your friend?' asked Jeffrey.

'He's Martin Rochester, roving reporter and leech. He'll come over to find out who you are and see if there's a story in you.'

Sure enough, we'd no sooner sat down than Martin was over, smiling, shaking hands, saying hello and blasting away without giving me the chance to introduce Jeffrey. He could do that himself, thank you.

'What brings you to Hong Kong, Mister, er ... ?'

'Pleasence, Ronald Pleasence, like the actor, but with no 'D' and no relation.'

'Mr Pleasence, good to meet you. Are you in publishing like Rich here?'

'Good Lord, no. I'm a missionary.'

That certainly floored Martin. No story here, you could see him thinking, better get going.

'Interesting,' he said absentmindedly. 'Rich, did you see the Marcos article? What did you think?'

'I'm worried about your source, that's all. You don't seem to care about protecting him.'

'He's fine. Don't worry about Chuck! He knows how to handle himself. I've told him to lie low for a while. Let the dust settle a bit, then we can do a follow-up, a more in-depth demolition job, once international opinion gets behind us. We might even get enough momentum for a change in the regime. Campaigning journalism at its best and most award-winning. Don't you just love it?'

When he didn't get the enthusiastic approbation he was seeking, he made his excuses and left.

'Why the nom de plume, Jeffrey, or should I call you Ronald, Ronald Pleasence?' I asked.

'I do it all the time. When you travel as much as I do, it's good to be able to go incognito sometimes, and that means I can be whoever I like, especially when I'm in a ghastly hotel, chewing the fat with A.N. Other bored international businessman. Gives me a kick. And anyway, why would I want a journo knowing who I am and what I do, giving me the third degree or fishing for a story about my company. Hell, I might give something away inadvertently. No, I pick a character and a cover I can stick to, and enjoy myself.'

Jeffrey insisted we both had what he called 'my version of a club sandwich', which was Hong Kong duck with barbecue sauce in a *bao*, which turned out to be a soft bread roll. With so many dishes on the menu, it's just as well to let someone order for you and see what happens, rather like a Chinese food version of Russian roulette. He'd just gone ahead and ordered the food and, he insisted on a couple of Tsingtao beers 'from China,' which came in big green bottles. He liked it, he said, 'because it has a hearty European taste and one of their spies, I like to imagine, got a large bonus for that bit of industrial espionage on one of our breweries back home. That's worth drinking to.'

Meeting Jeffrey had been just what I'd needed and I'd got past the first impression he gave me on the plane. He was knowledgeable and cynical, but, I guess, those two attributes go together, and, although he was still full of himself, he was also full of ideas for seminars and books.

He'd come up with a good way for me to start up in business, recommending that he put me in touch with a guy he knew, a former journalist with Jane's, the specialist military, aerospace and transportation publishers, who was looking to start a new monthly newsletter specialising in defence contracting around the world.

It would be a high-ticket item, on subscription of £1,200 per annum, payable in advance, which was a hefty ticket price, but would inspire confidence in subscribers that they were going to get worthwhile information if they were paying that much for it. He reckoned it would romp up to a level of five hundred subscribers around the world. A tidy, up-front, annual turnover.

The trick would be that his company would take, and pay for out of its Hong Kong marketing budget, thirty subscriptions, which would get us started and, once others came on board, we would have a healthy cashflow because of the advance payments.

Needless to say, I liked this idea more than Dickie's, as there'd be no sticky agreements and no obligations to Jeffrey or his firm. I told him that I'd had other offers, but I liked the sound of his. He was happy to let me mull it over.

He then told me to prepare a carefully worded proposal for the Chinese, and not to worry too much if I didn't hear their response for a while. They'll want to see what you're like, then they'll want another meeting to grill you further. I was urged to go in high with a decent profit share and not to call it a royalty.

'The Chinese don't like to be treated in a patronising way, which is how most businesses will approach them. A royalty is basically, in their eyes, a master:servant relationship – a big guy paying a little guy a percentage for his efforts. No, go in large and offer them 60:40 in their favour, once all costs have been met. And don't be too cute about loading costs on the project. Give them a joint venture deal, where they can get out of it more easily than you can. Your proposal should cover Heads of Agreement along those lines. Think you can do it?'

'I think so. I like being creative with contracts. People forget that often it's the contract that's actually the product, with all the rest that ensues being the after-sales service.'

'Well said, Rich. You're a man after my own heart.'

As we were winding up, I asked Jeffrey why he wanted to help me and his reply stunned me.

'Rodney told me about you. After I'd met you on the plane, I rang him to ask him if he'd ever come across you. He and I are old friends. What he said about you was good enough for me. "If you can give him a leg-up, Jeffrey, you'd be doing us all a favour", was how he put it.'

'Why didn't you say?'

'I thought I'd see how the meeting went first.'

We ordered a couple more beers and I told him more of what had happened.

When I'd told Jeffrey the news of Rodney's heart attack, it had come as a bit of a shock to him, and he, like me, was just as immediately suspicious about the causes, especially of the appearance on the scene of the mysterious Mr Ho. He knew about some drugs that were available that could instigate heart failure and, worryingly, knew of certain government agencies reputed to use them. It was a possibility, right enough.

I could tell that my brush with Jimmy, and all the other events were giving him some concerns about getting involved with me, but he wrestled a bit with that and urged me to take his advice on funding my business and leave all the rest of the complications behind me.

'And don't get too involved with Dickie Hart would be my advice. That's the thin end of the wedge. He tries to recruit anyone and everyone, no offence to you. Keep your independence if you can. They're a bit too keen on recruiting British businessmen and playing on their patriotism, to the extent that they forget about the risks they're being asked to take, and which their handlers simply ignore.'

I was going to press him further about all kinds of things, but the maître d' came over with a very elegantly dressed, middle-aged Chinese woman, with the reddest lipstick and the blackest hair I'd ever seen, who Jeffrey introduced to me with the words, 'Rich, meet Mrs Parker, she'll be our interpreter on our visit to China.'

I mumbled some stunned words as Jeffrey rose to greet her with a kiss. Clearly lunch with me was over and I was dismissed with a wave and a promise to contact me once he had the visa.

\*     \*     \*

I asked Simon to come round to the hotel as I thought I'd like to know more about what he'd discovered about Jimmy and any other rogues that Rodney's dossier had exposed.

I wanted to fill in time whilst I digested my resignation and, seemingly, my having jumped into the void of unemployment, a big black space into which I was falling, clutching only a parachute made of gossamer-thin dreams of a bright business future.

Seeing hard-nosed Simon had done the trick. After I'd filled him in on my proposed visit to China with Jeffrey and his wife, and we'd speculated on the nature of their relationship, we'd reverted to tax talk, guaranteed to get Simon fired up.

Did I know that Rodney knew where all the bodies were buried and all the cash was hidden?

'Like Captain Flint?'

'Certainly. As in a treasure tax haven island in the Caribbean or in the Pacific? Yes, just like that.'

'What sort of things have you found out?'

'For a start, Rodney says that Jimmy always boasted about keeping meticulous records – if only we could find out where they are, boy, would we have a field day. Even without them, we've got enough to go after him, for instance, for him manipulating the Hang Seng through falsifying his property company value with anonymous shareholders. Rodney names them and completely destroys the basis of any court action Jimmy could take to prevent newspapers printing anything about him. Jimmy meets any criticism of himself by using a big auditing firm to issue a whitewash report or by getting some fancy London law firm to sue for aggravated damages and costs. What we now know will counter those tactics.'

'That all sounds rather boring, Simon, and predictable.'

'All right, what about this revelation of Rodney's? Jimmy is shown as being the gateway to China and the sub-region because of the way he moves gold, diamonds, cash and untraceable bearer shares. He renders all that into cash, which he sends through Antwerp to a secret Swiss bank account via a Liechtenstein Anstalt, and then the Swiss bank lends the clean money back to the relevant client of Jimmy's.'

'OK, that's good. But any names?'

'Yes. And get this. One of Jimmy's couriers was stopped, not that long ago, at Heathrow carrying more than £670,000 in used notes. The cash was confiscated as suspicious, but was later returned as the courier said he was carrying it from a Swiss bank's strongbox to his bankers in Luxembourg.'

'The idiots!'

'You do realise, Rich, don't you, that Hong Kong is the most fabulous experiment in laissez-faire finance. Its status as a tax haven with its open-to-all-comers reputation and a conduit to China, has meant that, since the mid-70s, the place has grown exponentially. Corrupt officials and closet capitalists in China have set up Hong Kong companies with secret shareholdings.'

'Any names, again?'

'Enough to be starting with and plenty to prove that Hong Kong is where most of the corruption in China is carried out.'

'What type of people are we talking about?'

'I've got a team of investigators going through that now. Already quite a few names turn up as being involved in more than one scheme. There's one out of KL that's got things like deposit-taking cooperatives which, basically, are unregulated bank-like entities that take massive deposits from Malaysian and Chinese individuals and companies and channel the money offshore to Jersey. I'll bust that racket, and expose it for the scandal it is, for a start.'

'You are going to be popular, aren't you?'

'Why should I care, it's my revenge for having had to breathe the stench of corruption in this place for the past few years. Anyway my secondment ends soon. It'll be my swan song before I leave.'

'Or before you get bumped off!'

'Thanks, Rich. But I reckon I'll still be coming to your funeral and not vice versa, the way you're going.'

We carried on in that vein until it was time to start having an evening, which we'd decided would be some street food followed by, wisely or foolishly, a return visit to Club 97.

\*      \*      \*

As we strolled to Simon's favourite street food stall – or *dai pai dong* as he insisted we call it – in Staveley

Street, he had time to bolster Rodney's findings with a few choice items for my personal delectation and delight.

He'd found details of an elaborate scheme for smuggling ivory and gold through the Philippines that involved Tufty McMasters, but, as if that wasn't enough, he'd found out that Jimmy's partner in his shady Chinese art dealings was someone called Ferdy Graeme.

'Rodney clearly didn't know who he was, otherwise he might have told you. Of course, the name leapt out at me, but I only knew it because you and I had been talking about him,' Simon had said. 'Apparently, Ferdy worked with an old school friend of his who'd been the MD of the Hong Kong branch of a major London auction house run a bit like an old-style Swiss bank. You know, facilitating tax dodging and circumventing currency and export restrictions, all under the wrap of secrecy and anonymity. What's more, Ferdy's wife fronted up the London end of the whole thing. They're up to their eyeballs in Jimmy's shenanigans.'

'How can we get actual evidence of all that? I could have a field day with it as could the authorities here and in the UK, not to say the shareholders and main board of Langleys.'

'Rodney mentions a safe-deposit box that Jimmy uses at Honkers and Shankers. Just as well it's there, because I have a pet rat on the inside who works at weekends and we could, mind you I'm only saying we *could*, not *should*, feed him enough to open the box and let us take a look. If Rodney's right about meticulous records, then we might find them in the box.'

'Or, he might just keep his records under lock and key at home. What do we do then, a bit of Watergating? Simon, you're crazy. I think once you've been through all of Rodney's stuff and taken out what is relevant to you as a tax official, I think you've got to let the police see the evidence.'

'What, and risk them burying it? You've no idea how in with the local police Jimmy is. He's almost untouchable and that's why he is arrogant and thinks he can get away with anything, because he usually does.'

All that kept us going through our street food supper, the main challenge of which was stinky tofu. Simon assured me it was terrific, once you got past the stench, caused by it having been soaked in a brine of milk, meat and all sorts of vegetables for months.

'Come on, Rich. To thrive out here, some of us have got to overcome a natural revulsion to what we find when we arrive. If you can get past the humidity and smells of Hong Kong and its ruthless greed, you can certainly get past the honk of stinky tofu. And, once you do, it's delicious.'

It was, but after eating it I was in a bit of a hurry to have a whisky sour at Club 97.

\*　　　\*　　　\*

We hadn't been at Club 97 long when in walked Marie-Louise Audran and someone she introduced as her PA. They seemed friendly enough towards us and, as the DJ was on a break, we managed to talk. Simon surprised me with being able to converse in French, something about having been on secondment at the OECD based in Paris for a couple of years, working on the double tax treaty model convention. Simon had the ability to take something that sounded romantic, in this case working in Paris, and turn it into the mundane.

Still, it stood him in good stead with Joséphine – whose name he kept saying and pronouncing in the French way, which really irritated me, but clearly wowed her.

Joséphine was 'b for blonde', as an old friend of mine would say, but I thought, 'b' also stands for 'brunette', which maybe she was really. Who knew?

Marie-Louise, 'b for black-haired', as attractive as her namesake, the French actress Stéphane Audran who could have been her twin, was stuck talking to me in her fluent English, but even she pronounced any French word that cropped up in an exaggerated French accent. 'Pah-rhee', for 'Paris', that sort of annoying thing.

After what only seemed like a short while, Simon surprised me still further by saying he was taking

Joséphine off to the *dai pai dong* stall we'd been at earlier as she'd never tried street food in Hong Kong.

'That just leaves you and me,' breathed Marie-Louise, 'you'll have to take me home.'

'Fine by me,' I said, which was the understatement of the year, and I wasn't even slightly perturbed when she took me by the arm and led me out of the club.

She lived in the Mid-Levels area, and her apartment was, let's say, seductive. The sights and the lights of Hong Kong and Kowloon from the terrace were sensational and the ice, in the Negroni she mixed, sparkled along with the view.

I'd had to mention to her the off-hand tone she'd used when I'd first called her up, but she said, a bit too honestly for a diplomat, that she hadn't known quite who she was talking to, only realising it was me when it was too late. I believed her.

I said I'd thought it might have been because she'd been with Dickie Hart back in Cambridge, on the night we'd been for our skinny dip, and might find it awkward, now she wasn't with him, to meet up with me here in Hong Kong.

'Dickie? Don't be ridiculous. We were never together, even that night. He pretended to be with me and wouldn't let me out of his sight. But don't be absurd. Even though we were on the same summer school courses in Cambridge, and afterwards, on the Mandarin ones at

SOAS, he's never interested me. Actually, he stopped me meeting anyone I was interested in. He's a real control freak as well as being, what do you say, "a stuffed shirt"? That night by the pool, all those years ago in Cambridge, I kept hoping you would make a move. I'm still waiting for you now. After all, you've already seen me naked ... '

# 14

I DISCOVERED A LOT MORE about myself, about Marie-Louise, and a whole host of other things that night. I'd fallen asleep properly for the first time in ages and, like something out of a Chabrol or Truffaut film, had woken to the sound of Marie-Louise bustling about in the kitchen making us coffee that she brought back to bed. She was still naked. We sat up and talked and then one thing led to another, after which we talked some more.

She was interested in my exploits, talking about Chuck and the Philippines, and was particularly alert when I outlined my theories about Jimmy. She wanted to know my take on him, she said, as some of her people were investigating links they suspected he had in China, and there were concerns about how very close he was to the British.

'Don't tell me, you want me to do some work for you finding out more about it all. Is that what last night was all about?'

'Rich, you should trust me.'

'Now I am worried.'

'Just to show you, I won't ask another thing about Jimmy. After all, it was only when you brought him up that I asked about him. I had no idea what you've been involved in.'

'But surely you discuss all this with Dickie Hart, don't you?'

'Rich. It feels sometimes that we aren't on the same side as Dickie, but I can't say more than that.'

Perhaps it was a mistake, but I explained what I was going to do to set up my own business and that I had a trip to China planned with a business contact of mine. I told her I was after a business deal that Jimmy was trying to fix for my old boss at Langleys or for a rival company called Spreadworths. Her response was interesting to say the least.

'If I can be honest, we think that Dickie is somehow frightened of Jimmy, but, look, we don't have to talk about any of it, Rich, although it would help me if we could.'

That was a bit peeving, but, what was more discon-certing, was that she then walked to the bathroom, starkers still, and then, when the phone rang, answered it in the same state. She was more vice than consul.

I noticed that she was obviously gripped by the phone call. She walked to the bathroom with the handset, and proceeded to put on her robe with one hand while still holding and listening to the phone with the other.

Eventually, she put the phone down.

'You'd better get dressed,' she said. 'That was Joséphine on the phone. She's been with Simon and he's just had a call to say that Chuck Besky has been found dead.'

'What? Where? What's happened?'

'That's the thing. He was found dead, floating in one of those large fish storage tanks on the Jumbo restaurant at Aberdeen Harbour. One of the kitchen hands found him this morning. Simon wanted you to know. Will Tomkins is over there now and has asked for you to identify the body, although they're sure it's him from the ID they found at the scene.'

'How did he die?'

'His throat was slit, and then he was dumped in the tank. All the fish have died with him as he bled out into their water. What a mess. The body has now been taken out of the tank, but is still at the restaurant. You'd better make your way there. I'll order you a taxi.'

\*     \*     \*

Later, I met up with Marie-Louise at the French Consulate office on the twenty-sixth floor of Admiralty Centre, Tower II in Central. She had a corner office, just like head honchos in some Madison Avenue advertising agency would insist on as a measure of their status.

'How was that?' she asked, after formally greeting me. Considering I'd been shown in by a blushing Joséphine – who was whispering that Simon wanted me to call him as he'd been trying to get hold of me – Marie-Louise's hauteur seemed unnecessary, but protocol is protocol, I suppose.

'I'd like to know, Madame Audran, are you carrying out more than just consular duties whilst you are here in Hong Kong?'

'What a strange way to begin, Mr Rowlands,' she replied, 'I was expecting you to tell me what has happened since our last meeting.'

I'd spent most of the day over at Aberdeen, which had been a ghastly experience. What had happened at the Jumbo restaurant had put me off fish for life. I never wanted to see a tank of the creatures ever again and looking at Chuck, laid up on a marble slab as if he was waiting to be filleted, was a sight that will haunt me forever. I'd thrown up, of course. Who wouldn't, except of course the local police and forensic team who acted as if this was merely routine, which to them, I suppose, it was.

Will, battlefield-hardened, had been matter-of-fact and brusque once the ID-ing was done. Yes, it was Chuck. Silenced at last and forever at peace. I'd never seen a dead body before. The stillness, the palpable cold restfulness was profoundly affecting. I was stunned and horrified, tearful and angry, bitter and bereft, as I was given a few moments in quiet contemplation.

Then Will had led me to a shabby manager's office on an upper floor, thankfully away from the aquarium tanks full of mouth-popping fish awaiting their own fate.

I was questioned by Will and an over-enthusiastic Chinese detective for what seemed like hours and hours, over and over again. How long had I known Chuck? Who were his enemies? Where did I meet him? Who did he work for? What had happened in the Philippines? How did he get to Hong Kong? What had he been doing here? What were his plans? Who had he been seeing? When did I last see him? Had I seen him last night? What were my movements last night? Did I have anyone who could corroborate where I was last night? Did I spend any part of last night on my own? Who could support my story about Chuck in the Philippines? Can I provide names of anyone who knew Chuck in Hong Kong and in the Philippines? What did I know of Chuck's family? Did I know of his relationship with Martin Rochester? Did Martin Rochester tell me of any threats on Chuck's life? And so on, and so on.

I was going to have to go into the police station to sign a statement later and I was not to leave Hong Kong without authorisation. But the statement would be useless because Will and the police dismissed my accusations of Jimmy's likely involvement and his Manila connections as hearsay and they could not form part of my statement. Their investigations would get to the bottom of it I was told and I mustn't act like some private dick, nor should I discuss it with anyone other than, perhaps, people who asked me what had happened.

Which was what exactly? A friend had been murdered for trying to expose corruption on a mega scale in a country that has been propped up and tolerated by a West that is supposedly big on democracy and the welfare of ordinary people, even in far-flung places.

Before telling Marie-Louise what had happened, I thought I'd ask her a few questions.

'Look, I feel completely drained by what I've been through – the things I've seen and the questions I've been asked – and I think I ought to know a few things for myself, like, I think, you're probably with the SDECE and not just a humble consular official dealing with stranded tourists.'

'That's the SDECE you're talking about, Rich, but it's been replaced from 1982 by the DGSE.'

'Never mind the precise nomenclature. You know what I'm asking.'

'Then you'll understand why I can't answer.'

'Then I can't tell you what's been going on, because I've been told I can't discuss it with anyone. I might take a different view if I knew just who I'm dealing with.'

'Rich. I think I can help with your understanding of some of the things that might be happening to you and around you. I know things, let's put it that way. Does that help?'

'Tell me this? Who do you think killed Chuck?'

'I don't know.'

'Then you can't help me.'

With that I left the French Consulate and Marie-Louise made no effort to stop me.

\*　　　\*　　　\*

Back at the hotel, of course, Dickie Hart called me, immediately after I'd put the phone down on Simon, who couldn't meet for a drink as he'd arranged to see Joséphine. So much for *his* concerns for Chuck.

I was being urged on the phone, by Dickie, in his response to my theories, not to jump to conclusions. 'These things, more often than not, are not what they seem. Let the experts do their job. They'll ensure justice is done. We'll catch the bastards who did this, Rich.'

I knew it was all flannel.

I told him that he'd never really cared about Chuck or what could happen to him.

'He came to you in your in-tray and you just put him straight into your out-tray to see if he ever came back. Is that what you'll do to me?'

'Oh no, you're like the rest of us, an external file that becomes an internal one. You'll just go round and round the system forever. Anyway, Chuck is damn well back in my in-tray with a vengeance. The bugger has returned. A dead man reincarnated as a live file. I'll have to bloody do something with it now.'

As reception had informed me that Jeffrey had been trying to reach me, I'd called him back. He told me he'd organised our trip into China – to Shenzhen – for the following day, having obtained visas. It would be a day trip and he'd organised a car for him, Mrs Parker and me and it was going to be a quick in and out with it being a short drive of no more than an hour or so. How long it would all take would depend largely on border checks and the time taken for that.

Having told him that I'd need clearance to leave Hong Kong, I'd managed to get hold of Will at his office who said he'd square my absence with the police. They had my statement ready. An officer would be bringing it to the hotel in an hour's time for me to sign. 'No, they haven't played around with what you said, Rich,' he assured me when I asked.

'What's it like in China, Will?' I'd asked him, knowing he'd been in and out covertly and officially. After querying who I was going with and what I was going to be doing there, he'd replied in a relaxed way.

'You'll be fine. Just go along with what you're told and make sure you can provide your proposal in simple terms, in Mandarin and in English, I would suggest. And I take it this Mrs Parker is fluent in spoken Mandarin and not just Cantonese?'

Of course, I'd then checked with Jeffrey, who confirmed what Will had said and arranged to collect my proposal, which they'd get typed up and translated overnight.

\*     \*     \*

All of that had been done when I had a call from Marie-Louise. She offered to call for me on her way home and was going to cook for me. I'd, naturally, decided not to have anything more to do with her, so, of course, I immediately accepted her invitation. Weak? *Moi?*

We didn't talk 'shop,' as I'd told her we both should have a night off. All I can say about it was that it was a very, very pleasant and enjoyable evening, which I thought I'd deserved; good food – a kind of French Asian fusion, more coq in a wok than coq au vin, but you get the idea, conversation about French films and literature – better or worse than British or American – and then a few more intimate exchanges.

I'd left at a reasonable time, as I needed to be back at the hotel for the morning pick-up. When I hit the sack I was out for the count, not even having dreams about my nightmarish day.

\*       \*       \*

All went swimmingly until we hit the border checkpoint.

Mrs Parker was free to proceed, but Jeffrey and I were detained for questioning. As our interpreter, Mrs P wanted to stay with us, but was told she couldn't. We'd be questioned with their own interpreter and only then would we be sent back to Hong Kong. Routine questions, she was assured, but information had come to light, which meant my visa, and Jeffrey's, were revoked.

We had a hasty tête-à-tête, if that's even possible between three people, and Jeffrey was insistent that his wife continue on the trip, to keep the appointment with Khoo Ah Au and to be able to tell him what had happened and hand over the publishing proposal. He might even be able to help, especially if we were further detained and not returned to Hong Kong.

So, off she went, leaving us to be taken to a squalid office that had a simple table with two chairs either side.

Nothing was spoken in English, except for the interpreter's questions to us and our replies to him. They spoke to each other in what Jeffrey thought was Cantonese, but he wasn't sure. Fortunately, the official and his mouthpiece were both fairly pleasant in demeanour, and not as dour as their smart green military uniforms and caps, which they kept on, suggested they would be. Even so, everything they said sounded like they were sentencing us to death. And Jeffrey was one cool customer. All I kept thinking about was the way Jimmy had spat Cantonese out of the side of his mouth on that first lunch I'd had with him.

Surely not? Jimmy's dead hand behind this latest twist of fate?

The long and the short of it was that they'd received information we were both security risks – (who from? Jimmy?) – but they wouldn't name their sources, despite our requests. It was better for us not to be admitted to their country. They could arrest us for spying and have us put on trial, but their bosses had decided it was easier to refuse us entry. We were free to go, but first a few questions ...

What exactly did we do? What was Jeffrey's role for his company? Who did he know in China? Who did he know in Hong Kong? How did he meet Mrs Parker? What was her role? Was he now, or had he ever been working with British or any other intelligence agency?

That all took about an hour and a half, and jolly interesting it was too. I kept alert by thinking about what terrific books and seminars I could get out of Jeffrey based on what he told our interrogators.

Hey, maybe this was the way to interview potential authors and speakers in future, with no need to buy them a fancy lunch!

Then they started on me. Curiously, I wasn't the least bit frightened or fearful. When a great many unpleasant things happen to you, you reach a point where, hell, it's just one more nail in the coffin. If you're already in the coffin, why care about one more little old nail?

Who did I work for? What did I mean, that I was starting my own business? What publications did I produce or intend to produce? Was I planning works on China? Who did I used to be employed by? Was I now, or had I ever been, working with British intelligence? Did I know anyone who worked for British intelligence? Why did I run seminars on defence contracting? Why did I publish capitalist works on tax planning? Did the British government support the publishing of such books? Did I work with the CIA? Had I been to America? Who did I know in America? What American businessmen did I know in Hong Kong?

Did I know the publishers in Hong Kong who were publishing seditious material on China? A bookseller had been reported as being abducted from Hong Kong

– what were people saying about that? What was my relationship with Mr Parker? What did I hope to achieve by my visit?

All we gave away was that we'd met certain British diplomats, but did not know who may or may not have been with British intelligence, as we were simple businessmen with a legitimate interest in the amazing culture and opportunities that existed in their historically closed and fascinating country. Guff like that.

It had all taken such a lot of time that Mrs P, on her return from the meeting, was able to produce a note from Mr Khoo to our 'hosts', and we were quickly released to return to Hong Kong with her. Kung phew!!

\*       \*       \*

As we drove off, I noticed a large Mercedes going in the opposite direction, towards China. In the back, pretending not to look at us, were Ferdy and Jimmy. I waved, but they looked resolutely forward, ignoring us. Had they seen us? Yes, they had, I was certain. Did they know what had just happened to us?

Jeffrey speculated with me that it was a Jimmy trick, but how had he managed it? Khoo Ah Au had been appalled that we had been detained and had said he would try to find out, but even he couldn't raise too many questions without suspicion extending to him. He did what he could do, which was to send a note with Mrs P for the border guards to the effect that Jeffrey was well known to him and a friend to China and he would like to know what new information they had which cast doubt on that.

Jeffrey had been told via Mrs P, that subject to what he might later learn, Mr Khoo would personally try, if he could, to make sure any further visits by Jeffrey would not be a problem. That sounded a bit equivocal.

Me! That was another question.

Jeffrey surmised that the information they'd received was that I was a thoroughly disreputable publisher who was working against the interests of his former company and who was known to have relationships with anti-China political activists in Hong Kong publishing circles. That would be enough to get me blacklisted. Jeffrey had done that himself to some of his competitors. Charming!

Mrs P reported that although my proposal had been accepted, read and filed, 'That's the end of it, sorry.'

We could only agree that it smacked of Jimmy, but the deeper question that Jeffrey posed was this: we know Jimmy has influence in Hong Kong, but given China's opinion of Hong Kong and any successful businessmen based there, especially ones who had fled the mainland as Jimmy had done, why were they listening to anything he said?

'This is a deeply disturbing situation, Rich. Yes, your China publishing ambitions are dead in the water.'

'You mean, like poor Chuck was?'

'Exactly so.'

I'd given up trying to guess what next might happen to me.

\*       \*       \*

We'd got back to The Mandarin and Jeffrey and Mrs P came in with me, as we all agreed we needed a drink.

We were in the Captain's Bar and I'd signed for our drinks, consolatory doubles all round, when the waiter came back and asked me to go to reception. The duty manager wanted a word with me.

It transpired that Langleys had informed the hotel that I was no longer employed by them and did they realise that I would therefore have to be paying my own bill, without any expenses backup. Could I, the manager wanted to know, please assure the hotel that I had adequate funds to pay them myself, otherwise I would not be able to stay even for one more night.

Of course, I'd had to say I did, but at their rates, I would not be able to stay more than a couple of nights and still have enough to cover everything else.

Back in the bar, I reported this latest twist to Jeffrey, who calmly responded with the comforting words that I could stay in his company's flat over at Stanley for as long as I needed, and he'd arrange for me and my luggage to be collected in the morning.

As if that wasn't enough, he followed up with more generosity, saying that he and Mrs P had decided to back my business venture, privately and in a personal capacity. He could do it with his own slush fund that he held on deposit in Hong Kong and Mrs P would run the office out of Hong Kong for me, just as she did for him.

Strange! I had as many backers as enemies. Was a corner being turned?

I was just beginning to feel better about life and to start believing that maybe, just maybe, I was living out my grandmother's idea of a decent life: 'It's better to be born lucky than rich' – with no pun intended on my nickname.

That was a short-lived feeling of euphoria, because, just then, Miguel came into the bar in a complete fluster and told me that he'd met up with Nick Dale on his return from Manila, but over tea at his hotel, Nick had gone into convulsions and had had to be rushed to hospital.

He was at the Hong Kong Sanatorium and Hospital in Happy Valley, uncomfortably close to the private hospital I'd been in, the Hong Kong Adventist Hospital on Stubbs Road. That brought back unpleasant memories. Now it was Nick's turn. Coincidence?

Miguel and I headed off to see him with the blessing of the Parkers.

# 15

It turned out that Nick had been poisoned. Trouble is, they weren't quite sure at that stage exactly what substance he'd been given, or how much of it he'd ingested. The implication was that if he'd eaten all of the big breakfast he'd been provided with at his Manila hotel (echoes of the Aussies, but with murderous intent), he would probably be dead. Fortunately he'd been pumped and dosed and was already sitting up when we got there.

Although we were cautioned not to keep him talking too long, he managed to tell us that he'd been working with a banker doing a private audit of the Philippines Central Bank who'd identified payments that had gone offshore to private companies. Nick and the banker had been staying in the same hotel and they'd both had luxury breakfasts sent up to their room, courtesy of the bank. They'd had no time to eat it all, which was just as well, as they'd had to dash to get their flights.

He thinks the officials at the bank must have cottoned on to what the audit was about and had their food laced with some pretty toxic substance, which the hospital lab would have to test to find out its chemical structure. The banker had flown to Tokyo when Nick had gone to Hong Kong. Now, of course, Nick was anxious to find out how the other guy had reacted.

We left Nick with the promise we'd return the following day and I went off to try and see Dickie to see what we could do. We took our wait-and-return taxi back to Central and I dropped Miguel back at the Hilton. We'd had the chance to catch up a bit and for me to fill him in on what I was going to do to get the company up and running. I'd still not finally decided to jettison Dickie, but that was the way my mind was working. Miguel approved of this as, despite his initial excitement, like me he'd had enough of being involved in the clandestine world we seemed to have entered.

Dickie was not exactly pleased to see me.

'What now?' was his general bored tone.

I explained about Nick and basically asked him what he was going to do about it.

'Nothing,' was his curt reply. 'We can't exactly prove anything now, even if the Tokyo banker bod drops down dead, can we?'

'That's pathetic, Dickie, and you know it.'

'What did he expect? Nick knew that what he was doing in the Philippines was likely to get a reaction if the powers-that-be found out. After all, don't forget that what he was doing in Manila would be considered to be treason at home in the UK.'

'How can you say that?'

'Because it's what I believe! My job, like my oppos in the Philippines, is to defend the status quo, at all costs if necessary.'

'I can't believe I'm hearing this. That's not a belief. It's blind patriotism at best and shows a contempt for natural justice and moral rectitude.'

'I thought you'd lost all that self-righteous left-wing stuff when you embraced your Cambridge life, Rich. Seems I was wrong. My advice to you is to learn when to pick a fight. We can't go around accusing the Marcos regime of this or that without clear evidence that UK passport holders have been mistreated for no fault of their own. We can't say any of that in Nick's case.'

'Or in Chuck's case?'

'Chuck was American.'

'Same difference. How many deaths or attempted murders will there have to be before you can see a pattern, Dickie?'

'When you start taking a step back and taking a cool, hard look at the realities of operating in a third-world country.'

There was no point in arguing further. I could tell Dickie was getting irritated with me, and I didn't want to push my luck as I was beginning to realise that I needed all the friends I had. If I could count him as one, that is.

'All right, let's see what unfolds, but I want to ask you if you've found out anything about why Jeffrey Parker and I were stopped and questioned and turned back from entering China.'

'Look, Jeffrey is a colourful character and it's easy to be seduced by that. For all I know he's offended someone high up in the party and they want to unsettle him a bit. You probably got caught in the fine hairs of the net they'd thrown over him. Collateral damage, you could say.'

'Yes, but how do you account for the fact that I saw Jimmy and the Langleys lot sailing through.'

'Obviously they're after the same contract that you were and it's the usual case that the Chinese would schedule the meetings for the same day, partly so you could all see you had competition for their favours. They're not daft. You must have been part of a beauty parade before. It's no different out here. And I know for a fact that Nigel

Bland was going over even later still, because he sought some advice about a translator he'd have to take with him since Jimmy had spurned him at Spreadworths and jumped ship to Langleys. He's even more pissed off with Jimmy than you are.'

'Was he stopped then?'

'No, he wasn't, actually, but he's just seeing it as commercial competition and not getting all antsy about it as you are.'

'So, are you saying it could have been "commercial competition" that maybe caused Jimmy to leak some unpleasant stuff to the Chinese about us?'

'Rich, you have a vivid imagination, but it's born of a one-track mind. Look, it could have been Nigel Bland for all I know that fed some scurrilous stuff to the Chinese authorities. If it'll keep you quiet, I'll put out some feelers and try and find out what was behind your expulsion. But remember, Jimmy isn't exactly flavour of the month with the Chinese himself. I still don't think it could be him.'

He sounded more terse than ever. I eased off and said, apologetically, 'You can't blame me for trying to see a pattern in all this. It's been a pretty amazing trip so far.'

'How long are you staying?' he probed.

'Not much longer. I think I'll travel with Nick back to the UK, if that's what his intention is, probably not later than a week's time – even earlier if possible.'

'What about setting up in business? My offer still stands. You won't get a better one.'

'No offence, Dickie, although, of course, it might not work out and I'll have to come crawling back, but I think I want to fund it myself.'

'Don't make any rash decisions. I think it could work for both of us, however you're funded and set up. We could put all sorts of contacts your way, including in the Chinese Communist Party hierarchy, with China opening up the way it is – despite what's just happened to you. And even in the publishing world, we could see some deals directed to you from, say, the British Council.'

'That's tempting. How would you feel about talking to me again once I've set up the business and have got a proper commercial plan in place? After all, surely the attractiveness of an operation like mine is that it's a legitimate publishing entity in its own right and not completely and obviously a front organisation for an intelligence operation.'

'OK. OK. Let's do it your way. But will you do me a favour? Will you meet up with Bill Brumby and his sidekick Tong Lim. He still wants to talk to you about a tie-up on the book distribution and marketing side.'

'But he's CIA, isn't he?'

'Everyone is something in the intelligence services if you listen to the idle speculation of some people like your good self. Poor Bill gets painted in those colours, but he's been in publishing out here for most of his working life. He knows everyone, everywhere. You should hitch your wagon to his star because it's already risen and he'll take you higher than you could manage on your own.'

'I've got his card somewhere, I think. I'll give him a call.'

'Let me know how you get on. I can still contact you at The Mandarin, can't I?'

'Only until tomorrow. Langleys have turned off the tap, but Jeffrey Parker has offered me his company apartment over in Stanley.'

'Do me a favour, Rich. Don't do that. You don't know him well enough. Anyway, it's a faff to get to Central from Stanley. Stay on at The Mandarin. I'll speak to them and sort it out. Leave me to pick up the tab. It's only for another week. Even with our budget cuts, I think we can stretch to that. Just don't abuse the mini-bar or room service.'

That seemed like a good idea to me and he had a point, I suppose. I agreed to it and thanked him.

\*     \*     \*

That evening, once I'd phoned Jeffrey and made my excuses about his kind offer of accommodation, I'd managed to muster Simon and Miguel for a pow-wow and a few things were decided.

First of all, following advice from Miguel, backed up by Simon, I decided I was going to go back to the UK and fund any business start-up from there. Don't be beholden to a third party funding or holding shares in your business, otherwise you might as well still be an employee, was the thrust of their thesis. Basically, if I didn't take their money, they couldn't tell me what to do. I couldn't argue with that.

Miguel was happy to work freelance on his other commissions and be my link person in Asia, but he'd stay based in Singapore, thank you.

Simon was off to meet Joséphine and Miguel wanted to get back to his hotel to unpack and sort a few things out.

Just as I was planning a quiet night for myself, and maybe calling Marie-Louise, I had a call from Bill Brumby who was downstairs and wanting a chat.

I asked him to come up to my room, little knowing that he'd have with him not only his sidekick Tong Lim, but also another guy, whose name I didn't catch, or didn't register, and was too embarrassed to ask for it to be repeated so soon after the introduction.

It turned out he was the head of some locally based, but American-owned, security firm that Bill thought I'd like to meet.

'There's a lot, I think, we should talk about,' Bill kicked off, 'and I don't just mean publishing cooperation, which we're excited about, aren't we, Lim?'

'We need a new publisher who can produce many new titles, that's the only way we can make any money out of publishing distribution and marketing. Lots of new books coming through regularly,' Mr Tong had elaborated, 'that's what we need. What's your planned schedule? Do you even have one yet?'

'Other than subscription titles, I plan on ten titles in the first year, most of them with authors I know who can deliver quickly, some of them having already half-written stuff I can use. Thereafter I guess it'll be ten to twenty titles a year plus a solid-selling backlist and some major subscription partworks with ongoing sales. And, as all of my list will be high-ticket items, the commission should be good. I assume you use the usual percentages as the trade norm?' I replied.

'With some volume-stepped increases built in, of course,' Bill butted in. 'We'll leave you with our standard terms to read through and see what you think. When can you let us have your forward list?'

'I need to get back to London and sort out the finances, but I can give you a rough list before I leave.'

'Who is funding your operation?' Bill asked, looking from me to Tong Lim, 'I mean do you need any financial investment from us?'

'No thanks,' I replied. 'I've actually had quite a few offers, but I want to think about it before deciding the route to take. Knowing I've distribution out here is help enough. Incidentally, I'm hoping you can assist me with some direct mail, inserts and supply of lists, as well as representation into the book trade and professional firms.'

'Bread and butter to us,' said Tong Lim, using a British colloquialism as if he'd been born in England, which perhaps he had been, but I was too polite to ask.

'Where does the "security" side of it come in?' I asked, gesturing to the nameless elephant in the room.

'I understand, Mr Rowlands,' came the Southern States drawl, 'that you have had some bother with Jimmy Chan. We've been tailing him and we think he's thick with the Chinese.'

I couldn't help but reply, 'I think that's maybe because he *is* Chinese.'

Unabashed, Mr Nameless continued, 'I mean, he's thick with the mainland Chinese. The Commies,' he added by way of clarification. 'We know that you were barred from entering China the other day and we know from representatives we have over there that Jimmy tipped them off.'

'Fascinating. But that's not all I know about Jimmy. He keeps cropping up. Listen, do you know Mike Moreno?'

It was a deliberate attempt on my part to try and work out what Mr Nameless was doing there with Bill and Tong Lim and to see the connection between them all.

Mr Nameless looked at Bill, who nodded, before saying, 'Yes, I do, as a matter of fact and he's coming in to

Hong Kong tonight. We've been working with the French on something and Jimmy's a part of that too.'

This was all too much of a coincidence. I expressed a thought that came to me at that point.

'Look, can I ask you all to come to a meeting tomorrow. I think we should be pooling what we know about Jimmy.'

'Yes, of course,' Bill replied, but he then leant in, conspiratorially, 'it'll be good to share what we know about Mr Chan. Come to our offices on Nathan Road, the address is on my card here. Tomorrow afternoon at three?'

'Thanks for that and the enthusiasm for my publishing,' I said as we rose from our seats. When they moved to leave, I asked, 'And will our security expert here be able to come? Sorry, I've forgotten your name.'

'Call me Al,' he said informatively. Droll, right? 'Yes, it'll be my pleasure.'

I then felt the need to ring Marie-Louise, but there was no answer at her flat or from her office.

Room service would have to do.

*       *       *

The following morning, after breakfast, I'd found out from the hospital that Nick would be able to be discharged at noon, which was great to hear. He and I had some catching up to do. I rang Miguel with the good news and

I said, if he'd nothing better to do, that I was going to walk the famous jogging trail to try and exorcise the demons tormenting me about even going out in Hong Kong.

Funnily enough, I hadn't noticed anyone following me recently, and no strange taxi business either, but maybe I had just been careless. Perhaps nobody was interested any more in what I was doing.

Miguel and I walked to the Zoological and Botanical Gardens and it was much more enjoyable than jogging there, although I did run through my idea for the brainstorming meeting with all the key players for that afternoon. I said that it would give us all a chance to pool our resources on what we knew and what we could do about it.

I was enjoying chatting with Miguel, despite the heat and the humidity, but, as we entered the park, even with no Lane Crawford and none of Tufty's Filipino crew members making a beeline for me, I kept thinking I was going to get another whack round the side of my head at any moment.

The park was near Marie-Louise's apartment. I shouldn't have been surprised to see her strolling across on the opposite side from us, in that distinctive, easy, sashay walk of hers. And, given what Bill and 'Al' had said about working with the French, I shouldn't have been surprised to see that Marie-Louise was with Mike Moreno. But I was.

When they briefly held hands and kissed, for rather too long, before he turned and walked towards downtown and she turned to go back, presumably, to her flat, I was rather more than surprised.

'What's the matter, Rich? You've gone a bit pale,' Miguel asked. 'You look like you've taken another blow to the head.'

'I have, Miguel. Much, much worse than any mugger could inflict. Come on! Let's get out of here. I've realised I hate this bloody park.'

One too many unpleasant associations. And it dawned on me that she must have been in a relationship with Dickie Hart all those years ago, despite her denials, and still could be for all I knew. Just because I hadn't wanted to believe it, didn't make it untrue.

\*     \*     \*

We returned to The Mandarin and there was a message for me from Bill. The venue for this afternoon's meeting had changed. Fine. The new location? The French Consulate! Not so fine. But what could I say? Fait accompli?

Miguel and I needed to decide who was going to be there and what our tactics were going to be for the meeting. We could arrange to pick Nick up, but we needed Simon there. We couldn't agree on whether we should invite Dickie. Was he too close to Jimmy? Was there a relationship we didn't know of and which he'd kept quiet about? Would that irritate the Yanks? Would it piss off the French? I didn't care about the last one, but Miguel did have a case in raising that question.

We decided not to invite Dickie and, therefore, not to invite Will, as we couldn't, diplomatically, ask one without the other.

What exactly would the meeting achieve? What did we want it to yield? On the first, we thought that we might find out some interesting, new, incriminating evidence against Jimmy and his cronies and, on the second, we wanted to get to a point where the authorities would have no option but to take it all further. We would have to push for that, given that the track record was to 'do nothing'.

We spoke to the hospital and fixed a time of two o'clock to pick Nick up and, yes, he was in good shape, they assured us. Would he be able to make it through a meeting though? Yes, as he was functioning properly.

Simon was going to meet us at the hospital and then we'd all go on from there to the French Consulate at the Admiralty Centre. Miguel and I agreed there would be enough time to have a chat when we all met – in the hospital reception, if necessary.

So, that's what happened.

# 16

IMAGINE OUR SURPRISE THEN, when the four of us went to the meeting room on the twenty-sixth floor of Tower II of the Admiralty Centre and saw, seated around the conference table, Marie-Louise, Joséphine, Bill Brumby, 'Al', Mike Moreno, Dickie Hart and Will Tomkins.

I should have seen that coming. Was this a hijack and was it going to be a cover-up?

Not a bit. And that was what should have made us more suspicious.

I was distracted by thinking it odd that Marie-Louise and Mike Moreno could find it easy to behave as if there was nothing between them. There was the same lack of anything between her and me, whereas Joséphine and Simon would, every now and then – and perfectly normally in view of their intimacy – exchange coy looks. Marie-Louise was different, a natural dissembler, perfect to be a *chargé d'affaires*.

She and Mike, acting like joint-venture business partners and nothing more, revealed, after promptings from Bill, that they had evidence to believe that Jimmy had direct connections with organised crime as well as smuggling and money laundering throughout South East Asia.

That was condemning enough. When we added in the material from his connections in the Philippines and his suspected involvement in the attempted murder of one of his former tax advisors in Singapore, as well as his association with Tufty McMasters, who was also implicated in the attack on me, it was beginning to look like an open and shut case.

Nick, unfortunately, got a bit emotional at this point, and raised the issue of Marcos.

'Jimmy is implicated in financial scandals in the Philippines. I know he's assisting the Marcoses and their cronies to extract money and launder it. Chuck's death in a restaurant we know to be controlled by Jimmy's associates, means that Jimmy himself must be marked down as being behind that murder, carried out, probably, on the orders of the Philippine regime. It's obvious that Chuck's report is international dynamite and they couldn't afford to have him on the loose. That's why they've killed him.

What they don't know is that I've sent a copy of his report to the opposition in the Philippines.'

Looking at Mike, who blushed, Nick then said, 'I know too that the Americans have a copy. The original of the report is on film if anyone else wants to see it.' Then he thumped the table saying, 'And I've got a whole lot more information where that came from.'

Where did *that* come from?

This muddied the waters a bit with the others who seemed to make an allowance for Nick's emotional outburst at first until Dickie, who, with Will, had been silent up to this point, weighed in.

'I thought this meeting was going to be about hard evidence, not hearsay,' Dickie said, in such a nonchalant way that it really bugged me.

'We know what you think, Dickie,' I said, 'and we didn't even know you were going to be at this meeting, but since you are here, can you or Will tell us why no action at all has been taken against Jimmy. Neither he, nor Lane Crawford, have even been questioned, as far as I know.'

'You're talking about Ting Tack Chee, Rich, and I do wish you'd stop referring to him as Lane Crawford. That's the sort of idle, non-Hong Kong resident's way of dealing with local issues and it gets right up the noses of the Chinese.'

Will chipped in, trying to smooth things, with, 'We can't just haul them in. We need to build a case. That needs a proper investigation, which we'll consider when we've all the evidence. That's what this meeting is meant to be about, after all.'

'You've had long enough, Will, to start an investigation. The financial indiscretions,' Simon interjected, 'are surely blatant enough to merit getting him in for questions. You know, through our contacts, that we could get access to Jimmy's safe deposit box at the bank. That should give us quite a lot of incriminating evidence.'

'And,' Marie-Louise added, 'we've got an "in" with Jimmy's first wife, Betty Chan, and we think we can persuade her to give us access to what she says is a secret stash of his papers at the apartment she still occupies.'

Dickie was not his usual smooth self when he replied, saying, 'What you all need to get into your ... skulls ... is that Jimmy has the best lawyers in Hong Kong. And what you're actually discussing can't be done without special clearances, especially if we're trying to build a watertight case against him, conducted in a proper legal way. He regularly sues any journalist who even questions his actions in his Hang Seng listed companies. He would have a field day hanging us out to dry if we couldn't prove all accusations we made against him and were shown to have collected evidence by illegal means.'

Marie-Louise and Mike kept exchanging glances and, at that point, Mike coughed and gained our attention.

'Look, fellas, it's no secret to us and I think Dickie and Will ought to come clean, Jimmy works for British intelligence, doesn't he? That's the problem in all this.'

Although it perhaps shouldn't have come as a shock, this twist silenced our side of the table, except for Simon, who looked at Will in a rather contemptuous way, and asked, 'Did you know this, Will?' Will tried to assure him with, 'No, you have my word.'

Momentarily stunned, Dickie attempted a backhand return of the spinning ball that Mike had served.

Trying to recover his composure, Dickie addressed us all.

'First, Mike, that is a clear breach of protocol and I'm going to have to take it up with our superiors. It could even lead to a major issue between our sides. I can't tell you what Jimmy is to us. We see him as an asset, sure, but nothing more. Secondly, if Jimmy was guilty of criminal activity, we would be the first to take action, unless we felt that it was against the national interest.'

'That's bullshit, Dickie,' said Bill. 'We only *suspected* Jimmy worked for you, but now you've gone and come clean, in effect, that he does. And, for the record, I am one of those superiors you talk about on our side. Frankly, I think you're dragging your feet and I'm beginning to wonder if there isn't even more to all this than we thought.'

'That's an outrageous accusation. I'm going to have to ask you to withdraw it, or we're going to have to leave this meeting here and now.'

'Not only will I not withdraw it, Dickie, I'm going to make another one. We think Jimmy is probably in the pay of Chinese intelligence, an asset of theirs if you like.'

Bill continued, 'We've had a tip off that he is part of China's Ministry of State Security and supplies them with information on diplomats, businessmen and even members of the Chinese Communist Party. Everything he does is corrupt, from his business deals to his honey-trapping top senior commies with women and sex scandals, to helping others, even higher up, to remove opponents and to salt away money. One way or another, you've got to do something about him. The guy might be a double agent, for Pete's sake.'

It was now Dickie's turn to look stunned. He was momentarily completely nonplussed.

The silence that had greeted the end of Bill's little speech was total and then, the longer drawn-out it became, the more we all looked around at each other and the more embarrassing it was.

We were all glad when Nick broke in.

'That's put all the cards on the table. How do we play it from here? That's almost worth a seven no-trump bid. But who's going to take the lead role in all this?'

Will looked askance at Dickie. That was another relationship gone west, for sure.

Dickie was the first to respond.

'This meeting is breaking all rules. We must keep secret what we're saying about Jimmy. I believe that's what serves us best at this point.'

I couldn't help myself.

'The one thing I know you do believe in, Dickie, almost to the exclusion of all else, is the sanctity of secrets. But, in the light of this latest devastating development, I think we, on our side, can agree, at this stage, that we'll not say anything to anyone outside those here.'

Dickie was annoyed with us by then and he asked Simon for a copy of the dossier, so that everyone would have the two sources of information on Jimmy that we held, namely Chuck's report and the anonymous financial dossier. Simon held firm though, saying that he would reveal it only when he'd finished going through it in the detail that it warranted.

He then put his viewpoint clearly to the room by saying, 'I can and will take legitimate action against Jimmy and Craig McMasters for any breaches of the territory's tax code.'

'That's fine, Simon,' observed Dickie in a measured tone, 'provided nothing red lights to Jimmy the major issues that we're trying to link directly to him. Surely, in the next few days, you can furnish us with the salient features of the accusations that question Jimmy's financial integrity?'

Simon nodded in agreement, but in a way that didn't look legally binding to me. Dickie continued, calmly, looking at us all in turn.

'One thing for sure is that you, Rich, Simon, Nick and Miguel are sitting the rest of this meeting out. We can't discuss it anymore in front of you. This is now strictly a matter for the intelligence services as national security and the integrity of Hong Kong are at stake. We'll have to work together to decide what to do about Jimmy Chan.'

'Agreed.' 'Agreed.' 'Agreed.' 'Agreed.' 'Agreed.' Bill, 'Al', Mike, Marie-Louise and Will were like the yes-men and nodders in a PG Wodehouse story.

'Am I to write all this down?' asked the efficient Joséphine.

That broke the ice a bit and we all tried to laugh, but it was hardly convincing and nobody bothered to answer her question.

'At this point, I will show you out, I think,' said Marie-Louise, so, after looking round the table at each other, 'our team' got up, swapped mumbled goodbyes with the others and followed her out of the door she was pointedly holding open for us.

I was the last out and walked with Marie-Louise to the lift.

'I didn't even know you and Mike Moreno knew each other,' I said.

'We've worked together for years. We're old friends, that's all,' she glibly replied, but I could tell she was lying. I thought I might as well let her have it.

'I saw you in the Botanical Gardens this morning with Mike ... '

The dream of a perfect relationship with a beautiful woman, glimpsed by a pool at midnight all those years previously and given fresh imaginings in Hong Kong a couple of nights ago, had turned out to be unattainable after all, a promise killed by promiscuity.

All she could say was all I expected her to say.

'*Je suis désolé, Ree-chard.*' My name was pronounced in a very heavy French accent. How could I have lived with that?

As we went down in the lift, Simon asked me what I'd been talking to Marie-Louise about.

'Nothing really, Simon.' I said.

I could hardly say I'd been, in effect, asking whether her perfumed garden was as popular as Hong Kong's Tiger Balm Gardens on a Sunday afternoon.

\*     \*     \*

In the lift, we all agreed that it had been an unsatisfactory meeting with the assembled members of the intelligence community.

'Trouble is,' said Nick, 'none of us, with the exception of Simon, can do much about Jimmy.'

'We have learnt,' said Miguel, 'that Jimmy is likely a double agent, that CIA man Bill works for Langley and Rich has resigned from Langleys.'

'Witty, Miguel,' I said, 'very witty. But, Simon, what did you make of Will being out of the loop about Jimmy?'

Simon shrugged. 'That's Dickie for you.'

'Or how about Dickie? Missing that Jimmy was working for China. How bad is that?'

Simon shrugged again. 'Dicky'll squirm his way out of it. Wait and see.'

Miguel had then stated what had become obvious to each of us. 'We're not exactly going to go up against Jimmy ourselves, even if we've just cause.'

'I'll do my job,' said Simon, 'and to me Jimmy is just another taxpayer, or rather non-taxpayer, whichever.'

Nick took a Minolta camera out of his briefcase and handed it to Simon, 'You'd better have this for that safe-deposit stunt of yours.'

Nick explained he was feeling a bit weary, all the more so because he'd heard, before he'd left the hospital, that the banker in Japan was not making as rapid a recovery as he himself had done and was semi-conscious with the effects of a suspected form of botulism. That worried Nick because all he'd been told about himself in the hospital was that it looked like he had severe food poisoning.

'So, if you don't mind, I'd like to go back to my hotel and rest up.'

We went with him and chatted about what next over a coffee in the rather sterile lobby of the Hilton Hotel on Queen's Road.

We were all in a sombre mood. Simon was the most decisive and knew what he was going to do, which was to follow up all the financial leads he had and act accordingly, without fear or favour. He was going to keep away from Dickie and even from Will and just keep his head down.

Miguel was going to return to Singapore and follow up on his freelance contacts and await further instructions from me about the direction any business I set up was going to take.

Nick and I agreed we were going to leave for the UK in the next couple of days to reassess, in his case, what he was going to do to earn a living, and, in my case, for me to get a new business up and running.

# 17

THE NEXT DAY, I WAS back on the junk, courtesy of a kind farewell-to-Hong Kong invitation from the lovely Davina, which, if I was at all cynical, I would have thought was a themed, let's-make-sure-he-leaves-Hong Kong-for-good-this-time party.

Never mind what was in my head, by the look of the people on board a lot had happened since the first junket, and not just to me.

Davina had an airline pilot in tow, Cathay to be specific, and looked pleased with life and all it had to offer, whilst husband Laurence, slightly awkwardly, looking like he was in a documentary on open marriage, seemed to be partnered with Katy Covington. Chalk and cheese, the flamboyantly vivacious film-maker paired with the quiet

Laurence. She'd eat him alive, wouldn't she, like a version of 'video killed the radio star'?

Wait, is that Katy's work partner and ex-live-in partner, Clive Castle, over on the other side, kissing and cuddling with their employee, the luscious Elizabeth Chan, surely in clear breach of employment law, and, most certainly, against Jimmy's law.

What, no Tufty McMasters or Kenneth Minter? Don't tell me they've sailed off into the sunset together?

All I needed then was for Jimmy to turn up with Dickie and I'd have a full house.

I'd got to the boat nice and early and had a drink or two. Maybe the alcohol had gone straight to my head, or perhaps I'd taken auto-suggestion to a new level because, just as I was thinking about them, up the gangplank, larger than life, appeared Jimmy and Dickie, waving at one and all. Jimmy hadn't been arrested yet, that much was clear.

Oh no, they were headed straight for me.

'Hello, Rich,' said Dickie. 'You know Jimmy, don't you? Of course you do! Silly me.'

How many Martinis have you had, Dickie?

Whilst Jimmy tried to smile and scowl at me at the same time, making him look like a Chinese gangster who's about to be sick, Dickie charged on to tell me, 'I've persuaded Jimmy to put a good word in for you with a friend he's got in China. It might mean that your publishing proposal might be considered after all. With any luck your little misunderstanding at the border will be forgotten.'

Dickie couldn't resist some further self-promotion in boasting, 'I think they're keen to keep in my good books, what with 1997 on the horizon. Our intergovernmental discussions on that have reached a sticky stage and they know the Governor depends on my advice.'

'Thank you, Jimmy,' I felt I had to say, 'but can your friend in China tell you who tipped them off about my visit in the first place?'

Jimmy, by now distracted by the sight of Elizabeth canoodling with a *gweilo*, only grunted at me, so, just as Dickie moved off to greet Davina, I followed up with a question to Jimmy that had been bugging me.

'Do you know someone called Stanley Ho?' I asked, anxious not to let the opportunity pass for me to find out if there was any connection with Rodney's induced heart attack.

He came back with, 'Ho, Stanley, I presume you mean,' a witticism he surprised me with, that almost covered his lack of eye contact.

'Yes, that's him,' I pressed, expectantly.

'No. Never heard of him.'

'You'll remember Rodney Bolt, Jimmy. It seems like he had a heart attack after seeing your man, Stanley Ho. Doesn't that strike you as suspicious?'

'Not at all! Rodney an old man. He due a heart attack. That's what a man like him must expect. Perhaps fate thought he deserved one. Nature's way! That's what I believe.'

'Really? I've been wondering what you do actually believe in, Jimmy, especially when it comes to people? Perhaps you could enlighten me?'

'Only fools trust anyone but themselves. That is my number one belief. A good motto for you and your new business, yes? You must make your own luck and trust to fate.'

He was clearly bored with me. He finished our conversation with the comforting words, 'Come back to Hong Kong, by all means, if you can survive in the big world. Now, I must go! Talk to my daughter.'

That was my farewell to Jimmy and, thinking that nobody would miss me if I left, even before the party properly started, I walked the plank, just as the gangway was about to be drawn up by the deckhands for the harbour cruise on the junk to begin.

What a motley crew, was my thought as I drifted off without a backward glance and returned on the Star Ferry to Hong Kong Island and The Mandarin to relax, pack and make a few phone calls.

Only one call was disturbing and that was with Simon, who said that Will had just that minute phoned him to say that Betty Chan, Jimmy's estranged wife, had been found dead. She'd fallen accidentally, it had been reported by the police, from her fourth-floor balcony. Although we both knew who we each thought responsible, I told him I'd seen Jimmy on the junk where plenty of people could vouch for him and he'd arrived with Dickie. He couldn't have a better alibi, should he ever be questioned. But did he know she'd cut him out of her will? Perhaps it would turn out to be revenge from beyond the grave. Death, *there* is thy sting!

I was glad I was leaving in the morning.

What could I do about any of it?

# Afterword

**Benigno 'Ninoy' Aquino**, political opponent of Marcos, was assassinated on his return to the Philippines in 1983 from self-imposed exile in the US.

**Ferdinand Marcos** flew into exile with Imelda in 1986 and died in Hawaii in 1989. Imelda returned to the Philippines in 1991 and their son 'Bongbong' (Ferdinand Marcos Jnr) is active politically in the country. The current President of the Philippines (in 2019) is Rodrigo Duterte, who, because of the nature of his regime, has been dubbed 'Duterte Harry' by his biographer Jonathan Miller.

**1997** saw Hong Kong handed over and the New Territories handed back to China. Tung Chee-hwa, the first Chief Executive of Hong Kong under the Chinese, would not move into the Governor's House because it was thought to be comprehensively bugged.

**MI6** had one of the biggest listening stations on Hong Kong Island, in Siu Sai Wan, monitoring wireless communications from China. It was dismantled in the 1980s, when the inevitability of 1997 became obvious.

**Ferdinand 'Ferdy' Graeme**'s employment with Langleys was terminated and, with his generous severance package, he set up a China-specialist publishing house, based in Hong Kong, where he styled himself 'The Taipan of Type'. He divorced Mrs Graeme (who kept her lucrative Chinese art-importing business) and married **Elizabeth Chan**, with whom he went on to have five children, all educated at Stowe, and all of whom work in the family businesses.

**Nick Dale** set up his own forensic accountancy practice in the Home Counties, but still assists the Philippine PCGG (the Presidential Commission on Good Government) which, with its 94 lawyers, researchers and administrators, is still working to recover 'all ill-gotten wealth accumulated by former president Ferdinand Marcos, his immediate family, relatives, subordinates and close associates'. Only a small percentage of what was stolen has been recovered and nobody has gone to prison.

**Mike Moreno** became a campaigning journalist in Washington and foreign policy advisor to the Republican Party where he was known for his views on regime change.

**Richard 'Dickie' Hart** was knighted, later ennobled, and he successfully fought off sexual harassment claims by staff at the House of Lords. He lives in Godalming with his film-maker wife, **Katy Covington**.

**Kenneth Minter** lives in the Cotswolds, loves going to the opera and takes sex holidays in the Far East.

**Eric Old** was killed by natives on the Andaman Islands, when he tried to introduce a British Council book club to the local inhabitants.

**Jeffrey Parker** was arrested in China in 1990 and sentenced to twenty-five years on spying, bribery and corruption charges that he denies to this day. Released in 1997 as part of a swap, he and Mrs Parker moved to Aldeburgh, where he plays golf and entertains fellow club members with his colourful tales of the East and she runs an Asian deli. He wrote *Feng Ru, the Father of Chinese Aviation* and, currently, is writing a book about how he changed the aerospace industry in Asia Pacific.

**Rodney Bolt** and his wife moved to Canada where she had relatives and he still edits, even at his advanced age, his renowned tax planning encyclopaedias, now online. He assisted investigative journalists working on the so-called 'Panama Papers', in particular, identifying relatives of high-level Chinese officials who used **Jimmy Chan** to launder funds through Liechtenstein foundations that controlled businesses registered in the British Virgin Islands.

**Will Tomkins** became disillusioned with Military Intelligence and retrained for the priesthood, becoming known as 'the Vicar of Stanley' in Hong Kong.

**Simon Perkins** married **Joséphine** and lives in the West Country, where he is researching a PhD on 'Taxation under the Tudors'. His wife is a leading international interior designer, noted for her work with chinoiserie.

**Martin Rochester** is still a well-known journalist and author, who set up the **Chuck Besky Trust** that funds researchers working in the third world.

**Miguel Bentoz** worked with Rich Rowlands for several years until he was appointed Consul, in Hong Kong, for Paraguay and occupied Room 903, Hang Lung Bank Building, 8 Hyam Avenue, Causeway Bay, Hong Kong.

**Craig 'Tufty' McMasters** was for many years resident beyond the reach of the extradition powers of Hong Kong, but eventually paid the Hong Kong tax authorities a substantial sum in settlement of unpaid taxes before selling his company for many millions. He married **Davina Farmer** aboard his latest multi-million pound yacht, *NonDomIV*, and they live offshore.

**Marie-Louise Audran** left the French diplomatic service and was well known as the mistress of various senior French politicians before becoming VP (Europe) of a leading American social media company, based in Paris. She has been investigated recently for alleged historic offences undermining the security of the state and of aiding a foreign power, believed to be China.

**Richard 'Rich' Rowlands** sold his publishing company to Langleys and now writes novels that enjoy sales 'well into single figures'. He still uses the leather folder he bought in Hong Kong – the duplicate of the one he was mugged for in Singapore – to remind him of 'happy days'. Although active in publishing throughout Asia, using **Bill Brumby** and **Tong Lim** as his distributors, he never returned to the Philippines. He is currently writing *Meet me in Mogadishu*, inspired by his later undercover work with the intelligence services, which reunites him with Bill, Kenneth, Eric and Jimmy in a faction-based look at China's role in East Africa. He describes it as 'a genre-busting dystopian sci-fi crime noir spy murder mystery romcom'.

**Jimmy Chan** was a British 'asset' until arrested in 1987, as working for the Chinese. Released in 1997 as part of an amnesty and prisoner swap, he is now one of the wealthiest businessmen in the world, his empire having been handled, in his absence in jail, by **Ting Tack Chee (Lane Crawford)** and **Elizabeth Chan**. Prior to his arrest, he had reached a Back Duty settlement for an undisclosed sum with the Hong Kong tax service. His daughter refuses to allow Jimmy to take down a partition wall in the flat she inherited from her mother and which she uses as her bolt hole in Hong Kong. She considers it to be her pension and refers to it as the family nest egg.

*Sadly, nothing is currently known about the other characters featured in this book.*

# Also from Thorogood

www.thorogoodpublishing.co.uk

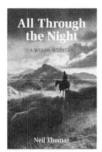

## All Through the Night

ISBN paperback: 9781854188960
ISBN eBook: 9781854188977

Written in the style of an old-fashioned Western, this tale of Welsh drovers taking a large herd of cattle from North Wales to London in the 1790s, stakes a claim for these engaging characters to be considered the first 'cowboys'.

Running through this 'Welsh Western', which is rich in adventures and incidents, the storyline has the strong cultural, emotional and human elements that make Westerns so appealing in exploring how people act in the drama of their own lives.

## Keeping the Lid On

ISBN paperback: 9781854188984
ISBN eBook: 9781854188991

Set in a private school a little in the past – at a time of turbulence following the death of the Old Headmaster – a sinister thread runs through the attempts to take the School forward. In whose best interests are the figures in authority acting; their own or those in their care?

Available at Amazon and all good retailers.